COVENTRY LIBRARIES

Please return this book on or before the last date stamped below.

132870

To renew this book take it to any of
the City Libraries
before the date
due for return

Coventry City Council

PRIVATE
NO. 1 SUSPECT

Since former US Marine Jack Morgan started Private, it has become the world's most successful detective agency. But when his former lover is found murdered in Jack's bed, Jack is instantly the number one suspect. With his team stretched to breaking point and Jack fighting for his life, he finds himself strong-armed by the mob into recovering $30 million stolen pharmaceuticals, and Jack realises he is facing his most powerful enemies ever.

PRIVATE
NO. 1 SUSPECT

PRIVATE
NO. 1 SUSPECT

by

James Patterson & Maxine Paetro

Magna Large Print Books
Long Preston, North Yorkshire,
BD23 4ND, England.

British Library Cataloguing in Publication Data.

Patterson, James & Paetro, Maxine
Private no. 1 suspect.

A catalogue record of this book is
available from the British Library

ISBN   978-0-7505-4006-3

First published in Great Britain by Arrow Books in 2013

Copyright © James Patterson, 2012

Cover illustration by arrangement with Random House Group Ltd.

James Patterson has asserted his right under the Copyright, Designs
and Patents Act, 1988 to be identified as the author of this work

Published in Large Print 2014 by arrangement with
Random House Group Ltd.

Magna Large Print is an imprint of Library Magna Books Ltd.

Printed and bound in Great Britain by
T.J. (International) Ltd., Cornwall, PL28 8RW

We dedicate this book to our nearest and dearest, Sue and John, Brendan and Jack.

Prologue

SHOTS IN THE DARK

ONE

A dark sedan turned off Pacific Coast Highway and slipped into the driveway of a gated Malibu beach house worth, had to be, seven or eight million.

The driver buzzed down his window and passed an electronic entry key over the reader.

The pair of high wrought-iron gates rolled open, and the sedan pulled up to the garage doors, the gates closing smoothly behind it. The driver got out of his car and looked around.

He was a medium-height white guy in his thirties, short brown hair, wearing a denim jacket, khaki pants, rubbersoled shoes, latex gloves. He saw that the cool modern house was screened entirely by shrubbery and protective fencing, hiding it from the road and neighboring homes.

He approached the alcove that framed the front door, noted the security camera focused on him and the biometric keypad.

Returning to the car, the driver opened a back door and said, 'Last stop, young lady.'

He leaned into the backseat and pulled out a slightly built female with long black hair. She was out of it, completely unconscious. Smelled like roses and soap. With a grunt, the man maneuvered the limp body, slung her over his shoulder.

When he got back to the door, he pressed the

female's finger to the pad, and the door lock thwacked open.

They were in.

The man in the denim jacket didn't turn on the lights. Sun came through the extensively glassed walls, bounced off the floor tiles, and made everything plenty bright enough to see.

The foyer led to a large skylighted living area with rounded walls and curved windows facing the ocean. To the left was a hallway to the master bedroom and bath. The man opened the bedroom door with his foot, and when he reached the bed, he eased the woman off his shoulder and arranged her on the blue-and-white pinstriped bedding.

He fixed a pillow under her head, then went to the window seat. Under the hinged lid was a metal box, and inside that, a custom Kimber .45 handgun. The guy in the denim jacket popped out the magazine, checked it, slammed it back in with his gloved hand. The gun was loaded.

He returned to the side of the bed and, aiming carefully, shot the woman in the chest at close range. Her body bucked, but when he pumped in the second and third shots, she didn't stir. He picked up the three spent shell casings and pocketed them.

The shooter took the receiver from the phone beside the bed. He dialed while looking out the windows to the beach.

The killer hung up the phone without speaking. Then he left the bedroom and found the media center in the living room. He opened all of the cabinet doors, rifled through the compartments,

14

and located the security system hard drive at the back.

He unplugged the drive and tucked it under his arm, then he exited the house through the front door. Once outside, he scraped away some mulch at the foot of a bougainvillea vine that scrambled thickly over the fence. He buried the gun in the shallow trench and covered it up with chipped bark.

He got back into his vehicle, started it up, and passed the electronic key across the reader on the opposite post. Once the gates had opened, he backed his car slowly into the emergency lane. Then he edged out onto the highway and headed north.

He was already thinking about this seafood restaurant in Santa Barbara called Brophy Bros. He loved that place. The clam bar had steamers, a Dungeness crab platter, and oysters on the half shell. He'd get a bottle of something worthy of his first-class day's work.

The shooter popped a Van Halen CD into the player and smiled as the dark sedan blended into the stream of traffic.

TWO

A. J. Romano was driving the white transport van west on I-15, a hundred fifty miles east of Vegas. The van was a late-model Ford. On both sides and across its rear cargo doors were decals saying

'Produce Direct' over a basket of red, green, and yellow vegetables.

Benny 'Banger' Falacci was slumped in the passenger seat, his new eel-skin cowboy boots up on the dash. Rudy Gee was in the back, taking his shift in the air-conditioned cargo section, his sleeping bag wedged between the cartons.

A. J. liked night driving anyway, but especially on those crystal clear nights you got at high altitudes out west. Bright stars. No traffic. A strip of road cutting through miles and miles of grazing land and desert terrain with a dusky backdrop of foothills like crumpled packing paper rising high and wide in the distance.

He was saying to Banger, 'I made this stew, you know, me cooking for her for a change.'

Banger broke the filter off a Marlboro, lit up with his lucky silver butane, opened the window.

'Jeez,' Romano said, opening his window too. 'Ever heard of secondary smoke? You're smoking for two here.'

'It's been three hundred sixteen miles,' said Banger. 'That was the deal. One smoke every three hundred miles.'

'Awright.' A. J. went on, speaking louder now over the rush of air past the window, 'So I make some noodles and a little chocolate cake. It's nice.'

'Fascinating, A. J. You got the major food groups covered.'

'So I'm full but not stuffed. We go to bed and at about two-thirty I wake up. I'm literally freezing.'

Banger plucked a shred of tobacco off his tongue. There was no CD player in the van, no radio signal this far from any fucking thing. In a

16

few hours he was going to be sitting at a black-jack table. He'd be sleeping in a triple-wide bed tonight. He could call Suzette at the last minute. He was thinking about that and how much talking she'd do before he could get her panties off. Or he could go to the Sands and find someone new. He was feeling lucky.

'I dial up the electric blanket. Still my nips are hard as diamonds.'

'Christ,' Banger said. 'Change the subject, do you mind?'

'I notch the heat up to nine. That's *weld*,' said A. J. 'I'm still freezing my ass off. When I wake up again, I'm sweating like I ran a couple of miles–'

'What's happening there?' Banger asked.

'I don't know. That's what I'm asking. Is my heart acting up on me?'

'What's happening *there*,' Banger said, pointing through the windshield at the red lights up ahead.

'That car, you mean?'

'It's slowing down.'

'Asshole should have filled up in Kanarraville.'

'Pull around him,' Banger said.

But A. J. was decelerating, saying, 'Guy runs out of gas on this road, he could get eaten by a bear.'

But the car in front of them wasn't running out of gas. It was crawling, giving a Chevy in the left lane, headlights off, a chance to catch up and pull alongside the van.

'What the fuck is this now?' A. J. said, staring at the Chevy six inches from his door. 'What's *this* asshole doing?'

'*Brake. Brake!*' Banger yelled. 'Pull around him.'

A. J. Romano leaned on the horn, but it had no

17

effect. Their van was hemmed in, being shunted toward the Pintura exit, and he had to either slam into the car beside him or barrel down the ramp.

A. J. jerked the wheel to the right, sending the van down the exit ramp, while Banger was digging under his seat for his piece. Next thing, metal was grinding against his door and the van was off the exit, forced onto some kind of spur road.

Banger was yelling, *'You mother,'* as A. J. stood on the brakes. The van skidded in dirt and plowed through a wire fence into the middle of fucking nowhere, dust shutting out the view and filling the cab.

Car doors banged shut in front and behind. Banger gripped his piece with one hand and undid his seat belt with the other, ready to bolt out the door, but a man's face was in the window, a punk he'd never seen before, yelling, 'Grab the ceiling.'

A. J. had his hands up. 'Banger,' he yelled, 'do what they say.'

Banger pulled up his gun from below the window opening. There was a bright flash and a loud report. Banger slumped, exhaled, and didn't move again.

Inside his head, A. J. screamed, *Oh, my God. They killed Banger.* A .45 was pointed at his left ear.

'Listen to me,' A. J. said. 'I don't know you. I didn't see nothing. Take what you want. I got six hundred bucks—'

A. J. didn't even hear the gun go off. He twitched, but that was all.

THREE

The van's rear cargo door blew open, and Rudy Giordino jumped down from the back. His right leg buckled, but he had played ball in high school and had good balance. He came out of the stumble into a dead run.

His head was clanging from the tossing he'd taken in the back, but his instincts were intact. He ran under a black sky, across the flats and parallel to the road.

His blood whooshed across his eardrums and he still felt the aftershocks of gunfire.

Christ. Guns had gone off in the cab. They'd been jacked.

Rudy Gee ran, flashing on his gun, lost under the cascade of boxes in the back of the truck. He thought about Marisa and Sparky and how he wasn't supposed to die yet, not gunned down out fucking here. He had so many plans. He was still a kid.

It felt good to run. He was making distance, could almost hear the cheering in the stands.

Behind him, a guy name of Victor Spano took careful aim with his .45, bracing against the side of the van. The dude was making it too easy, running in a straight line.

Victor squeezed the trigger, felt the kickback as the round found its mark. The guy making a break for it stopped running like someone had called his name. Then he dropped to his knees and did a face-plant in the dirt.

Victor walked up to the dead guy and put a shot into the back of his head just to be safe. If you fired a gun and no one heard it, had you still fired the gun?

Yes. Definitely.

'Is he dead?' Mark called.

'He says he wants to go have pizza with us,' Victor yelled.

'Get back here, okay? We need help with these two.'

Victor helped stash the first two dead guys in the Chevy. Mark backed up the car, and Victor and Sammy stuffed the third stiff in with the other two.

Then, as planned, Victor got behind the wheel of the transport van, and all three vehicles motored off the dirt road and back out to the highway.

Ahead of him, the Chevy peeled out, taking off toward Highway 56 and Panaca, Nevada. Victor Spano, a guy with a future, headed for LA, and Mark, in the Acura, for Cedar City. From there, Mark would be doubling back to Chicago.

It had been a good night. The jacking had taken a total of nine minutes including the cleanup.

He'd kept his mind on the business until this minute. Now, as the van made good time toward LA, Victor Spano started to think about his paycheck.

He was a millionaire and a made man.

This had been the most incredible day of his life.

Part One

I DIDN'T DO IT

Chapter 1

The car was waiting for me at LAX. Aldo was out at the curb, holding a sign reading, 'Welcome Home Mr. Morgan.'

I shook Aldo's hand, threw my bags into the trunk, and slid onto the cushy leather seat in the back. I'd done six cities in three days, the return leg from Stockholm turning into a twenty-five-hour journey through airline hell to home.

I was wiped out. And that was an understatement.

'Your packet, Jack,' Aldo said, handing a folder over the divider. The cover was marked 'Private,' the name of my private investigation firm. Our main office was in LA, and we had branches in six countries with clients all over the map who demanded and paid well for services not available through public means.

I had worried lately that we were growing too big too fast, that if big was the enemy of good, *great* didn't stand a chance. And most of all, I wanted Private to be great.

I tucked the folder from Accounting into my briefcase and as the car surfed into the fast lane, I took out my BlackBerry. Unread messages ran into triple digits, so I chose selectively as I thumbed through the list.

The first e-mail was from Viviana, the stunner who'd sat next to me from London to New York.

She sold 3-D teleconferencing equipment, not exactly must-have technology, but it was definitely interesting.

There was a text from Paolo, my security chief in Rome, saying, 'Our deadbeat client is now just dead. Details to follow.' I mentally kissed a two-hundred-thousand-euro fee good-bye and moved to texts from the home team.

Justine Smith, my confidante and number two at Private, wrote, 'We've got some catching up to do, bud. I've left the porch light on.' I smiled, thinking that as much as I wanted to see her, I wanted to shower and hit the rack even more.

I sent Justine a reply, then opened a text from Rick Del Rio. 'Noccia wants to see you pronto, that prick.'

The text was like a gut punch.

Carmine Noccia was the scion of the major Mob family by that name, capo of the Las Vegas branch, and my accidental buddy because of a deal I'd had to make with him six months before. If I never saw Carmine Noccia again, it would be way too soon.

I typed a four-letter reply, sent it to Del Rio, and put my phone back into my pocket as the car turned into my driveway. I collected my bags and watched Aldo back out, making sure he didn't get T-boned on Pacific Coast Highway.

I swiped my electronic key fob across the reader and went through the gate, pressed my finger to the biometric pad, and entered my home sweet home.

For a half second, I thought I smelled roses, but I chalked it up to the delight of standing again in my own house.

I started stripping in the living room and by the time I'd reached the bathroom, I was down to my boxers, which I kicked off outside the shower stall.

I stood under water as hot as I could stand it, then went into my bedroom and hit the wall switch that turned on the lights on either side of the bed.

For a long moment, I stood frozen in the doorway. I couldn't understand what I saw – because it made no sense. How could Colleen be in my bed? Her sweater was soaked with blood.

What the hell was this?

A tasteless prank?

I shouted her name, and then I was on my knees beside the bed, my hand pressing the side of her neck. Her skin was as warm as life – but she had no pulse.

Colleen was wearing a knee-length skirt and a blue cardigan, clothes I'd seen her wear before. Her rose-scented hair was fanned out around her shoulders and her violet-blue eyes were closed. I gripped her shoulders and gently shook her, but her head just lolled.

Oh, Jesus. No.

Colleen was dead.

How in God's name had this happened?

Chapter 2

I'd seen countless dead while serving in Afghanistan. I've worked murders as part of my job for years, and I've even witnessed the deaths of friends.

None of that protected me from the horror of seeing Colleen's bloody and lifeless form. Her blood spattered the bedspread, soaking through. Her sweater was so bloody I couldn't see her wounds. Had she been stabbed? Shot? I couldn't tell.

The covers were pulled tight and I saw no sign of a struggle. Everything in the room was exactly as I had left it four days ago – everything but Colleen's dead body, right here.

I thought about Colleen's attempted suicide after we'd broken up six months ago – the scars were visible: silver lines on her wrists. But this was no suicide.

There was no weapon on or near the bed.

It looked as if Colleen had come into my bedroom, put her head on the pillow, and then been killed while she slept.

And that made no sense.

Just then, my lagging survival instinct kicked in. Whoever had killed Colleen could still be in the house. I went for the window seat where I kept my gun.

My hands shook as I lifted the hinged top of the

window seat and grabbed the metal gun box. It was light. Empty.

I opened the closet doors, looked under the bed, saw no one, no shells, no nothing. I stepped into jeans, pulled on a T-shirt, then walked from window to window to door, checking locks, staring up at skylights looking for broken panes.

And I backtracked through my mind.

I was certain the front door had been locked when I came home. And now I was sure that every other entry point was secure.

That could only mean that someone had entered my house with an electronic gate key and biometric access – someone who knew me. Colleen had been my assistant and my lover for a year before we'd broken up. I hadn't deleted her codes.

Colleen wasn't the only one with access to my house, but maybe I wouldn't have to guess who had killed her.

My house was watched by the best surveillance system ever made. There were cameras posted on all sides, over the doorways, sweeping the highway, and taking in 180 degrees of beachfront beyond my deck.

I opened the cabinet doors on the entertainment unit in the living room and flipped the switch turning on the six video monitors stacked in two columns of three. All six screens lit up – and all six screens were blank. I stabbed the buttons on the remote control again and again before I realized the hard drive was gone. Only a detached cord remained.

I grabbed the phone by the sofa and called Justine's direct line at the office. It was almost seven. Would she still be there?

She answered on the first ring.

'Jack, you hungry after all?'

'Justine. Something bad has happened.'

My voice cracked as I forced myself to say it.

'It's Colleen. She's dead. Some *bastard* killed her.'

Chapter 3

I opened the front door and Justine swept in like a soft breeze. She was a first-class psychologist, a profiler, smart – hell, brilliant. Thank God she was here.

She put her hand on my cheek, searched my eyes, said, 'Jack. Where is she?'

I pointed to the bedroom. Justine went in and I followed her, standing numb in the doorway as she walked to the bed. She moaned, 'Oh, no,' and clasped her hands under her chin.

Even as I stood witness to this heartbreaking tableau, Colleen was still alive in my mind.

I pictured her in the little house she had rented in Los Feliz, a love nest you could almost hold in cupped hands. I thought about her twitching her hips in skimpy lingerie, big fuzzy slippers on her feet, sprinkling her thick brogue with her granny's auld Irish sayings: 'There'll be caps on the green and no one to fetch 'em.'

'What does that mean, Molloy?' I'd asked her.

'Trouble.'

And now here she was on my bed. Well beyond trouble.

Justine was pale when she came back to me. She put her arms around me and held me. 'I'm so sorry, Jack. So very sorry.'

I held her tight – and then, abruptly, Justine jerked away. She pinned me with her dark eyes and said, 'Why is your hair wet?'

'My hair?'

'Did you take a shower?'

'Yes, I did. When I came home, I went straight to the bathroom. I was trying to wake myself up.'

'Well, this is no dream, Jack. This is as real as real can be. When you showered, had you seen Colleen?'

'I had no idea she was here.'

'You hadn't told her to come over?'

'No, Justine, I didn't. *No.*'

The doorbell rang again.

Chapter 4

The arrival of Dr. Sci and Mo-bot improved the odds of figuring out what had happened in my house by 200 percent.

Dr. Sci, real name Seymour Kloppenberg, was Private's chief forensic scientist. He had a long string of degrees behind his name, starting with a PhD in physics from MIT when he was nineteen – and that was only ten years ago.

Mo-bot was Maureen Roth, a fifty-something

computer geek and jack-of-all-tech. She specialized in computer crime and was also Private's resident mom.

Mo had brought her camera and her wisdom. Sci had his scene kit packed with evidence-collection equipment of the cutting-edge kind.

We went to my room and the four of us stood around Colleen's dead body as night turned the windows black.

We had all loved Colleen. Every one of us.

'We don't have much time,' Justine said, breaking the silence, at work now as an investigator on a homicide. 'Jack, I have to ask you, did you have anything to do with this? Because if you did, we can make it all disappear.'

'I found Colleen like this when I got home,' I said.

'Okay. Just the same,' said Justine, 'every passing minute makes you more and more the guy who did it. You've got to call it in, Jack. So let's go over everything, fast and carefully. Start from the beginning and don't leave anything out.'

As Mo and Sci snapped on latex gloves, Justine turned on a digital recorder and motioned to me to start talking. I told her that after I got off the plane, Aldo had met me at British Airways arrivals, 5:30 sharp.

I told her about showering, then finding Colleen's body. I said that my gun was missing as well as the hard drive from my security system.

I said again that I had no idea why Colleen was here or why she'd been killed. 'I didn't do it, Justine.'

'I know that, Jack.'

We both knew that when the cops got here, I would be suspect number one, and although I had cop friends, I couldn't rely on any of them to find Colleen's killer when I was so darned handy.

I had been intimately involved with the deceased.

There was no forced entry into my house.

The victim was on my bed.

It was what law enforcement liked to call an open-and-shut case. Open and shut on me.

Chapter 5

If you're not the cops on official business, processing an active crime scene is a felony. It's not just contaminating evidence and destroying the prosecution's ability to bring the accused to trial, it's accessory to the crime.

If we were caught working the scene, I would lose my license, and all four of us could go to jail.

That said, if there was ever a time to break the law, this was it.

Mo said, 'Jack, please get out of the frame.'

I stepped into the hallway and Mo's Nikon flashed.

She took shots from every angle, wide, close-up, extreme close-ups of the wounds in Colleen's chest.

Sci took Colleen's and my fingerprints with an electronic reader while Mo-bot ran a latent-print reader over hard surfaces in the room. No fingerprint powder required.

Justine asked, 'When did you last see Colleen alive?'

I told her that I'd had lunch with her last Wednesday, before I left for the airport.

'Just lunch?'

'Yes. We just had lunch.'

A shadow crossed Justine's eyes, like clouds rolling in before a thunderstorm. She didn't believe me. And I didn't have the energy to persuade her. I was overtired, scared, heartsick, and nauseated. I wanted to wake up. Find myself still on the plane.

Sci was talking to Mo. He took scrapings from under Colleen's nails, and Mo sealed the bags. When Sci lifted Colleen's skirt, swab in hand, I turned away.

I talked to Justine, told her where Colleen and I had eaten lunch on Wednesday, that Colleen had been in good spirits.

'She said she had a boyfriend in Dublin. She said she was falling in love.'

I had a new thought. I spun around and shouted, 'Anyone see her purse?'

'No purse, Jack.'

'She was brought here,' I said to Justine. 'Someone had her gate key.'

Justine said, 'Good thought. Any reason or anyone you can think of who could have done this?'

'Someone hated her. Or hated me. Or hated us both.'

Justine nodded. 'Sci? Mo? We have to get out of here. Will you be all right, Jack?'

'I'm not sure,' I said.

'You're in shock. We all are. Just tell the cops what you know,' she said as Sci and Mo packed up their kits.

'Say you took a very long shower,' Sci said, putting his hand on my shoulder. 'Make that a long bath and then a shower. That should soak up some of the timeline.'

'Okay.'

'The only prints I found were yours,' said Mo-bot.

'It's *my* house.'

'I know that, Jack. There were no prints other than yours. Check the entry card reader,' she said. 'I would do it, but we should leave.'

'Okay. Thanks, Mo.'

Justine squeezed my hand, said she'd call me later, and then, as if I had dreamed them up, they were gone and I was alone with Colleen.

Chapter 6

The Beverley Hills Sun was one of three exclusive hotels in the chain of Poole Hotels. Located on South Santa Monica Boulevard, a mile from Rodeo Drive, the Sun was five stories of glamour, each room with a name and an individual look.

The Olympic-sized eternity pool on the rooftop was flanked with white canvas cabanas, upholstered seating, and ergonomic lounge chairs – and then there was the open-air bar.

Hot and cool young people in the entertainment business were drawn like gazelles to this oasis, one of the best settings under and above the Sun.

At nine that evening, Jared Knowles, the Sun's night manager, was standing in front of the Bergman Suite on the fifth floor with one of the housekeepers.

He said to her, 'I've got it, Maria. Thank you.'

When Maria had rounded the corner with the bedding in her arms, Knowles knocked loudly on the door, calling the guest's name – but there was no answer. He put his ear to the door, hoping that he would hear the shower or the TV turned on high – but he heard nothing.

The guest, Maurice Bingham, an executive from New York, had stayed three times before at the Sun and never caused any trouble.

Knowles used his mobile phone to call Bingham's room. He let it ring five times, hearing the ringing phone echo through the door and in his ear at the same time. He knocked again, louder this time, and still there was no answer.

The young manager prepared himself for best- and worst-case scenarios, then slipped his master key card into the slot and removed it. The light on the door turned green, and Knowles pushed down the handle and stepped into the suite.

It smelled like shit.

Knowles's heart rate sped up, and he had to force himself to go through the foyer and into the sitting room.

Lying on the floor by the desk was Mr. Bingham, his fingers frozen in claws at his throat.

A wire was embedded in his neck.

Knowles put his hands to the sides of his face and screamed.

The horror was in the present and in the past. He had seen a dead body almost identical to this one when he had worked at the San Francisco Constellation. He had transferred here because he couldn't stand thinking about it.

That night, five months ago, the police had grilled him and criticized him for touching the body before they let him go. He'd heard that there had been other killings, strangulations with a wire garrote; in fact, there had been several of them.

That meant a serial killer had been in this hotel, standing right where he was standing now.

So Jared Knowles didn't touch the body. He used his cell phone to call the hotel's owner, Amelia Poole. Let her fucking tell him what he should do.

Chapter 7

Amelia Poole was just getting home when she got the phone call from Jared Knowles, her night manager at the Sun. She asked him to hang on until she got out of the garage, closed the door, and stood in her yard overlooking Laurel Canyon.

'It happened again,' Jared said. He was speaking in a hoarse whisper, and she could hardly make out what he was saying.

'What are you talking about?'

'It happened again. A guest in the Bergman Suite. His name is Maurice Bingham. He's dead. He's been killed. Just like – I can't remember his name, but you know who I mean. At the Constellation. I'm scared because I'm a link, Ms. Poole. The police are going to think I could have done it.'

'Did you?'

'Hell, no, Ms. Poole. *Believe me.* I would *never.*'

'How do you know Mr. Bingham is dead?'

'His face is blue. His tongue is out. There's still a wire around his neck. He's not breathing. Anything I've forgotten? Because I didn't learn anything in hotel management school that covered things like this.'

He was screeching now.

And Amelia Poole was suitably frightened.

This killing made five – and it was the third in one of her hotels. The cops had come up with nothing. She hadn't heard from them in weeks. And this murder struck her as personal. Maybe some kind of warning. Any of her guests could be killed. It was too sick.

'Jared. Listen to me,' she said. 'I'll try to keep you out of it. Flip on the "Do Not Disturb" light. Can you do that? Use your elbow, not your fingers.'

'Housekeeping called me to say that Mr. Bingham had ordered an extra blanket and pillows. That he didn't open the door.'

'Did you bring bedding into the room?'

'No.'

'Did you touch anything?'

'No.' Jared was crying now. This was too much.

36

'Jared. Flip on the light and go back down to the desk.'

'Isn't that breaking the law?'

'I'll take responsibility, Jared. Just go down to the desk. Do not call the cops. Okay?'

'Okay.'

'If you can't do your job, say you're getting sick and take the night off. Ask Waleed to take over.'

'Okay, Ms. Poole.'

'I'll call you tomorrow.'

Amelia Poole disconnected the line and thought again about a private investigation agency she'd heard about. The head guy was Jack Morgan, former CIA and US Marines. His agency promised 'maximum force and maximum discretion.' It was called Private.

It was late, but she'd call Private anyway. Leave a message for Jack Morgan to call her as soon as possible.

Chapter 8

I called my friend chief of police Mickey Fescoe at home. He got on the line, said, 'My dinner is on the table. Make this good, Jack.'

'I can't make it good, Mick. Colleen Molloy, my ex-girlfriend – she was killed in my house. I didn't do it.'

I was looking at Colleen's body as I answered Mickey's questions in monosyllables. He said he would send someone over, and after hanging up

I sat down in a chair at an angle to the bed, keeping Colleen company as I waited for the cops to arrive.

I thought about how close Colleen and I had been, that I had loved her but not enough.

With a jolt, I remembered what Mo-bot had told me to do before she left the house. I went to the living room, booted up my computer, and drummed my fingers as the key entry program loaded.

A long list of times, dates, and names appeared on the screen, and I scrolled to the last entries. Colleen's key had been used thirty minutes before I had walked in the front door.

I was starting to get a piece of the picture. That this whole ugly deal had gone down as I was on my way home from the airport meant that someone was keeping tabs on me, knew my schedule to the minute. But dozens of people knew my movements – coworkers, clients, friends. Anyone with a computer would have known when my plane was landing.

I got to my feet as a siren screamed up the highway. I hit the button that opened the gates, stood in the doorway, and shielded my eyes against the headlights pulling into my drive.

Two cops got out of a squad car. I focused on the closest one: Lieutenant Mitchell Tandy.

Mickey Fescoe hadn't done me any favors. Tandy was a smart-enough cop, but he had a crappy take-no-prisoners attitude.

Tandy had arrested my father, who had owned Private before me. Dad was tried and convicted of extortion and murder. He had been doing his lifetime stretch at Corcoran when he was shanked in the showers five years ago.

Tandy didn't like me because I was Tom Morgan's son. Guilt by association. He didn't like me because Private closed a higher percentage of cases than the LAPD. It wasn't even close.

And then there was the most obvious irritant of all. I made a lot of money.

I watched and waited as the two cops came up the walk.

Chapter 9

Tandy was forty, tanned, a gym rat. His shoulder holster bulged under the tight fit of his shiny blue jacket.

Tandy said, 'You know Detective Ziegler.'

'We've met,' I said.

Ziegler had a swimmer's build: broad shoulders, a long torso. He wore a copper bracelet on his right wrist. Gun on his hip. I remembered him now. We'd mixed it up once when he was harassing one of my clients. I'd won. His hair had gone gray since I'd seen him last.

Tandy said, 'Where's the victim?'

I told him and he told me to stay where I was. Ziegler smiled, said, 'Sit tight, Jack.'

I stared out the windows toward the beach. All I could see was foam on the dark waves. My head pounded and I wanted to be sick, but I held everything down as Tandy and Ziegler went to my bedroom.

I heard Tandy's voice on the phone but not what he said. And then he and Ziegler were back.

Tandy said, 'I called the ME and the lab. Why don't you tell us what happened while we wait for them to come?'

We all sat down, and I told Tandy that I didn't know who could have killed Colleen or why.

'I haven't slept in more than twenty-four hours,' I said. 'I was a zombie. I started taking off my clothes the minute I walked in. I used the hallway entrance to the bathroom.'

I told him about walking into my bedroom after my shower, expecting to fall into bed. Finding Colleen.

'Very convenient, you taking a shower,' Tandy said. 'I suppose you did a load of wash too.'

'My jacket is on that chair. My shirt is on the hallway floor. I threw my pants over the door. My shorts are outside the stall.'

I gave Ziegler the names of Colleen's next of kin in Dublin and told the cops that the entry log showed that Colleen's code had been used a half hour before I came home.

'Colleen had the access key to the gate. But it's not here,' I said. 'Someone had to have coerced her, used her key, pressed her finger to the pad at the front door.'

Ziegler said, 'Uh-huh,' then asked me to talk about my relationship with Colleen.

'We used to go out,' I said. 'And Colleen worked for me. I was very fond of her. After we broke up, she went home to Ireland. She came back a couple of weeks ago to visit friends in LA. I don't know who. I had lunch with her last Wednesday.'

Tandy didn't read me my rights and I didn't ask for a lawyer. I hoped he would have a break-through, find something I had missed, but when he asked me to tell him if Colleen and I had had a fight, I excused myself, went to the bathroom, and threw up.

I washed my face and returned to my inter-rogation.

Tandy asked again, 'You have a fight with the girl, Jack?'

'No.'

'You shouldn't have taken a goddamn shower. That was either insulting or a mistake. We *will* take your clothes and we *will* take your drains apart. We'll check the airport surveillance tapes and dump your phones. That's just tonight. To-morrow we'll do background on the victim. I'm thinking her body will tell us something interest-ing.'

'Do your best, Tandy. But even you and Ziegler have to know that I wouldn't kill my ex-girlfriend in my house and then call the cops. It's a setup.'

'I only want one thing. To find that girl's killer.'

'I want the same thing.'

I gave Tandy my boarding pass and Aldo's con-tact information. I said I wouldn't leave town. I said I wouldn't take a piss without asking him first.

The ME came and the CSIs arrived after that. I gave the lab techs my prints, some fresh cheek cells, and my dirty clothes.

'Am I under arrest?' I asked Tandy.

'Not yet,' he said. 'You have a friend in high

41

places, Jack. But you can't stay here.'

I called Rick Del Rio.

Twenty minutes later, I got into his car.

'What the hell happened?' he asked me.

I told the story again.

Chapter 10

Rick Del Rio lived in a one-bedroom house on the Sherman Canal, one of four parallel canals bounded by two others at the ends, a whimsical interpretation of Venice, Italy.

The houses were small but expensive, built close together, fronting the canal, backed by little alleys. Rick drove down one of those alleys, lined with garbage cans, telephone poles, garage doors, and the occasional row of shrubs along a back fence.

Del Rio's garage door was painted green. He pointed the remote, the door opened, and he drove in.

'I don't have much in the fridge,' he said.

'That's okay.'

'Half a chicken. Some beer.'

'Thanks anyway.'

We went up a few steps, through the door in the garage that led to the kitchen.

Del Rio said, 'No one knows you're here. Go into the living room. Try to relax.'

I'd been here before. The three-room, cabin-style house was pristine inside. White walls, dark beams, every chair and sofa down filled. Centered amid the furnishings was a coffee table made from a wooden boat hatch, polyurethane-protected against beer and scuff marks.

I collapsed into a chair wide enough for two, put my feet up on the table, and hoped to hell the world would stop spinning.

I heard Del Rio puttering in the kitchen and just closed my eyes. But I didn't sleep.

I thought about a night seven years before. I'd been flying a CH-46 transport helicopter to Kandahar, fourteen marines in the cargo bay, Rick Del Rio in the seat beside me, my co-pilot.

It had been a bad night.

A rocket-propelled grenade fired from the back of a 4x4 hit our aircraft, taking out the tail rotor section, dropping the Phrog into a downward spiral through hell. I landed the craft upright, but the bomb had done its work.

Men died horribly. A lot of them. I knew them all.

I was carrying one of the barely living out of the cargo bay when a chunk of flying metal hit me in the back.

It stopped my heart – and I died.

Del Rio found me not far from the burning wreck and beat on my chest, brought me back to life.

I was out of the war after that, worked for a small PI firm out in Century City. Then my crooked, manipulative bastard of a father sent for me.

He grinned at me through a Plexiglas wall at Corcoran, still giving me the business, but this time literally. He handed me the keys to Private and told me that fifteen million dollars was waiting for me in an offshore account.

'Make Private better than it was when it was mine,' he said.

A week later, having been shanked in the shower, he died.

Rick didn't have a rich father. He was fearless and knew how to use a gun. After his tour, he came back to LA. He did an armed robbery, got arrested, convicted, thrown into jail. When he was released early for good behavior, he came to work at Private and I bought him this house.

I knew everything about Rick. I owed my life to him, and he said he owed his to me.

My friend came into the room, saying my name. I looked up, saw the face only a bulldog's mother could love. He's five foot eight inches in his bare feet, an ex-con and a highly trained former US Marine. He was carrying a tray – a *tray*. Like he was a nurse, or maybe a waiter.

He kicked my feet off the table and put the tray down. He'd made sandwiches out of that leftover half chicken, spread some tapenade and honey mustard between the long slices of a baguette, thrown in a few leaves of romaine. And he'd brought two bottles of beer and a church key.

'Eat, Jack,' my wingman said. 'You take the room upstairs. Don't fight me on this. It's dark up there, and if you try, you can sleep for nine hours.'

'I can't take your room.'

'Look,' he said. He opened the lid of an ottoman. It folded out into a bed. 'Take the bedroom. You've got a full day tomorrow.'

'Colleen.'

'Colleen for sure. And you got my text? You've got an appointment first thing. Carmine Noccia is coming to see you.'

Chapter 11

My assistant, Cody Dawes, stopped me at his desk, said, 'Morning, Jack. We need to go over some things–'

'Just the red flags, Cody. I'm still dragging my tailpipe.'

'Sure, okay, uh. I'm giving you my notice.'

'What? What's the problem? I thought you were happy here.'

'I got a speaking part in a Ridley Scott film. I've got *lines.*'

He grinned broadly, clasped his hands together, and maybe jumped off the ground. I stuck out my hand, shook his, and said, 'Good for you, Cody. Congratulations.'

'I'm not leaving you in the lurch. I've lined up people for you to see. I screened them all myself.'

I sighed. 'Okay. What's next?' It was half past eight a.m. in Los Angeles, meaning it was half past five p.m. in Stockholm. My circadian rhythms were still on Central European time.

'Mr. Noccia is here. I had to put him in your office.'

'I thought I'd have a little time before he got here.'

'He was waiting at the curb, Jack. Inside a Mercedes with three other guys you wouldn't want to marry your sister. I opened the front door. He said he wanted to come in, so I brought him upstairs. Judgment call.'

'Do you still do coffee?'

'Yes, I do,' Cody said with a grin.

I went into my office.

It's got two sections; my work space at one end, a seating and meeting space at the other. Carmine Noccia was sitting in a chair by my desk.

'Carmine,' I said. I shook his hand, went around my desk, took my seat. All the phone lines were flashing. A three-inch-high pile of paper was stacked to my right. My schedule was up on my computer monitor, just waiting for me.

'You're looking good, Jack. Like you spent the night in a gym locker.'

'Jet lag,' I said, 'feels just like that.'

Noccia smiled. He was a handsome guy, mid-forties, perfect teeth, salt-and-pepper hair, wearing a custom-made suit and hand-stitched Italian loafers.

Carmine was what a modern-day Mafia rock star looked like. You looked at him and saw the Ivy League-educated businessman, not the son of a sitting don, the Mafia capo and killer.

Cody brought in a large silver thermos of coffee and a plate of biscuits, and when he left, I said, 'Del Rio told me you had to see me urgently.'

I tried to keep it out of my voice, but what I was saying was, What the eff do you want?

Chapter 12

Carmine Noccia said, 'It's a fucking disaster, Jack. One of my transport vans was jacked in Utah. Three of my guys were killed, dumped in the desert. I don't think the cops are going to help me recover my property – which needed to be done yesterday. It's a good thing I've got you in my corner.'

I don't do business with mobsters.

Make that past tense. I didn't do business with mobsters until my identical twin brother, Tommy Jr., racked up a six-hundred-grand gambling debt and I paid it off to keep Tommy's sweet wife from becoming a widow.

A few months ago, Del Rio and I had flown to Vegas to see Noccia in his over-the-top, Spanish-style manse complete with racehorses and a man-made recirculating river located about five miles from the Vegas Strip.

I'd brought a cashier's check for the full amount of my brother's debt, and Noccia and I had exchanged favors. We realized that day that we'd both been in the Corps. As marines liked to say about themselves, 'Never a better friend. Never a worse enemy.'

Carmine Noccia and I had shaken hands on that.

Now Noccia poured coffee for himself, used the cream, passed it to me. He said, 'My guys were good. The highway robbers were better. And that's all I know about the sons of bitches.'

'When did this happen?'

'Last night,' Noccia said. 'Our van was coming west from Chicago. We had a tracking device in there. No one knew anything was wrong until the van passed Vegas and kept pinging until it got to LA. The jackers must have discovered the GPS and trashed it when they stopped to check the inventory.'

'So you think the van is in LA?'

'I would say yes. LA is a big distribution hub. It's a valuable cargo, Jack.'

'Drugs?'

He nodded. 'Prescription variety.'

'How much?'

'Street value of thirty million.'

Now I understood why Noccia had been waiting for me before our doors opened. In the past, the Mob had frowned on the drug trade, but pharmaceuticals were a fast-growing and highly profitable business, just too good to pass up.

Pharmaceuticals were also easy to steal at any point along the distribution chain. Even a mom-and-pop store with a twelve-dollar padlock on the gate could have a hundred fifty grand worth of Oxy in stock on any given day.

Every pill was a tiny profit center, 100 percent FDA approved. The largest tablets of OxyContin were 80 milligrams. At a buck a milligram, one 80 mg pill was worth eighty bucks, and they came in bottles of a hundred. That meant one little bottle was worth eight thousand dollars. A truckload – thirty million or more.

Noccia had a big problem. He was desperate to control the damage and at the same time he couldn't let anyone know he was dealing in pharmaceuticals. So instead of turning his own crew loose on the underground, he'd come to me.

More people died from illegal prescription drugs than all the street drugs combined. This was a very bad business and I wanted no part of it.

Noccia leaned in toward me, fixed me with his big brown eyes. 'I've been waiting thirty years to say this, Jack. I'm gonna make you an offer you can't refuse.'

Chapter 13

I gave Noccia a smile I didn't mean and said, 'Carmine, I don't do drug-recovery missions. We do corporate work. Government contracts. You know.'

'You do more than that, Jack, but that's your business. I'll give you ten percent of the street value. That's three million dollars – cash. All you have to do is find the merchandise. With your connections, it'll take you a few days, tops. Three million dollars, Jack. How many cheating husbands do you have to tail to make that?'

Cody buzzed me on the intercom. 'Mr. Morgan, your nine o'clock is here.'

I said to Carmine, 'I wish I could help you, but this isn't my kind of work.'

49

I ran my eyes over my schedule; my appointments were stacked up like incoming aircraft at LAX, every half hour to the end of the day. I thought about Colleen, lying on a cold slab, the medical examiner slicing her open from her collarbone to her bikini line.

As I sat here, cops were going through my house, putting my life under their Slap Chop while Carmine Noccia dangled millions of dirty dollars in front of my face.

I lifted my eyes and looked at the mafioso with a big future, a future that had now been compromised by the loss of a monumental inventory and three men.

Carmine's expression was cold. No more kiddin' around with *Godfather* lines. He interlaced his manicured fingers on my desk.

'I'll double your take to twenty percent,' he said. 'Tax free, six million in cash.'

The bigger the offer, the more I wanted nothing to do with it – or him.

'Thanks, but I'm not interested, Carmine,' I said. 'I'm sorry, I've got another meeting.' I got to my feet.

Noccia also stood up.

We were the same height.

'You misunderstand me, Jack. You've got the job. What you want to tell me is how fast you can recover my merchandise – because very soon those goods will be all over the country and I'll be out thirty unacceptable million. Call me when you have the van.'

'No, Carmine,' I said again. 'No can do.'

'What part of "can't refuse" don't you get, Jack?

You know where I'm going. "Never a better friend." I'm calling in my marker. Here's my number,' he said, writing it across an envelope. 'Stay in touch.'

He tossed the pen down and it skidded across my desk as he walked away.

I heard Noccia say to Cody, 'I can find my way out.'

I sat back in my chair and looked out at the wide cityscape of downtown LA. If I didn't take the job, what would happen? Was I prepared to go to war with the Noccia family?

I got Del Rio on the line, kicked it around for a few minutes: what was possible, what was the wisest, safest plan of attack. Rick said his piece. I said mine. And then we kicked it around a little more.

When we had a working plan, I asked Cody to show my nine o'clock appointment into my office.

Chapter 14

The attractive woman sitting in a blue armchair made me think of old black-and-white gumshoe movies adapted from novels by Chandler, Hammett, Spillane.

Amelia Poole looked like Sam Spade's new client: glamorous white female, late thirties, short brown hair, no bling on her ring finger.

In place of a cigarette holder and a fox fur around her neck, Ms. Poole gripped an iPhone and had a fine necklace of gold chains and diamonds at her throat.

'Looks like you pulled an all-nighter, Mr. Morgan,' Ms. Poole said with a quick grin, stashing her phone in her handbag. 'I know because I just pulled an all-nighter myself.'

'I'm sure yours was more interesting than mine,' I said, flashing on Del Rio's bedroom with its military mattress and plain white walls.

Amelia Poole had a pretty smile, but it was forced. Her eyes were somber.

Why had she come to see me? Was she being sued? Stalked? Did she need me to find a lost child?

I knew from her dossier that Amelia Poole had bought and renovated three old hotels in choice locations into first-rate, five-diamond Poole Hotels. I had been to the rooftop bar at the Sun, stayed a couple of times at the Constellation in San Francisco. I agreed with the ratings.

Also in her dossier was mention of some unsolved robbery-murders in her hotels and a couple others that had sent a shiver through the California Chamber of Commerce.

The cases were still open, but tourist slayings didn't make the front page in the current political-economic climate.

'I'm sorry, Ms. Poole, but I wasn't told why you wanted to see me.'

'Jinx,' she said.

'I'm sorry?'

'Call me Jinx. That's the name I go by.'

'I'm Jack,' I said.

I poured coffee, and she told me that she had

heard about Private and that she knew we were damned good. She continued to look nervous, as if she were trying to keep whatever was bothering her under wraps.

Ms. Poole played with her diamonds, took snapshots of me with her darting eyes.

I said, 'So, what brings you to Private?'

And then she blurted it out. 'A guest was killed in his room at the Sun last night. I haven't told anyone. I haven't even reported it to the police. I'm scared. This is the third guest who was killed in one of my hotels, and I don't know what to do.'

Chapter 15

Hotel robberies weren't rare, but hotel murders were. Jinx Poole told me that all of the murder victims – three at her hotels, two at other California hotels – were businessmen, out-of-towners traveling alone.

'The police are worse than hopeless,' she said. 'The last time they came, they shut the place down, closed the bar for forty-eight hours. They interviewed every guest, freaked out my staff, and didn't come up with a suspect, not one!

'Our bookings tanked. We've got empty rooms in high season – I mean, who's going to stay in a hotel where someone was murdered?

'Jack, I'm desperate. People are being killed. I don't know why. I don't know who is doing this. But all I have are these hotels. I need your help.'

I wanted Jinx Poole to have the LAPD work the crime and hire Private to set up an airtight security system going forward – but the woman was getting to me.

She was vulnerable, but she was bravely working hard to solve her problem. I liked her. I understood her feelings. Completely.

Still, we didn't have the manpower to take on a multivictim crime spree on the wrong side of law enforcement. We were booked to the walls, and now our number one job was finding whoever killed Colleen Molloy.

I asked Jinx questions, hoping that her answers would help me decide what to do.

She told me that the dead guest at the Sun was Maurice Bingham, midforties, lived in New York, an advertising man who was in LA on business.

No sounds of a fight had been reported. The hotel staff knew Bingham. He paid his tab by credit card, didn't make extraordinary demands. He wasn't due to check out until tomorrow – which was promising news.

It meant that no one was looking for him yet in New York and that it was reasonable to assume that this early in the day, with the 'Do Not Disturb' light on, housekeeping hadn't yet found his body.

'Tell me about your security system.'

'Cameras are in the hallways, of course. And we have a few at the pool.'

'I need you to shut down the cameras on the murder floor for about an hour so we can get in and out. Can you do that?'

'Yes. So you'll take the job?'

'I can't make any promises, but we'll check out the room and the body. Call it a consultation.'

'I understand.'

'I'll need access to the room.'

Jinx Poole opened her handbag, took out a master key card, and handed it over.

'I need a place to stay for a couple of nights. I can check into the Sun,' I said.

'Great idea,' said Jinx Poole. 'The Coppola Suite is empty. Be my guest.'

Chapter 16

With the exception of city dumps, hotel rooms are the worst places on earth for gathering forensic evidence. Even in five-diamond hotels, DNA, fibers, and fingerprints from a few hundred previous guests will all be present.

But it was worth a try.

Carl Mentone, a high-tech geek known at Private as Kid Camera, manned the laptop with the Delta program that mapped out the Bergman Suite from every angle. My laptop came to life with streaming video that bounced off a satellite and delivered crystal images to my office.

As if I were standing inside the doorway, I watched Sci, Del Rio, and Emilio Cruz enter the suite, the Kid giving me the video tour of what $1,500 a night looked like in a Beverly Hills hotel.

Gold silk curtains framed the windows. Cozy

furniture was grouped around a mahogany table, and good art hung on the walls. The lamps were standing upright. Throw pillows were in place. There hadn't been a struggle. So what had happened here?

By the desk, looking like a particularly grotesque sculpture, was the dead man.

Sci stooped beside the body of a white male wearing dark trousers and an unbuttoned white shirt. His hair had been recently cut, businessman-style. He wore a wedding band. His wrist was white where his watch used to be.

Sci peered at the dead man's neck. 'A garrote,' he said. 'It's a thin, coated copper wire, commonly found in hardware stores. The victim tried to claw the wire loose but failed.'

'Has he got ID?'

'Wallet's gone,' said Sci.

Cruz leaned in toward the lens and said, 'Jack, there's no problem with the lock. The victim either let the killer in or had a key. There's an open bottle of Chivas on the table, two glasses. Dregs of scotch in the glasses.'

'Let's go into the bedroom,' I said.

The Kid led the others, set the laptop on a table. The quality of the images I received was so fine that I could see the weave in the jacquard bedspread lying in a tangle on the floor. Pillows had also fallen to the carpet. The sheets were twisted toward the foot of the bed.

'Looks like sex to me,' said the Kid.

Sci set his scene kit on the floor and went to work running an alternate light source with variable wavelength filter over the sheets.

'Right you are. We've got sex,' he said.

'No wallet in here either,' said Cruz, pawing through a small pile of personal items on the night-stand. A ballpoint pen, spare change, rental-car keys.

The Kid took his webcam into the bathroom. I saw swim shorts and goggles on a hook behind the door, toiletry kit on the vanity, towels on the floor.

Emilio Cruz took a seat on the closed toilet lid and spoke into the lens.

'Jack. This killer was cool, maybe professional. There's no sign of a fight. Like I said, the dude let his killer into the room. Had a drink with him, and then maybe he said or did something to piss the guy off. The killer got behind him and strangled him. Bingham never had a chance.'

Chapter 17

While I viewed the Bergman Suite from ten miles away, Cody kept me informed about incoming phone calls, his messages popping up on the left-hand side of my screen.

I typed back to him as I watched Del Rio scrutinize the scene for evidence. He was only feet from the deceased when something caught my attention.

'Kid, what's on the desk?' I asked.

'Phone book,' he said. 'Local type. Beverly Hills.'

He moved in tight on the phone book, which

57

was open, face down, and lifted the book with his gloved hand, showing me the pages the book was opened to.

I could read the print as clearly as if the book were in my hand.

The category was Escort Services.

'Interesting,' I said. 'Maybe Mr. Bingham paid for the party in his bedroom.'

'Could be, Jack. You think a woman did this? She had to be strong to strangle a guy this size, though.'

'Sci, you've got Bingham's prints?'

'Yep. Couple hundred other prints on the furnishings that could belong to anyone. DNA up the wazoo.'

'Need anything else?'

He shrugged as if to say, 'What can I do?'

If the cops found us at this crime scene, Private was out of business.

'Okay. I'm calling it time to go,' I said.

My people snapped their cases closed and headed to the door. The Kid turned the camera on his own intense, heated, twenty-two-year-old face and said he was going to shoot the hallway and the exits.

When the video feed was shut down, I called Jinx Poole.

'Jinx, you can turn the security cameras back on. And I need a backup of last night's tape of the fifth floor.'

'I already made you a copy.'

'Fine. Leave it for Rick Del Rio at the desk. It's time to have housekeeping discover the body and call the cops.'

'Oh, no.'

'It's got to be done.'

I was telling my new client that I'd be at the hotel's bar tonight, when another of Cody's instant messages popped up on my screen.

The text read, 'Lieutenant Tandy and Detective Ziegler are here to see you.'

My stomach dropped to the basement. What was this about? Did they have a lead in Colleen's murder?

I told Jinx I'd see her later.

Then I asked Cody to send in the bad lieutenant and his partner.

Chapter 18

Mitch Tandy and Len Ziegler entered my office and looked around as if they'd just bought the place at a blind auction and were seeing it for the first time.

I showed them to the seating area, and Tandy and I sat down. Ziegler wanted to look around – at the view, the bookshelves, the photos on the wall.

Tandy said to me, 'Why did you mess with the crime scene, Jack? It's just a little too neat, you know what I mean?

'Girl dies in the middle of the bed with her shoes on. Doesn't leave any fingerprints, not even in the bathroom. In my experience, the girl always uses the bathroom.'

The cops hadn't come to bring me news. They were here so that they could read me, scare me, catch me in lies or deviations from what I'd told them last night.

'She was dead when I got home,' I said. 'What you saw is what I saw.'

'Jack, I'm a fair guy.'

Aside to self: No, he wasn't. He was a poisonous human being. His unexamined lack of self-respect and his envy of others made him that way. Dangerous.

He said, 'Tell me what really happened so you can get ahead of this thing.'

'Mitch, I told you everything I know.'

'Okay.'

He leaned over the coffee table, straightened a stack of books, and said, 'Now I want to give you my theory of how this girl got killed. Colleen Molloy was in love with her boss. That's not in dispute. Not unusual. Happens all the time. But this particular girl, Colleen, she tried to kill herself after you and she broke up. That's a fact. Attempted suicide tells me she was emotional. Unstable.'

'Slashed her wrists about six months ago,' Ziegler said from across the room. He had a pocket knife, about six inches long, pearl handle. He tossed it in the air and caught it. Did this throughout as he went on. 'Colleen survived. Quit her job and moved back to Ireland, returned to LA two weeks ago to see friends.'

'That's right,' said Tandy. 'Now we're up to date. So last Wednesday, Colleen has lunch with you at Smitty's, but whatever went down wasn't

60

entirely satisfying to Colleen. She knows your schedule, when you'll be coming home, et cetera, and last night she takes a cab and shows up at your house uninvited.'

His tone was even. No rough stuff. No threats. But Tandy was laying out his theory, that it was me, and he was setting it in concrete.

I said, 'You've got a good imagination, Mitch. But Colleen had a boyfriend in Dublin. She wasn't stalking me.'

'Not saying she was stalking. She wanted to talk. She knew when you'd be home. She uses her access code and waits for you. You walk in. She says, "Surprise, I still love you, Jack. I'll always love you."'

'Tandy, you're making me sick, you know that? Nothing like that happened. Colleen and I were friends. Just friends.'

'You were tired when she showed up. That's what you told us. That long flight, all those layovers. You're not in the mood for the needy ex-girlfriend, but maybe you try to be a gentleman.'

Ziegler was on his feet, knife in his back pocket now, moving around toward my desk. I got up, went over to my desk, shut down my computer, and said over my shoulder to Tandy, 'Nothing you've said is true.'

'It's just talk,' Tandy said pleasantly. 'Just talk. When I've finished telling you my theory, you can tell me yours.'

Chapter 19

Tandy enjoyed spinning his 'Jack Morgan did it' storyline. He sat there on my couch, smelling like curry, moving his hands around as he got to the crux of his 'theory.'

'So now the girl is crying, I don't know, or maybe she's giddy. Was that it? Was she all lit up? Manic?

'At any rate, Colleen is worked up. And here's where it gets painful,' Tandy said. 'You say you're not interested in her anymore. "Thanks but no thanks. Let's be friends." And she doesn't want to be rejected by you again. So she's going to kill herself. That'll show you.'

What Tandy was saying hurt. Yes, Colleen still had feelings for me. I'd still had feelings for her too.

I said, 'Very theatrical, Tandy, but as I keep telling you, I didn't do it.'

'So, as I'm telling *you*, Colleen knows where you keep your gun. She goes for it. You struggle with her. The two of you fall on the bed – and the gun goes off. Hair trigger. *Bam. Bam. Bam.* She takes it in the chest.'

'That never happened.'

'Colleen has been shot. It was an accident. I know you well enough to say that, Jack. But you can't change the events. And now this poor mixed-up girl is dead in your place. Sure, you could dump the body, but you gotta ask yourself. Maybe Colleen told a friend she was coming to see you; you can't know. Or maybe you're scared. You panic. You lose it–'

'Ziegler, stay away from my desk.'

'What's wrong, Jack? Is there something here I'm not supposed to see?'

Ziegler meandered over to where I was sitting with Tandy. I imagined putting my fist into his jack-o'-lantern grin.

'If I've got this wrong, make me a believer and I'll work with you,' said Tandy.

So polite. Covering his ass because the chief of police and I were friends.

I said, 'My turn to talk?'

'You're on,' Tandy said.

'Okay. You've got to look at me for the crime. I get that. But you're wasting time. I've been set up. Someone doesn't like me. He kidnapped Colleen, got her to give up her key fob, and used her print to open the door. He brought her into my house and shot her in my bed.

'The shooter left before I got home. He figured that the cops wouldn't look very hard at anyone but me. That was his plan.'

Tandy smiled. 'But here's where your story goes off road, Jack. There's a gap in your timeline. You left the airport at five-thirty-something. Hit some traffic. You arrived home at six-thirty. So you say.

'At eight you call the chief. Time passes as Fescoe calls the precinct and the call goes down the line. By the time Ziegler and I arrive, almost two hours have gone by since you walked in your door.

'You had plenty of time to shoot the girl, get rid

63

of your gun, throw it and your security system hard drive into the ocean. Then you shower, shampoo – hell, you could have had your guys come in and do a professional cleanup, like it never even happened.'

I said, 'Mitch. The card reader shows Colleen's key was swiped at six. At six, we were just getting clear of the airport.'

'So what? She waited for you. Or you screwed with the security program after the fact. Look, I'm a fair guy, Jack. You tell me. Who do you think killed Colleen?'

'I don't know. I wish I did.'

'Well, think about it. I could use your thoughts on this. Why don't you put together a list of your enemies. I'll check them out. Personally. Okay? Call me, Jack. Anytime.'

'Thanks, Mitch. I will.'

I shook hands with the cops, then Cody walked them out to the elevator. Bastards. It was absolutely clear. I was going to have to find Colleen's killer.

It was up to me to save my own life.

Chapter 20

I swallowed some aspirin, then stole a few minutes at my desk, attacking the backlogged avalanche of e-mails and phone calls. When I looked up, Sci was sitting in front of me. I hadn't heard him come in. Had he materialized out of the air? If anyone could do that, it was Dr. Sci.

'What the hell?'

'I've been thinking,' he said.

Sci was wearing a red shirt, tails out over his jeans, bowling shoes up on the edge of my desk. He had the face of a cherub and the brain of Einstein – if Einstein had lived in the digital age. Since he hadn't, Dr. Sci was arguably smarter.

'Thinking about what?'

'I've got news, Jack. I can't find anything good in it.'

'Let's hear it.'

'I spoke to someone.'

Along with Sci's advanced degrees, he'd worked in the LA crime lab for a couple of years, doing rotations in ballistics, fibers, DNA. He had deep contacts at LA's hundred-million-dollar lab, and his tech friends were close to the cops. One of those friends was hoping that Sci would bring him over to Private.

We had agreed long ago that Sci would give me off-the-record intel and I wouldn't ask any awkward questions.

'There was a witness,' said Sci.

'Someone saw Colleen?'

'Someone saw *you*, Jack. On the beach. A neighbor, Bobbie Newton. You know her?'

'Slightly. She lives a couple houses down the beach.'

'She said she was jogging last night and she saw you on the beach, talking on your phone. She waved at you and you waved back.'

'When was this?'

'Approximately six something. She doesn't

know for sure. She wasn't wearing a watch.'

'She saw *me?*'

'So she says.'

'For Christ's sake, Sci. I wasn't on the beach.'

I didn't want to have the thoughts that were turning in my mind, but the tumblers were clicking into place. A riddle. Who was me yet not me?

My womb-mate. My enemy.

'*Tommy,*' I said. 'What else?'

'The fingerprints in your room were all yours.'

'We're identical,' I said.

'Yes, but your fingerprints aren't identical. They're shaped by the currents in utero. Tommy's prints will be a little different than yours.

'Jack, you really think Tommy killed Colleen?'

'He knows her. He knows me. He could get close to her and he could force her to give up her key, press her finger to the biometric lock. He has motive. He fucking hates me.'

Chapter 21

I took the stairs down to Justine's office, which was directly under mine. Three associates were arrayed around her semicircular desk: Kate Hanley, Lauri Green, and our sixty-year-old virtual chameleon of a sleuth, Bud Rankin.

Justine was assigning them to collect background on all five of the hotel murder victims.

She looked up, her long dark hair hanging to her shoulders, framing her lovely face.

She thanked the troops and they filed out.

I sat down and told Justine about Noccia's offer that I couldn't refuse.

'We're not taking the job, are we?'

'I don't want to.'

'I vote, no, no way, and not in a million years.'

'Duly noted.'

'Now, bring me up to date on Colleen.'

About me and Justine. A few years back, we bought the beach house where I live as a future wedding present to us both. We made a lot of love and had a lot of good times in that house. Truth is, we fit together in every way – but one.

I don't like to spill my guts. And Justine is a shrink. I'm guarded, or what she calls 'too well-defended,' and she gets pissed off. Then she closes up. And she stays mad.

We were lovers. We broke up, then tried it again with the same result. After we split up the second time, more than a year ago, I started seeing Colleen – and Justine dated a guy not half good enough for her.

A few months ago, we were both unattached again, and we'd started dating in a noncommitted way. I still couldn't open up. She still couldn't tolerate that. So for good and for bad, not much had changed.

Sitting here looking at her, I couldn't understand why I had to talk when Justine could pretty much read my mind.

She was peeling back the layers even now.

'There's a witness,' I said. 'A neighbor says she saw me on the beach around the time Colleen was killed.'

'I don't understand.'

'It wasn't me.'

I leaned back in the chair without breaking eye contact with Justine.

'God. It was Tommy,' she said.

We were both thinking about my evil twin. Would he dare set me up to be tagged for Colleen's murder? Did he really hate me that much?

Justine asked, 'What do you think happened?'

'I think she was walked in, maybe at gunpoint. She had the electronic gate key, and whoever killed her pressed her finger to the pad at the door.'

'Colleen still had access?'

'She's not the only one. You've got access too.'

'I'm sure it's a pretty big crowd of insiders,' Justine said, swiveling her chair away from me.

'I'm not hiding anything from you,' I said – but that wasn't entirely true.

She swiveled back. 'You're not telling me everything, Jack.'

She was right. But the part I was leaving out had nothing to do with Colleen's murder.

'Colleen and I had lunch. There was a lot on my mind. I had to catch a plane. She was in a good mood. She seemed okay to me, but we didn't talk about anything important.

'Someone has gone to a lot of trouble to set me up.'

'Okay.'

'I'm staying at the Sun for a few days. Until the cops give me back the house. Let's have dinner there.'

'Not tonight,' she said. 'I have plans.' That was

a lie.

She said, 'What are you going to do about Tommy?'

'What would you do?'

'I'd go back in time and loop the umbilical cord around his neck. Make a slipknot and pull it tight.'

'I wish I'd thought of that.'

We both laughed loud and long.

It felt really good to laugh.

Chapter 22

Cruz and Del Rio were in Del Rio's office, working their case, comparing the phone calls Maurice Bingham had made from his cell phone with the list of escort services in the Beverly Hills yellow pages.

'I had a girlfriend once who was an escort,' Del Rio told Cruz.

Cruz said, 'This I've got to hear.' He moved his chair to Del Rio's side of the desk so he could see the computer screen.

'I signed up for the "special-gift daddy" section,' Del Rio said. '"Special-gift girls" want a hookup with one guy until they earn enough from him to buy this so-called gift.

'Her name was Chelsea,' Del Rio went on. 'Very pretty, very smart. On her way to becoming somebody in the fashion business when a friend of hers told her she could make a bundle being an escort. That she could make enough to get her business off the ground.'

'When was this? Before or after you got out of the joint?' Cruz asked.

Cruz was a good-looking guy of twenty-seven. Dark hair pulled back in a short ponytail. Clean shaven, dressed in black. Former middleweight boxer. Former cop and investigator for the DA. Currently a senior investigator on the fast track at Private.

'After. I was so starved for a woman by that time, I can't tell you. A kiss could send me to the moon,' Del Rio said.

'Here's our match,' said Cruz, pointing to the number on the screen. 'Bingham called an escort service called Phi Beta Girls.'

Del Rio tapped the name of the escort service into his browser, and a website filled the screen.

Cruz read the sales pitch at the top out loud: '"Beautiful girls of every ethnicity. Not just beautiful but very intelligent," blah, blah. "Each one loves her work as an escort," har-har. "Matched by our placement experts." Oh, sure. Matched to your credit card, more like it.'

Del Rio said, 'Chelsea wanted implants, so, you know, took about three dates for her to pay for those, and then she wanted another "special gift." She wanted a *car*. I didn't have a spare fifty grand, so Chelsea dumped me for a gift daddy who owned a luxury-car dealership. Now she drives around town in a Bentley.'

Cruz laughed. 'Not bad for a few hours' work.'

'You woulda thought my looks and my fine skills in the rack would've meant something to

70

her,' Del Rio said. 'I was a definite keeper.'

'You're not still hooked on this girl?' Cruz asked.

'Yeah. She was the love of my life,' Del Rio said. 'I'm kidding, you jackass. Chelsea was a ho.' He laughed and turned his attention back to the screen. 'Okay, Phi Beta lists about a hundred escorts. Look at these girls. Jessie. Six hundred an hour. Two-hour minimum. Three grand for an overnight. "Diana, Playboy Bunny, a known celebrity..."'

'Here's Phi Beta's address,' said Cruz. 'Let's take a ride.'

Chapter 23

Del Rio got out of the passenger seat of the Mercedes fleet car. He walked between the six-foot-high concrete gateposts dripping with flowers and up the crescent-shaped brick drive to the glass front doors of the Beverly Hills Sun.

The doorman opened the door, and when Del Rio got to the desk, he said to the girl in the black suit with the choppy hair, 'There's a package waiting for me. Rick Del Rio.'

The girl, name of Amy Kang pinned to her jacket, said, 'May I see your ID?'

Del Rio thought that Cruz could come in here and say the same thing and the girl would pout and hint around for his phone number. If he looked like Cruz, or like Jack, for that matter, he could own the world.

He showed the girl his driver's license. She ducked under the black marble and came up with a sealed manila envelope with his name on it.

He said, 'Thanks, little Amy,' swiped the package off the countertop, and a moment later got back into the car with Cruz.

As the car shot west on Wilshire, Del Rio slid the CD into the tray of the dash 'puter and booted up the twenty-four-hour-long surveillance video of the fifth floor of the Sun.

The video was time dated, so Del Rio fast-reversed to Sunday afternoon, five o'clock, put it in fast-forward, and watched people getting in and out of the elevators, walking woodenly up and down the hallway, taking the one-way exit up to the pool deck.

'Christ,' he said to Cruz as the car took a right onto Westwood Boulevard. 'They call this security?'

'Did ya see that?' Cruz said.

'What?'

'I think that was Sandra Bullock shot past me like I was stopped at a light.'

'The exit to the roof. Supposed to be one-way only, but it's two-way if someone holds the door open for you. Like they all do.'

'Red Jag,' said Cruz. 'I'm pretty sure that was her.'

'Room 502 is kinda far from the camera,' Del Rio said, 'but I think this is our vic. Gets out of the elevator, walks away from us. Dark pants. White shirt, sport jacket. Yeah, that's him. He was alive at five-thirty-eight last night.'

'Let me know when you see the hooker,' said Cruz.

'Here she comes,' said Del Rio. He slowed down the fast-forward to normal speed, watched the female come off the elevator. She was wearing a short blue dress, a push-up bra hoisting her ta-tas out of the neckline. Envelope-style purse. Stilettos. Long brown hair.

'I'll give her a nine,' Del Rio said, his eyes following her as she went to 502 and knocked on the door.

Maurice Bingham opened it. The girl smiled, said something, and went inside. Time: six-thirteen.

'Couldn't see her face too well,' Del Rio said. 'But it matches with the timeline. He made the call to Phi Beta at what time?'

'Five-forty-five.'

'Right. So the girl arrives at six-thirteen. Let's see how much time he paid for.'

Del Rio cranked up the speed, watched people doing little Charlie Chaplin walks up and down the hallway, taking the exit door up to the roof, coming down from the roof, then at eight-fifteen, the blue-dressed girl left 502 and headed to the elevator.

Del Rio froze the tape at the best shot of the girl's face, which was not too good. But it was something.

'That's it,' said Del Rio. He attached the still shot to an e-mail and sent it to Jack, copying himself. 'Bingham got his last two hours of bliss,' he said to his partner, 'before doll-face killed him. Roll credits. Go to black.'

73

Chapter 24

Phi Beta girls operated from a small three-story house on Hilgard Avenue in Westwood, also known as UCLA's Sorority Row. Cruz pulled the Mercedes up to the curb next to a gatepost where the Greek letters phi beta gamma were screwed into the wood.

Cruz and Del Rio got out of the car and went through the gate and up a path to the front door of the old earth-colored stucco house. Del Rio pressed the buzzer.

A twenty-something Hispanic male answered the door, hair slicked back, eyebrows waxed, wearing flip-flops, spotless white yoga pants, and a white tunic.

Cruz flashed his badge. Gold shield in a leather wallet. Looked like the real official thing.

'Can I help you?' the man asked.

'We need to see the lady of the house. Susan Burnett. We're investigating a homicide.'

'Please wait here,' said the guy in white.

Cruz said, 'Might be better for us not to stand on your doorstep.'

'I'll be back in a minute.'

Cruz turned away from the door and stood with his chin tilted up, hands clasped behind his back, taking in the smells of jacaranda and banana trees, while Del Rio stood on one foot, then the other until the guy came back.

'Miss Burnett will see you now.'

The madam or booker or whatever she called herself had a cappuccino complexion and a Pilates build. She was jogging on a treadmill in the gym at the back of the house, jalousie windows overlooking the pool.

Del Rio thought she was smokin', probably a hooker herself a few years back. He tapped her shoulder and she turned, hit the power button, and got off her Nordic Track. Draped a towel around her neck.

Del Rio held up his badge again, not saying he was with the LAPD but implying it. No crime called 'implying,' although impersonating a police officer was a felony.

'I'm Rick Del Rio. This is my partner, Emilio Cruz. We're investigating a homicide. We're not here about your business activities. This is all about a homicide last night at the Beverly Hills Sun.'

'We may have a witness, a girl who works for you,' Cruz said. 'If I can put my CD into your player.'

'Oh, my. You're very forward, Mr. Cruz,' said Susan Burnett, giving him a dry smile. 'Let me see that badge again?'

Cruz took it out of his jacket pocket, preempting her indignation by saying, 'We're investigators with Private. We're not going to talk to the cops. If we don't have to.'

Burnett said, 'I should call the cops just to see what you would do.'

'You want to turn this little inquiry into an official case, go ahead,' said Del Rio. 'The tabloids will love it.'

Burnett thought for a second. 'I wouldn't want to play cards with you, Mr. Arroyo,' she said. 'Follow me.' She went up a spiral staircase ahead of Cruz and Del Rio.

Chapter 25

The room where the business was done had once been a bedroom but was now outfitted with a conference table. Three women over thirty, and in one case over fifty, sat around it wearing headsets, each with a Sony workstation.

Travel posters were on the wall. St. Barts. Cozumel.

The older woman was making flight arrangements, saying, 'I've got you two first-class bulkhead seats on the fifteenth, Mr. Oliver.'

Decent cover for an escort service, Del Rio thought.

The two other women just stared back at him.

Burnett was saying, 'So, let's have that CD.'

Del Rio handed it over and went to stand behind Burnett as she brought up the video.

'What am I looking at?'

'May I?' Del Rio asked.

He leaned over Burnett's shoulder and reversed the CD to the time and date just before the hooker got off the elevator.

He hit 'pause' and said, 'We have Mr. Maurice Bingham entering room 502 of the Sun at five-thirty-eight last night. He called Phi Beta seven minutes later, at five-forty-five. Call lasted three minutes. Credit card transaction at five-forty-eight for twelve hundred dollars plus tax, payable to Phi Beta Girls.'

'I don't know that Mr. Bingham was a client,' Burnett said. 'Our clients don't always use their real names.'

'Bingham used his real name and a real Master-Card. We checked. What you're looking at is the fifth floor at six-thirteen p.m. last night. This is Mr. Bingham's "date,"' Del Rio said, hitting 'forward,' showing the girl walking to the room.

'Miss Cutie Patootie was in 502 for two hours on the nose, and now' – he sped up the action – 'we see her leaving. Bingham was never seen alive again.'

Del Rio froze the image of the six-hundred-dollar-an-hour escort, then ejected the CD and handed it to Cruz.

Del Rio said, 'We need to talk to this girl. If she didn't do it, you're done with us.

'I want to remind you that if you don't help us, we will turn this disk over to the cops. So let's play nice, okay, Susan? Who is the girl in the blue dress? And how do we find her?'

Chapter 26

'Party girl at two o'clock,' Cruz said to Del Rio. They were parked illegally on Charles E. Young Drive, right outside the UCLA Geffen School of Medicine.

'You go first,' Del Rio said. 'I'll bring up the rear.'

The escort's name was Jillian Delaney and she was between classes, coming up a path between the brick buildings and geometric-shaped greens of the campus.

Cruz walked up to the pretty young woman, brunette, slim, walking by herself, books in her arms, knapsack on her back. He showed her his badge and the girl backed up a couple steps, looked around for a way out, but by then Del Rio was behind her, his badge in his hand.

'What's this about?' she asked.

'Last night. Room 502 at the Beverly Hills Sun,' said Cruz.

'Oh, my *God*,' she said.

Talk about a deer in the headlights. But, Del Rio thought, here again was where playacting got tricky. You couldn't say to the girl, 'Get into the squad car. Let's discuss this downtown.' Just had to bluff and hope for the best.

He and Cruz walked Jillian Delaney toward a bench, and Cruz introduced them as 'investigators.' They all sat down.

The girl was petite without the five-inch heels and looked much smaller sitting between them than she had on the surveillance tape. She weighed maybe a hundred and ten pounds with her clothes and shoes on.

Cruz said, 'Let me hold your books, okay, Jillian?'

The girl looked at him. 'Are you arresting me?' When Cruz didn't answer, she handed them over.

Del Rio said, 'Please hold out your hands.'

Jillian did as instructed, and Del Rio checked out her perfect nails, pale pink polish, no chips, no breaks. She turned her hands over, palms up.

There were no cuts or bruises on her baby-soft hands.

Even if she'd been wearing gloves, there should have been some physical signs from strangling a man to death with a wire.

'What classes are you taking?' Cruz asked.

'I'm studying emergency medicine,' said Delaney. She folded her arms and furrowed her brow as she looked at Del Rio.

'What were you doing at the Sun?' Cruz asked. 'Don't bother to lie, Jillian. We have a record of the phone calls from the john to Phi Beta. And we have you on time-dated surveillance tape. So how about it? Tell us about your date last night.'

Chapter 27

The college girl who was moonlighting as an escort still looked afraid, but she was getting her stuff together, Del Rio thought. In fact, she was getting huffy.

'So, are you going to charge me with prostitution? Because look,' Jillian said to Del Rio. 'I'm putting myself through medical school. That's not an insignificant achievement. In a couple of years, I'll be saving lives. You really want to get in the way of that?'

'We're not here to bust you for your extracurricular activities,' Del Rio said. 'Tell us about the guy last night.'

'Maurice? He was nice enough. No rough stuff. Nothing weird. He just wanted a good time. The kind he doesn't get at home.'

'What happened after the good time?'

'Nothing. All the financials are handled through the service.'

'And how did he seem to you when you were leaving?'

'He was happy. He said maybe he'd see me again next time he was in town. I said good-bye. The limo was waiting for me out front.'

'There's not going to be a next time for Bingham,' Del Rio said. 'He's dead. He was murdered.'

'But how could that...? Oh, no. After I left?'

'Did he get any phone calls while you were there?' Cruz asked. 'Did he say he was worried about anything? Did anything about him seem unusual?'

'Nothing at all. Clean guy. Wore tighty-whities and a wedding ring. A normal date in every way.'

Back in the car, Del Rio put the CD into the player and ran it through all the way to the end once more.

There were long stretches of emptiness, interspersed with individuals going to their rooms. And there were crowds of people who got off the fifth-floor elevator on their way to the roof, their bodies blocking the camera's view of 502.

Someone in one of those crowds had to have gone down the hallway, gained access to 502, and killed Bingham. But Del Rio never saw the door to 502 open after Jillian Delaney left.

'You think that girl could have killed the john?' Del Rio said to Cruz.

'I don't see it.'

'Me neither. Someone came to his door and Bingham let him in. I'm calling this lead a dead end,' Del Rio said.

'Maurice Bingham's last ride,' said Cruz.

Chapter 28

Cruz spoke into his phone to someone named Sammy as he headed the car toward the Hollenbeck area of East LA. When he hung up, he said to Del Rio, 'I've known Sammy his whole life. I didn't expect to know him this long. I thought by now he'd be just a memory in his grandmother's mind.'

Cruz knew a lot of Sammys. He could have become a Sammy himself. He had grown up in Aliso Village, a notorious, crime-ridden housing project in the Flats. He became a boxer, went pro, was a middleweight on his way up until a bad concussion made him see double for a while. Maybe it cleared his mind enough for him to look for a way out.

He joined the LAPD for a year, then Bobby Petino – DA Petino – his second cousin twice removed, gave Cruz a job in the investigative branch of his office. A hard-ass ex-cop named Franco became his boss, and Cruz learned. He saw a lot of dead bodies, got to know people, learned what to look for to help the DA make a case. In three years, Franco was working for him.

Two years back, Jack Morgan told Bobby Petino he needed another investigator, and Petino gave Cruz another break of a lifetime. Sent him to meet Jack.

It was a good fit.

Working at Private, teaming up with Del Rio, a genuine war hero, was the greatest job Cruz ever had. The only thing better would be to head up Private, LA – if or when Jack promoted himself off the line.

Del Rio asked, 'So, this Sammy. He's on our payroll?'

'No. Strictly freelance.'

Whittier Boulevard was a four-lane strip through a broken neighborhood. In daylight, vendors stood outside their shops, hawking T-shirts and tube socks, and families shopped with their little kids. At night, drug dealers worked the dark places. Hookers worked their strolls.

But there was no time of day or night when a Mercedes looked right on Whittier. Right now, it was sticking out like patent leather shoes at a hoedown.

Cruz would have liked to be driving a Ford. A gray one. Like he had when he was working for the DA. But Jack had a weakness for good-looking cars.

Cruz said to Del Rio, 'I want to park the showboat in the Kinney on South Soto. Two blocks up.'

After the car was stowed, Cruz and Del Rio walked past a minimall with run-down shops and barred windows. Crossing the street at Johnny's Shrimp Boat, Cruz saw Sammy waiting outside La Mascota Bakery.

Sammy was thirty, white, shaggy black hair, goatee, turquoise boots with pointy toes, enough metal piercing his face to start a hardware store.

Sammy said, 'Who's this?' indicating Del Rio.

'This is Rick. He's my partner. He's cool,' Cruz said.

Sammy was high, eyes dilated, agitated, but ready to do a transaction.

Cruz said, 'You hear anything about a big shipment of Oxy and shit, came into town last night?' He took a twenty out of his pocket, held it out with two fingers.

'A 'frigerated van?'

Cruz nodded. 'What do you know about it?'

Sammy snatched the twenty, flashed a gappy smile, said, 'I know that the van is locked up, off the street. There's a lot of chatter 'bout how to get in on the score.'

Cruz said, 'That tip wasn't worth twenty cents, Sam.'

'I can't tell you what I don't know, man. Hey, you know Siggy O?'

Cruz said, 'I know Sig. I haven't seen him in a while.'

'Another twenty and I can text him for you,' said Sammy.

Chapter 29

Siggy O was a black kid, six-foot-plus, two hundred pounds, Rasta hair tied back with string. A third-generation druggie, the kid was hooked before he was born.

'Duuude,' Siggy called out to Cruz. 'Been so long, man. How you shaking?'

They clasped hands, patted each other's backs, Siggy going into boxing stance, doing some feints and jabs and footwork, Cruz catching the jabs with the flats of his hands. Siggy said, 'I saw you on the TV, man. On Sports Classics, you know? The MGM Grand. You and Michael Alvarez. He put you down so hard in the eighth round.'

'I know,' said Cruz, laughing. 'I was there.'

'You good now?'

'I'm good. How 'bout you?'

'I've been straight for thirty-eight days,' Siggy told Cruz. 'I'm in a program. I don't miss a meeting,' he said. 'Very cute women there. They want to take care of me. But that's cool. I want to be taken care of.'

More laughing, and then Siggy said, 'So, whatchoo need, 'Milio?'

'We're looking for a van that was jacked last night. Shitload of pharmaceuticals inside.'

'It's air-conditioned? With vegetables and shit on the outside?'

'That's right,' Cruz said.

'I gotta live, bro. What's in it for me?'

'Fifty for the location. Two hundred more if we recover the goods.'

'Two fifty? 'Milio. There's millions in that truck, homes. Millions.'

Siggy worked Cruz up to a hundred in advance, and when Cruz gave him the money, he said, 'Warehouse on South Anderson. A flowerpot company, or, more like, looks like a flowerpot company. High-tech security all around. I hear the van is parked inside, and 'Milio, if you cut me in, I'll cut *you* in.'

'We're not going into the drug business, Sig. Thanks anyway. What else have you heard?'

'I heard the van was stolen from the Eye-talians and it's not going to stay in that warehouse too long.'

Cruz said, 'Thanks, Siggy.'

'Good seeing you, bro. You got my number now?'

'Give it to me.'

Siggy tapped his number into Cruz's phone. Then the two clasped hands, bumped shoulders. The big kid lumbered off down an alley.

And Cruz called Jack.

'We've got a lead on the van,' Cruz said. 'It's stashed inside a warehouse. Sure. Okay. Really? No kidding.'

Cruz told Jack where they would be and closed his phone. He said to Del Rio, 'Jack has a new guy he wants us to work with. He used to be a ballet dancer.' Cruz paused. 'Does that mean he's gay?'

'Haven't you ever heard of don't ask, don't tell?' Del Rio said.

Chapter 30

Del Rio had parked on South Anderson, across from the Red Cat Pottery warehouse. The warehouse was red brick that had been whitewashed a few times; whitewash was flaking off, revealing partial names of previous, now defunct, businesses.

From their spot on South Anderson, they could clearly see the loading dock around the corner on Artemus. There was a sixteen-wheeler parked in the bay, a guy with a forklift loading pallets into the back. A couple of brothers were on the sidewalk smoking, then they flicked their butts into the gutter and climbed up into the cab of the big rig.

At five in the afternoon, vans and small trucks were making their last drops in this mixed-use light-industrial area. Gates were closing, people leaving for the day.

Twenty minutes into their wait, Del Rio heard a motorcycle coming up the street behind him, then the motor cut out. In the rearview mirror he saw a guy get off the bike and disappear into his blind spot.

Del Rio heard the back door of the fleet car open.

He jerked around to see a guy get into the backseat with a black-and-silver helmet. He was about thirty, blond, blue eyes, five-ten, 160, and tight. Muscles rippled under his T-shirt.

Had to be the ballet dancer.

Dude reached a paw over the seat, said, 'I'm Christian Scott. Scotty. How ya doing?'

Del Rio shook his hand. 'Rick Del Rio. This is Emilio Cruz. My sidekick.'

Cruz said, 'Yeah, I kick him in the side from time to time. Nice to meet you, Scotty.'

'Thanks. You too. Is this the place?' he asked, looking out at the Red Cat warehouse.

'We've been told it is.'

'Have you checked it out?'

87

'Nah, we're just watching the paint fall off. They should be closing up in about a half hour.'

'Okay with you if I do a little reconnaissance now?'

'No problem,' said Del Rio.

Scotty got out of the car. There was a little spring in his step as he crossed the wide street, went over to the loading dock on Artemus, and shouted something up to the forklift driver.

The driver pointed to a door up a flight of metal stairs and Scotty waved at him, took out his phone, sprinted up the steps, and pulled the door open.

'I don't know if he's gay,' said Del Rio. 'A little bouncy on his feet, maybe.'

'Bet you a hundred this Scotty was a cop.'

'How do you figure?'

'I know eleven hundred cops. He feels like one of them.'

'Then I'll keep my money. And I'll ask him,' Del Rio said.

Another fifteen minutes had passed – Del Rio feeling uneasy that the guy had been in there for so long, wondering what Jack knew about him and how Scotty was supposed to fit into the team – when Scotty came around the corner, a piece of paper rolled up in his hand.

He looked both ways as he negotiated the street traffic, then he got back into the car.

'I inquired about a job,' he said, grinning. 'This is my application form. I got a little tour of the place.'

Del Rio was laughing inside, but he didn't show it. The kid was smart.

'What did you see?'

'Very decent security,' he said. 'Got cameras over the doors, wires in the windows. The van, gotta be the one we want. It's white, scraped all to hell on one side. Parked in the back northeast corner. I didn't want to be too obvious, but I walked by it.'

'Jesus,' said Cruz. 'You do a lot with fifteen minutes, dude.'

'Let's get this fifty-thousand-dollar ride off this block,' Scotty said. 'I got pictures.' He showed his phone. 'Maybe we can work up some ideas.'

Chapter 31

I drove the Lamborghini into my short stub of a driveway and swiped the key fob across the pad. The iron gates rolled open, and I saw a notice taped to my front door. I wasn't close enough to read it, but I knew what it said.

'Do Not Enter by Order of the LAPD.'

I turned off my engine and sat for a couple of minutes, trying to imagine my brother walking Colleen up to the door at gunpoint. I saw him jabbing a gun into her back, going into the house with her. And then I couldn't see any more.

Was Tommy so sick, so morally corrupt, he could actually kill Colleen? Honest to God, I didn't know.

I got out of my car and walked down the narrow side yard, along the fence and out to the beach. The sun was still bright at five p.m. Yesterday at about this time, someone had been readying Colleen for her last mile.

I headed south, parallel to the shoreline, passing two enormous houses and one small one that had resisted the real estate brokers and the bulldozers. The fourth house had a hybrid Victorian-contemporary design with a high profile and a wide deck.

It was where Bobbie Newton lived.

Bobbie was a gossip columnist, the queen of prime-time celebrity news, and the ex-wife of some Wall Streeter back east. She was sitting out on her deck, tall drink in her hand, feet up on the railing. She wore an open shirt over her hot-pink bikini, a white visor in her blond curls, dark glasses, and a Bluetooth cuddling her left ear.

She was talking and watching the waves.

I called to her and she took down her feet, sat upright.

'Bobbie – can I come up? I need to speak to you.'

'I'll come down,' she said. 'Call ya later,' she told whoever she was talking to. 'I gotta go.'

She set her drink on the deck and came down the short flight of wooden steps, holding on tight to the handrail.

I thought about my history with Bobbie. It had happened after my first breakup with Justine, way before Colleen. I thought it had ended okay – no-fault incompatibility. But when I found the envelope at my back door without a note, my key inside, it was a crystal-clear 'Screw you.'

Bobbie was combustible, and I didn't like that

about her. I'm sure there were a few things she didn't like about me. But we'd been neighborly since our split.

Now, as she crossed the beach and came toward me, seabirds flew up from the sand. And I saw from her expression that we weren't friends.

She put her hands on her hips and said, 'If you want to know if I told the police I saw you last night, the answer is yeah, Jack, I damn well did.'

Chapter 32

'I wasn't on the beach last night,' I told Bobbie Newton. She had taken off her glasses, and I was looking into her little bloodshot eyes. She drank early and often. Another thing I hadn't liked about Bobbie.

'I wasn't hallucinating,' she said. 'You were on your phone. I heard it ring. I ran by and called out to you, "Hey, Jack." You pointed to your phone, like, "I'm talking." And then you *waved*. That signature wave of yours.'

'What? You're saying I have some kind of … wave?'

'Like this.'

She lifted her right arm, cocked her hand back, fingers spread like she was holding a football.

I used to play college ball. Tommy didn't.

'Nobody ever told me I have a unique wave.'

'Yeah, well, I'm telling you. I've seen you wave, what? A hundred thousand times?'

91

'It was past six o'clock, Bobbie. That's what you told the police.'

'So?'

'The sun was going down. Maybe you thought it was me because you expected to see me. It wasn't *me*, Bobbie.'

'Tell it to the judge,' she said.

Bobbie raised her hand above her head, cocked it in a football hold, and trotted up the beach.

I stared after her. What the hell was she talking about?

I hadn't been on the beach the night I found Colleen's body in my bed. But Bobbie was unshakable. And as a gossip reporter, she was well-connected. She had to be the one who'd set the Internet wildfire naming me as the number one suspect in Colleen's murder.

I hiked back up the beach, twenty yards behind Bobbie, wondering if she'd actually seen Tommy, thinking he was me. Or had she seen *no one?*

Had she made this story up to show me payback is a bitch?

I walked from the beach to my driveway and got into my car. I took off, south on PCH toward Santa Monica. I wanted to see Colleen's closest friend. Through her, he'd become a friend of mine. I had to be with someone who knew her, felt what I felt, who would understand my grief.

My mind churned, and the next time I checked, I was on the 10 going east, not knowing if I was driving the Lambo or it was driving me.

But I knew exactly where to find Mike Donahue. I pictured him as I had last seen him, standing behind the bar.

Chapter 33

Mike Donahue's Tavern was an Irish pub with a restaurant that could have been transported from Galway or Cork and simply planted in Los Feliz.

When Colleen first came to Los Angeles, she was determined to get her citizenship. In the hours between quitting time at Private and going home to study, she stopped at Donahue's. It was where everyone knew your name, and nearly everyone in front of the bar and behind it had relatives in Ireland.

Mike Donahue came from a town only a few country miles from where Colleen grew up. He had gone to school with Colleen's father, and when they met, Donahue became an uncle to her in the City of Angels.

I was outside Donahue's Tavern, the red-painted, gold-lettered sign hanging above the doorway, patrons spilling out to the curb.

Inside, the place was throbbing with loud music and the shouts of customers trying to be heard. The horseshoe bar was packed three deep all the way around. There was a raucous dart game going on in the back.

Mike was at the taps, serving up the suds. He was a heavyset man with a thick beard and deep lines around his eyes and across his forehead, grooves that came from smoke and sun and laughter.

But when he lifted his eyes and recognized me in the doorway, I saw terrible sorrow there.

He threw a cloth down on the bar and came out from behind it. I lost sight of him as he worked his way through the crowd, then he broke through a knot of drinkers and approached me.

I never saw the punch coming.

I was taken down by a fist like a two-by-four. The pain in my jaw seemed to shoot to all points: my nose, neck, shoulder, out to my fingertips. When I opened my eyes I was staring up into a circle of angry faces. Mike's was one of them.

I wasn't welcome here.

I'd gotten it all wrong. And so had Donahue.

I was enraged – with everything and everybody. I wanted to strike, fast and hard. I could take Donahue. I thought I could take the three bruisers standing around him too. And if I couldn't, it might even feel good to take a beating.

Turn the emotional pain into the physical kind.

I struggled to my feet, and Donahue put his hand on my chest and pushed me into the wall. He said, 'You shouldn't have come here, Jack. I'm mad enough to do bloody murder in front of God and witnesses.'

I clenched my fists at my sides. 'Mike. I didn't do it. It wasn't me.'

'Is that your story, then?'

'Story? I was crazy about Colleen. Why would I want to kill her?'

'Maybe she was cramping your style, Jack.'

'Listen to me.'

I felt desperate for him to believe me. I grabbed

94

both his biceps and shook him, shouted into his face. '*I didn't do it.* But I *promise,* I will find out who killed Colleen. And I will hurt him.'

Chapter 34

I held an ice pack to my jaw with one hand, a Guinness in the other. Donahue sat across from me at a small table in his dark restaurant, a candle flickering between us. After twenty minutes of shouting at each other, I had managed to convince him of my innocence.

'Did I say I'm sorry, Jack?' Donahue said in his Irish brogue.

'Yes. You did.'

Donahue sighed.

'It's okay, Mike. I understand. And no harm done.'

A waiter brought my dinner, a plate of chops and chips, and put it down in front of me. I refused another drink, looking at my plate with two minds.

One, I hadn't eaten in a long time.

Two, I wanted to throw up.

The dinner was Donahue's peace offering, so I put down the ice and picked up my cutlery.

'She was sad,' Donahue said. 'We talked about this boyfriend of hers, in Dublin, and I think she loved him in a way, but he didn't make her heart race. You understand what I'm saying?'

'Not in love with him.'

Donahue nodded. 'Do you want me to cut your meat for you, boy-o?'

I smiled painfully, speared potatoes with my fork, and said, 'She didn't tell me that. She said she was happy.'

'Putting on a brave face, more like it,' said Donahue. 'Or maybe looking to see if you'd changed your mind. If you still loved her.

'But anyway,' he continued, 'I'd stopped worrying she was going to hurt herself. I never thought that someone would do this terrible thing to her.'

'Everyone loved her, Mike.'

'So *why?*' Donahue asked me. He thumped the table with his fists. China jumped. Beer sloshed. 'Why am I sending her back to Dublin in a box?'

I laid down my knife and fork, pushed my plate away.

'It had nothing to do with Colleen,' I said. 'Someone killed her to hurt me. Someone who hates me.'

'Who was it, Jack?'

'I don't know. Yet. I'm working on it. Whoever he was, he was a pro. He could have found a way to kill me without putting Colleen in the middle. But that wasn't what he wanted.

'He set me up so that I would get taken down one step at a time. First, this ... loss. Then humiliation. Then I'd be locked up for life. Or get the needle. That was the plan.'

'May the cat eat him. And may the divil eat the cat.'

'Copy that.'

We sat silently as the dishes were cleared.

When we were alone again, I looked into Mike's

sad eyes. 'I'm sorry, Mike. I'm the one who owes you an apology. If Colleen hadn't been involved with me, she'd still be alive.'

Chapter 35

I pulled up to the Beverly Hills Sun, Jinx Poole's flagship hotel, at just after ten. I stepped out of my two-hundred-thousand-dollar car looking as if I'd been dragged behind it for a couple of miles. I gave my car keys to the valet and checked in at the desk.

The clerk said, 'Mr. Morgan, I believe the woman on the red sofa is waiting for you.'

It was Justine.

Thank God.

I was so glad to see her, my eyes got wet. Thinking about stretching out on clean sheets, Justine lying beside me, of feeling her skin against mine, flooded me with relief.

But why was she here? I called her name. She looked up, and I crossed the plush and glittering lobby to her, saying, 'How long have you been waiting? Are you okay?'

I couldn't read her expression.

'What's going on, Justine?'

'It's just – we have to talk. Gloves off. Nothing but the truth.'

'Let's go to my room,' I said. I turned my head, pointed to my bruised jaw, and said, 'I've got to lie down.'

'You stink of beer. You were in a bar fight?'

'You don't miss a thing.'

'Sit down. Please. This won't take long.'

It didn't sound good, whatever was coming. I eased myself onto the sofa next to Justine.

'I'm just about brain dead. Maybe we should talk tomorrow.'

'Very little of your brain is required.'

I looked at her and she hooked me in with her eyes. I loved Justine. I loved her.

'When you saw Colleen last week, before you left for Europe – what happened?'

'We had lunch at Smitty's. I have a receipt somewhere. I haven't had time to go over my credit card bill.'

'Did you sleep with her?'

'Christ. You shouldn't do this. Do I ever grill you? Can't you just trust me?'

'Did you say "trust me"? I'll take that to mean it wasn't just lunch. Oh, Jack.'

She shook her head.

I threw up my hands. 'If you don't believe me about this,' I said, 'then what's the point? How can we work things out if you don't trust me?'

Justine got up, hooked the strap of her handbag over her shoulder, and without looking back, left the hotel through the revolving doors. I watched her through the glass. She gave her ticket to the valet and faced the street as he went for her car.

Justine could read me like an FBI polygraph. Lying to her was futile. I could chase after her, but what more could I say?

The valet brought her car, and Justine slid in behind the wheel, strapped in, and took off fast

98

down South Santa Monica.

This time I was sure I'd lost her. It wasn't what I wanted, but it was pretty much what I deserved.

Part Two

LOVE YOU,
LOVE YOU NOT

Chapter 36

The next morning, I walked from my office across the hall to the 'war room,' thinking about Colleen. I wondered what she'd been doing in her last hours, trying to see through her eyes how she'd been trapped by a man with murderous intentions. I imagined her horror when that gun – probably *my* gun – had been aimed at her chest, her killer taunting her before he squeezed the trigger.

I had a horrifying thought.

What if she'd believed her killer was *me?*

I stiff-armed the door, saw that the conference room was packed: Sci, Cruz, Mo, and Del Rio, arrayed around the black table, hunched over coffee, texting and phoning, looking up when I came in.

Associates filled the row of swivel chairs around the perimeter, buzzing about a hot case that had been resolved at four this morning when a team of Private investigators caught a runaway teen and her user boyfriend withdrawing funds from an ATM with her mom's bank card.

Justine's seat was empty. Justine was never late for a meeting. Had never been late in five years.

The chatter stopped as I pulled out my chair.

Cody brought in my Red Bull and a list of names.

'What's this?'

'Candidates for my job. I'm setting up appointments for you to meet the best three. Best three in my humble opinion.'

I nodded. 'Let's get started.' I introduced Christian Scott, said that Scotty had been with the Joffrey Ballet, suffered a knee injury, joined the California Highway Patrol as a motorcycle cop.

'Scotty was one of three guys who brought down a major doper, four hundred pounds of weed in the trunk. It was Scotty who pulled him over on a hunch–'

'A hunch and the rear of the car was sending up sparks on the freeway,' Scotty said.

'He's got good hunches and, I've been told, a pretty decent pirouette,' I said into the laughter. 'Scotty has just finished his six thousand hours as an investigator at California Casualty, so his license is in the mail.

'Stand up and show us your face.'

There was applause. Scotty stood and said he was glad to be here. Then investigator Lauri Green raised her hand and said, 'Jack, I gotta go in a minute. Just to let you know Mara Tracey is out on bail.'

Lauri was talking about our shoplifting movie star, made ten million a picture and still lifted a hundred-dollar sweatshirt from a boutique, attracting tabloid headlines, paparazzi popping up out of the shrubbery, and a publicized date next week in front of a judge.

Mara's husband had hired us to keep eyes on her. We discussed tailing Ms. Tracey, then Cruz got up and filled the group in on the dead businessman at the Beverly Hills Sun. He sketched in the backstory: the string of four other dead men in other hotels, and the dead-end lead to an escort service. He talked about research he was doing now, interviews with hotel staff, and so on. He was keeping himself in the background, he said, now that the cops were on the case.

He didn't mention the Noccias' stolen van full of boosted pharmaceuticals – I was keeping that one off-limits to the group.

When Cruz sat down, I tapped keys on my laptop and Colleen's photo filled the center flat screen on the wall.

My ears hummed and my heart rate shot up when I saw that picture. Only two days ago, Colleen had been alive and well.

I dropped my eyes to the keyboard, trying to get a grip on my emotions. When I spoke, my voice cracked.

'Most of you knew Colleen. She was most likely killed to torment me and to implicate me in her death.'

Del Rio said quietly, 'Dude.'

I swallowed hard and kept going.

'As you've probably heard, I'm not only the prime suspect, I'm the only suspect. Meanwhile, Colleen's killer is out there somewhere – laughing his ass off.'

Chapter 37

I leaned back in my seat at the conference table. I was aware of my colleagues looking at me as I stared at Colleen's face on the screen. Her expression was sunny, luminous, and it wasn't a portrait, just a snapshot for her ID card taken on her first day of work at Private.

I remembered how an hour after that photo was taken, Colleen was sitting outside my office, going through my mail. She had looked up when my shadow crossed her desk and said, 'Is someone wanting to harm ye, Mr. Morgan?'

'A dozen people I can think of. Why?'

She showed me a padded envelope marked up with red grease pencil, block letters reading, 'Time Dated Material. Open Upon Receipt.'

An arrow pointed to the pull tab. It wasn't ticking, but the envelope had no return address and the lettering looked insane.

We had evacuated the building, eighty of us standing out in the glaring sun on Figueroa while the bomb squad took the envelope out with a robot and x-rayed it in the bombmobile. The contents were shredded newspaper and a note, same red letters with a lot of rays coming out from the words 'BANGETY-BANG-BANG-BANG.'

Fingerprints were traced back to a repeat offender, Penn Runyon, a psycho who'd been incarcerated for the illegal sale of weapons and

106

had been released a few months before.

Runyon was interrogated, said he'd read about me in the paper, how I'd tracked down and brought in an escaped con who was a friend of his.

Actually, it was *Tommy* who had brought down Runyon's friend, not me.

Common mistake: Jack Morgan, Private Investigations. Tom Morgan Jr., Private Security.

Runyon wanted to know if he'd killed me. Really? You sent a nonexplosive paper bomb, buddy.

So Runyon got it all wrong.

Colleen, on the other hand, had gotten it all right. She was the best assistant I ever had. And more. I'd cared about her deeply.

I stopped reminiscing about Colleen and brought my attention back to the present. I said to my investigators, 'Colleen worked here at Private for over a year. We started going out. It wasn't a secret.'

'She was a great girl,' Del Rio said.

'Yes, she was. She was visiting friends here in LA and somehow she was captured or tricked, then murdered in my house.'

I talked about the terrible scene I had found in my bedroom, then turned the floor over to Sci, who looked fifteen years old in his pineapple-print aloha shirt, painter's pants, and tennis sneakers.

He read from a report citing the cause and manner of Colleen's death, homicide by gunshot to the heart. And he said that there was evidence that she'd had sex sometime before her death.

107

'We'll have the DNA profile later today,' Sci said.

I said, 'No matter what we find, the LAPD isn't going to buy it because we can't tell anyone that we processed the crime scene. So we'll have to use what we've found to trap the doer and then lead the cops to him.'

There were questions about the time of Colleen's death, where I was when it happened, whether the murder weapon had been found, and if the killer had written, called, or left a message for me to find.

'The killer was a pro. This was a well-planned murder, and it can only have been a setup to frame me. We're working overtime until we nail the shit who killed Colleen.'

At that, the door to the conference room opened and Justine came in, tall, slim, elegant in navy-blue suit and cream-colored silk blouse.

'Sorry,' she said, taking the seat next to mine.

'We're just wrapping up,' I said. 'You want to report on Danny Whitman?'

'Possible new case,' she said to the group. 'Young movie star with a criminal zipper problem. I'm meeting him today.'

'Thanks, Justine. Anyone else?'

'I need a few minutes with you, Jack,' Justine said. 'If you can spare the time.'

I adjourned the meeting. And after the room emptied, I closed the door and sat down next to Justine.

Chapter 38

Seven years ago, after I returned from the war, I went into therapy, saw an excellent guy, Josh Moskowitz, who specialized in vets like me. That is, ex-military who'd gone through bloody hell and weren't adjusting too well back home.

Like many of us, I had night terrors.

I kept hearing those boys in the bombed-out rear section of the CH-46, screaming as the helicopter went up in flames.

Dr. Moskowitz had an office in Santa Monica, a little office in a tall building on Fifteenth Street. I didn't know it then, but Dr. Justine Smith worked in the same building.

I ran into her in the elevator one night, was thunderstruck in a way that you can't explain by describing hair and eyes and curves. I rode up ten floors just staring at her before I realized that the elevator wasn't going down.

She'd laughed at me, or maybe she just enjoyed seeing me go from zero to smitten in sixty seconds. Next time I saw her, I held the elevator door open, told her my name, and asked her to have dinner with me.

She said okay.

It was as if she'd cupped her hands around my heart.

Justine was a couple years younger than I was and maybe a decade wiser. Beautiful. Smart.

Worked in a mental hospital most of the week, had a private practice and saw a handful of patients on Mondays and Wednesdays.

We had dinner together at a little Italian place out at Hermosa Beach, and I talked through it all. I told her more about myself over that one dinner than I'd told her since. I sensed she was a safe person, trustworthy, accepting, and she must have thought I was the kind of person who could open up.

Later she said that I was like a clam. With a rubber band around my shell. I laughed it off, said that she'd now met my real self when not in crisis. By the time we had that conversation, we were already in love.

Now Justine sat in a leather chair, swiveling gently from side to side. I came around the table and sat down next to her. Her face looked stiff.

She was so angry at me.

'I have a job offer,' she said. 'A good one.'

'That didn't take long.'

'I'll complete my cases, including the new one if it's a go. I didn't give an answer yet, but that's just negotiation. I'll probably take the job.'

'I know this is a long shot, Justine, but imagine that I'm actually innocent here. Imagine that I never needed you more than I need you now.'

'Okay, Jack. Now you imagine that I just don't care anymore.'

Chapter 39

Justine was at the wheel of her midnight-blue Jaguar, Scotty in the passenger seat beside her. They turned off Melrose, passed under the arched gates of the Harlequin Pictures lot, and stopped at the guard booth.

Justine said to the guard, 'Justine Smith to see Danny Whitman.'

The guard ran his finger down a list on his laptop, did a visual match between the picture on Justine's driver's license and her face. He said her name into a phone, then turned back to her and said, 'Take a right, then left on Avenue P. Keep going until you see 231 on the corner of Eleventh.' He waved her through.

Scotty said, 'I've seen everything Danny Whitman has ever made. I saw his first film, *Badger*. Played the kid with the wild dogs? I knew he was going to take off.'

Justine flashed him a smile, slowed for a speed bump, took a left at the second intersection, and headed down a street lined by soundstages and two- and three-story white stucco buildings once used as studio homes for writers and actors, now mainly production and administration offices.

Her mind ranged as she drove, thinking about Jack, about Jack with Colleen, about how she was sure he'd lied about what had happened at lunch with Colleen. Justine also thought about the job

111

she'd been offered, which wouldn't be as good as the one she had now – except for one important detail. She wouldn't be seeing Jack five days a week.

Scotty was looking at her. She recalled what he'd said. Excited about working with Danny Whitman.

'We don't have a check yet, Scotty. But if we take the job, bet you ten bucks you'll be happy when it's over.'

She lifted the visor, downshifted, and said to Scotty, 'He's just starting this new film. Action-adventure, of course. The question is, will he get to finish it?'

'*Shades of Green*,' said Scotty. 'I read about it. Spies and counterspies in the twenty-first century.'

'Okay, I'm impressed,' Justine said. 'You do your homework.'

Justine's mind flicked over this assignment. She wished she hadn't told Jack she would do it. It could drag on. And the one thing you could absolutely count on with movie stars, it was going to get messy.

Please, God. Let this one be the exception to the rule. Let this one be easy.

'Sorry?' she said to Scotty. He was speaking again.

'So you missed the meeting. Jack was talking about Colleen Molloy. People seemed to like her.'

'She was adorable,' Justine said. 'What number is that?' Scanning the nearly identical white buildings.

'*Adorable.* Interesting word choice.'

'Genuine. Funny. Unaffected.'

'And you dated Jack too?'

'Boy, you're quite the background checker,' Justine said. 'There it is. On the corner. Now listen, Scotty, I don't even know if we're going to get this job, so just watch and listen.'

'I can do that.' He grinned. 'But you didn't answer my question.'

Justine braked the car at the curb, turned off the engine, and looked at the new guy on the team. He was young, regular features. Probably a little German, a little Brit, a little American Indian. Nice looking and kind of full of himself, but he was also curious and dogged. Good-natured too. He was going to be a fine addition to Private. As long as he stayed optimistic.

'Jack breaks hearts,' Justine said. 'That's what he does. I don't even know if it's his fault. Women want to fix Jack, and they think they can. I thought I could too.'

She reached into the backseat for her shiny leather handbag, opened it, and found a makeup kit in there. She took out her lipstick and a mirror, put fresh color on.

Scotty said, 'So it is as Jack says. He was framed.'

'Jack is a lot of things, but he's not a killer.'

Justine snapped her handbag closed and opened the car door. Scotty was saying, 'But wasn't he in the war? Wasn't he a marine?'

Chapter 40

Scotty stood beside Justine as the door to the building marked 231 opened and a barefoot Johnny Depp look-alike introduced himself as Larry Schuster, Danny Whitman's manager.

Justine shook Schuster's hand and introduced Scotty. They stepped inside, the air smelling of pot, burned toast, and air-conditioner coolant.

Scotty looked around the spiffy modern office, hardwood floors, round chairs in bright colors, desktops off to one side of the room littered with fruit baskets, stacks of scripts, half-eaten breakfasts on trays, and opened gift bags with watches and other loot spilling out, cornucopias of excess.

On the walls were framed posters of Whitman's four previous action films, every one of them a blockbuster.

A man of about forty came toward Scotty and Justine. He had a crumpled brow and graying hair. He wore a wrinkled blue linen shirt with a monogrammed pocket, the sleeves rolled up. 'I'm Mervin Koulos,' he said. 'MK Productions.'

Koulos was the man who was making *Shades of Green*.

Justine handled the introductions, and they all took seats, the manager, the producer, Justine, and Scotty, in the squat chairs around a low table that made them all look like kids.

A girl came out and asked if anyone wanted

anything. Schuster said, 'Pass,' Koulos said, 'Fiji, no ice.'

Justine said, 'Coffee, please. Milk and sugar.'

Scotty took a pad and pen out of his pocket. 'Okay if I take notes?' he asked, and everyone nodded yes.

Scotty understood that Schuster, the manager, was the hands-on guy responsible for the actor's career, took 10 percent. The producer, Koulos, the scruffy older guy, had a big stake in whether or not the film got made. No wonder he looked worried. His star was in trouble.

Justine was explaining how Private worked, their methods, billing, et cetera, and what she proposed to do in this case. Both the manager and the producer agreed to 'Whatever it takes to contain this thing.'

Everyone stood up. Schuster went to the back door and held it open, saying, 'Dr. Smith, I think you should talk to the rest of the guys.'

Chapter 41

Scotty was the last one out the back door. He saw a basketball hoop high on a wall forming an angle with another building. The asphalt court still had lines on it showing where to park.

A basketball sailed across Scotty's sight line and went into the basket. Someone yelled, 'Yeah!'

It was a guy about five-ten, short brown hair, shirtless, barbed-wire tattoo around his right biceps. He was grinning, triumphant, and he looked about twenty-two.

Schuster said that the guy, now dribbling the ball, was Rory Kovaks, Danny's school pal from Nebraska. They'd grown up together, Rory coming out to LA to keep Danny company.

Schuster pointed out Alan Barstow, Danny's agent at CTM, a big talent agency with top, top clients. Barstow was in his thirties, medium height and thin.

Last, Schuster pointed out Randy Boone, assistant to Danny, and Kevin Rose, Danny's fight coach, all members of the Whitman entourage.

Schuster called out, 'Time out, people. We have guests.'

The ball swished into the net and bounced off the asphalt onto the grass, where the various players gathered around. Schuster told the four guys that Justine and Scotty were from Private and that they had been hired to do damage control.

Some stood, some sat on the ground as Schuster gave Justine the floor. Scotty hung around at the sidelines, just watching.

Justine said hello to everyone and introduced herself as a senior investigator at Private. 'The tabloids are watching for anything that they can exploit,' she told them. 'Katie Blackwell, the girl in question – well, her parents have probably also hired private investigators. They could be following Danny, and any of you who are associated with him, just to find a questionable moment they can blow up, leak to the tabs, and use to tar Danny's character.

'It's critical to Danny's case that he, and really all

of you, keep the party down until after his trial. That means no drugs, no drinking, and especially no girls.'

'Sure, and no eating with your mouth open, no bare feet when entering this establishment,' Kovaks said.

Rose, the fight coach, said, 'Dr. Smith, no offense, but we don't need a PI dogging us. Come on,' he said to Larry Schuster. 'You can't be serious.'

Scotty watched Justine, fingers interlaced in front of her, smiling. She said, 'Mr. Rose, it's all of you or none of you. If you can't go along with us on the terms, we'll leave in peace. No problem.'

Scotty saw the job going south. Not what he wanted at all.

He said to the whiners gathered around the ball court, 'What's going on here? Danny Whitman needs our help. He's being tried for the rape of a fourteen-year-old girl, isn't that right? You want to help him with that? Or are you goons just out to suck his blood?'

Chapter 42

After Schuster chilled down the ensuing scuffle with a garden hose, after Justine said, 'Scotty. *Watch* and *listen*,' Justine sat with Scotty and Danny Whitman in the music room on the third floor with its nice view of the Harlequin lot, one of the oldest film studios in Hollywood.

Danny was at the piano, plinking out 'Lay Down Sally.'

Justine said to the movie star, 'Tell us what happened, Danny.'

Danny sighed, came off the piano bench, fell into a cushy chair. Justine thought how much younger he looked than he did on the big screen. And he was bigger too, well proportioned, the famous dimple on one cheek, thick brown hair, could have been a high school ball player, although he was twenty-four.

She noted the number written in ballpoint pen on the cleft between thumb and forefinger of his right hand. Looked like a phone number.

Danny said, 'This is going to sound idiotic, but I honestly don't know what happened. We were at Alan Barstow's house. My agent?'

Justine nodded. 'I met Mr. Barstow.'

Danny said, 'Alan was having a party. There were a lot of girls there. Dozens. I woke up in my own house in my own bedroom – alone. Next thing, before my alarm went off, the police are at the door. They say this ... Katie Blackwell is lodging a complaint against me.'

'You say her name like you didn't know her,' Scotty said.

'I know who she *is*,' said Danny. 'I've seen her around, but that's all. I didn't date her. I sure don't know her age. I can't even say she was at Alan's that night, except that my boys saw her hanging on to me.'

'And Katie's story is what?' Justine asked.

'She says we left the party together, that I made her have sex with me in my car, and that I

118

dropped her off at her front door. You should see my car. Sex in that thing is physically impossible. But she has a girlfriend who says she saw us drive off together. Otherwise it would be strictly he-said, she-said.'

'Did Katie go to the hospital?'

'No. In her deposition she said she was embarrassed, took a shower, didn't say anything to her parents until the next morning, then they called the police.

'Here's the thing,' Whitman went on. 'I was so stoned that night. If I did it, I deserve to be punished. But I really don't think I had sex with that girl. I'm pretty sure I would have remembered.'

Justine said, 'Pretty sure?'

'It's all very sketchy. I just remember laughing. Falling down. Girls pawing me. That's it. And none of my boys saw me leaving with Katie.'

'She could've been lying to get out of trouble,' Justine said. 'If she was out late, that sort of thing.'

The star pulled on his lower lip, looking to Justine as if he was searching his memory, not making up a story.

Then again, Whitman was an actor.

'Dr. Smith, I might as well tell you, this wasn't the first time I lost track of myself. My life's kinda unreal, you know? I was just a kid when I came out here. A normal kid. Here there's too much of everything and my time isn't my own. Half the time it feels like someone else is running my life and I have no control over what happens to me.'

Justine said, 'All I want to do is help you so that

things don't get worse, so that you can get through your trial without any more bad press. Do you want me to advise you?'

'Yes. Hell, yes. Tell me what you want me to do.'

Justine thought, *Oh, crap*. Danny was likable and now she was responsible for keeping him clean and celibate so he could make the hundred-million-dollar blockbuster.

She handed Whitman two cards, saying, 'Here's how to reach me and Scotty. It's really simple. Don't go out with girls at all. That way there will be no pictures, no headlines. Don't spend the night out with anyone. Go to work, go home alone, keep your phone on, and stay in touch with us.'

'Done deal.'

'Whose number is on your hand?' Justine asked.

'I don't know. This is what I'm talking about. Look. It's gone,' Whitman said, spitting on his hand, wiping it against the leg of his jeans.

'Okay,' Justine said. 'Starting now, pretend you're a monk. And we'll dig up what we can on Katie Blackwell.'

Chapter 43

The staircase at Private was a wide, winding spiral, five stories wrapping around the core of the reception entrance on the ground floor. The stairs were inspired by the cross section of a nautilus shell. And by a stone staircase I once walked

120

down at the Vatican.

I was going up the stairs to my office when Sci loped up the steps, caught up with me on four, and said, 'Hold on, Jack.' He had a sad look on his face.

My guts took the down elevator.

'What is it, Sci?'

'You're looking at the bad-news messenger,' he said. 'Bruno just called.'

Bruno was Sci's friend, the high-level tech at the city lab, the one with cop connections who hoped that Sci would one day bring him over to Private.

We walked past Cody into my office.

Sci dropped into a chair, put his feet up on the edge of my desk, and said, 'Between us, okay? Or else we're going to have to hire Bruno. Lose a good contact at the lab.'

'Go ahead. No, wait. I want Justine to hear this.'

'Are you sure?' said Sci.

'Absolutely.'

I got Justine on the interoffice line. She said she'd be right up, and in a minute she came into my office, barely looking at me. She took the chair next to Sci.

Sci said, 'The LA crime lab found semen in Colleen's body. The DNA is consistent with yours.'

'Come on,' I said.

Justine didn't say it, but I could read it in her face– *Why am I not surprised?*

Sci went on, 'And apparently the cops have a timeline for the murder. Here's what I've been told. On the day it happened, Colleen used her

121

credit card to buy gas and a few random pur-
chases at the Sunoco on La Cienega. She had
lunch alone at the Newsroom Café on North
Robertson, and her car was just found at the
adjacent parking garage.'

I was seeing it as Sci laid it out. I tried to block
out the issue of the semen in Colleen's body.

'Cops have dumped your phone records, Jack,'
said Sci. 'Your landline was used during the time
period when Colleen was killed, and you say you
weren't home.'

'The killer used my phone?'

'Yeah. Seems like he used it to call a number
that was answered and then disconnected after
two seconds. That call was to Tommy's cell.'

'*Christ.* What the hell does that mean?'

What *did* it mean?

'That semen,' Justine said. 'If Tommy had sex
with Colleen, the DNA would be the same.'

'Right,' Sci said. 'His DNA and Jack's are
identical.'

'So the cops are saying what? I had sex with
Colleen, killed her, and then called my brother?
Or we killed her together?'

'Jack, what I know is that Mitch Tandy wants to
get you for this, and if he can get Tommy too it's
a very big day for Tandy.'

Chapter 44

Tommy.

I had to face it. My goddamned brother could have been involved in Colleen's death. Had he gone insane? Had he killed Colleen to hurt me?

I thought back to the break that had divided us for good. It had happened when Tommy and I were in the ninth grade, fourteen years old.

April Lundon was a year older.

She was charming and flirtatious and spontaneous. She could walk on her hands and ride a horse bareback, and she'd been to Paris. She'd had a French boyfriend the summer before and knew bedroom French.

She liked to walk between me and Tommy with her hands hooked into the backs of our pants. She said she liked us equally – and we were both crazy for her. April wouldn't choose.

We agreed, Tommy and I, that only one of us could have the girl. April set the terms, a kissing contest. She would be blindfolded. The best kisser would win. And there was the implied promise that the winner would take *all*.

We were testosterone fueled and cocky. The idea of a 'kiss off' was delicious. We both thought we would win, and we never considered the consequences. It never occurred to either of us to just walk away.

The competition was on for a Saturday morning, and a dozen kids showed up at the beach behind the juice bar to cheer us on in this wicked and daring contest.

April kissed Tommy, then she kissed me. I put my whole heart into that kiss, as if I would never kiss a girl again. April picked me.

Then, best two out of three, she picked me again.

Tommy didn't forgive April and he didn't forgive me. Our dispute was encouraged by our father, who would favor one of us, then, for no reason we could see or understand, favor the other. He was unpredictable and cruel.

Our bitterness escalated, got dirty, got physical, and lived on after April Lundon was in college, married, a mother of four. Continued even after my father gave me fifteen million dollars and the keys to Private.

Continued even after he was dead.

So there was bad history between Tommy and me, but could he, would he, get revenge by committing murder?

I thought he was capable of it.

But I didn't know if he had done it.

I stared through Sci and Justine, thinking that I'd go to his office, drag him out, do whatever it took to get him to talk.

I called to Cody, 'I need Del Rio and Cruz. Now.'

But Justine reached across my desk and put a hand on my arm.

'Wait,' she said. 'Wait until you have enough evidence to box Tommy in.'

Chapter 45

Jack Morgan's multimillion-dollar crime lab took up the entire lower level of Private: twenty thousand square feet of cutting-edge forensic laboraory, regarded as one of the top independent labs in the country. A service for Private clients, Private's lab was also a profit center, hired by police departments across the country when they needed fast results and only the most advanced technology would do.

Dr. Seymour Kloppenberg, Private's own Dr. Sci, was the proud head of this lab, but right now he and Mo-bot were in Mo's office, a dark cave of a room that Mo liked to call her 'cozy hole.' She was burning incense, had scarves draped over the lamps, and photos of her husband and kids saved screens on the dozen computer monitors banked above her desktop.

The local news was on video six, tight close-up of a talking head reporting on the sensational 'Murder in Malibu.'

Sci reclined and rocked in a swivel chair, but Mo was on the edge of her seat, visibly angry and agitated. An accomplished warrior on a multi-level, real-time online combat game, Mo sometimes felt the lines blur between game and reality.

The feeling was coming over her, that rush of being in a warrior frame of mind.

As she watched the reporter speak to the camera, Mo assumed her avatar's personality, thought about weapons in her arsenal, and assembled her virtual army.

The reporter staring back through the screen was Randi Turner, who had been a fixture on Channel 9 for the past couple of years. Turner said to the camera's eye, 'Jack Morgan, CEO of Private Investigations, is widely viewed as the prime suspect in the murder of his former lover and personal assistant Colleen Molloy.'

Pictures of Jack flashed on the screen, and then shots of Jack, his arm around Colleen, running through rain from a restaurant marquee to his car. After that, there was a film clip of them at a Hollywood party, whispering and laughing.

Turner spoke throughout the slide show.

Turner said, 'Jack Morgan's father was the late Thomas Morgan, convicted of extortion and murder in 2003, died in prison in 2006. Like his father, Jack Morgan is said to have links to organized crime.'

Mo had had enough.

She sprang up from her chair and yelled at the TV, 'Links to organized crime? Paid off his brother's gambling debt, you mean.'

'Take it easy,' Sci said. 'All this means is that the press is reaching. If they had something on Jack, they wouldn't need to refer to his father. They wouldn't have to imply anything.'

Turner spoke from the high-def screen on the wall above Mo's desk. 'Sources close to the police tell Channel 9 that physical evidence found on the victim implicates Jack Morgan, but the nature of that evidence is being withheld from the press.'

'Damn you. Die, bitch!'

Sci grabbed the remote from Mo's hand and shut the TV off.

Mo said, 'I could cut off her head, slice her below the knees, and leave her standing in sections. She wouldn't even know she was dead.'

'Maureen, emotion is counterproductive.'

'Jack could *never* have killed Colleen.'

'No, he couldn't, he didn't, and he won't get charged. This is just the free press at work, churning the news.'

'Oh, and you're saying no innocent person has ever gone to prison? That never happens?'

'What do you say? What if you put all this energy into working the case?'

'Sure, I will. But you and I both know,' Mo-bot said, 'the only thing that can save Jack is a confession from the killer. A confession that includes an explanation of how he got Jack's semen into Colleen's body.'

Chapter 46

I went through my voicemail as I drove.

I listened to a message from an edgy Carmine Noccia, heard from Del Rio and Scotty, then got an update from Cruz about the murder at the Beverly Hills Sun. I talked at length to our Rome office, during which time Justine returned my call. I called her back and got her voicemail.

127

'I'm on the road,' I said. 'I'll try you again later.'

At just after eight p.m., I pulled into my driveway. I was undoing my seat belt when a police cruiser drove up behind me and parked on the shoulder of the highway. The cruiser's grill lights sent bursts of color across the gates and the stucco wall.

The lights came on in my mind too. I'd been driving on autopilot for the past forty minutes, had driven myself home, although I hadn't meant to come here at all.

The squad car door slammed behind me. I buzzed down my window, and a flashlight beam blinded me so that I could only see the patrolman's silhouette.

'License and registration, please.'

I couldn't swear to it, but I was pretty sure I hadn't been speeding. I got my license out of my wallet, handed it out the window, reached across the seat to the glove box, and located my registration. Handed that out too.

'I'll be back in a minute,' said the cop.

I waited. Stared at the yellow tape and the notice on my front door. I listened to the crackling and chirping of the cop's radio, remembering how two nights ago, right about this time, I'd gotten out of the car right in this spot.

I'd signed the voucher, said good night to Aldo, passed my fob across the gate card reader, entered the house, and stripped down as I made for the shower.

A couple hours after that, I was being grilled by two hardened LA cops who'd determined I was guilty of killing Colleen before I'd said a word.

As I waited for the cop to come back to the car, I thought about being interrogated that night. Detective Tandy's theory, part of it, anyway, seemed plausible.

Had Colleen come to my house to surprise me?

I could see her doing that. She would have known it was risky, but it was in her character to take a chance that after all we'd had together she could change my mind.

I pictured Colleen curled up in a chair in my living room, waiting for me to arrive. Maybe she'd heard a car stop outside the gate.

I could see her going to the window, peering out into the dark, hearing the whirr of the gates rolling back. Maybe she'd opened the door, called out, 'Jack?'

Had someone said, 'Hey, Colleen.'

Had he looked just like me?

Had Tommy caught her by surprise, backed her into the house, made her lie down on the bed? Maybe Colleen went for my gun – she knew where it was. But she wasn't fast enough. Wasn't strong enough. The gun was snatched out of her hand. And she was shot three times.

Did Tommy really do that?

Another set of images spooled out in my mind's eye. In this scenario someone had been tailing *me*.

Say he was watching when I left Colleen's hotel room the week before. He knew me. He knew Colleen. He wished me harm, and he'd come up with a plan.

I saw Tommy.

Let's just say he'd kept his eye on Colleen while

I was in Europe. At some point in that four-day period, he'd kidnapped her, and an hour before I was due to land at LAX, he'd restrained her somehow and driven her to my house. He'd used her gate key, pressed her finger to the biometric lock...

My thoughts were interrupted by a car door slamming behind me. I heard the cop walking back to my car.

The flashlight beam was pointed at my face again as he handed me my identification.

'Mr. Morgan, do you know why I stopped you?'

'No. I live here. You know that, right? This is my house.'

'This is a crime scene. Why are you here?'

'I need a change of clothes.'

'That's not happening, Mr. Morgan.'

'Okay,' I said. I started up the engine. It roared.

But the cop wasn't letting me go. Not yet. He scrutinized my face from behind his light.

I understood why he'd stopped me.

The cops were watching my house in case the killer came back to the scene of the crime.

The cop looked at me as if that was just what I'd done.

Chapter 47

Jinx Poole's flagship hotel was set like a diamond tiara at the top of the intersection of South Santa Monica and Wilshire.

I drove my Lambo around the generous, curving driveway to the front doors of the Beverly Hills Sun, handed my car keys to the valet, and went directly through the busy marble-lined lobby to the elevator bank.

A gang of partygoers broke around me, and when they had dispersed, I got into the elevator. I leaned against a cool stone-paneled wall as it rose to the fifth floor, where Marcus Bingham had been strangled to death and where I was staying until my house was mine again.

I headed toward my room, but instead of going in, on impulse I opened the fire door and walked up a flight of stairs to the bar on the roof.

The air was cooling down, and looping strands of pin lights twinkled like stars, illuminating a scene rich with possibilities of sex with a stranger or maybe even romance.

A jazz trio was playing 'Polka Dots and Moonbeams' at the far end of the deck, the music wafting across the swimming pool. Couples flirted at the bar, leaned toward each other on the chaises around the pool. Flaps were closed on the white canvas cabanas.

I stood at the edge of all this hazy, hedonistic optimism, then took a seat at the freestanding bar. I asked the bartender, 'What am I having?'

He looked at me, then answered by pouring me a double Chivas straight up.

I'm not a big-time drinker. But if I ever needed hard liquor, this was the night.

I lowered my head so that there was no mistaking my purpose at the bar. I didn't want company. I wanted oblivion.

But I felt someone's eyes on me. When I looked

up, a woman at the end of the bar was staring at me intently. She was in her late twenties, dark hair tied back into a ponytail, the lines of her slight frame camouflaged by loose clothing that was too dark for California and too big for her.

The woman looked familiar, but I didn't know her. I looked away, got the bartender's attention, and ordered another double.

When I looked up from my drink a few minutes later, the woman was gone.

Chapter 48

Two young business guys in neon-colored shirts sat down in the empty seats at the end of the bar. They ordered screwdrivers, talked about the stock market and their shrinking expense accounts that wouldn't cover a free weekend at the Beverly Hills Sun.

I blotted out their voices by concentrating on the music and the glowing scotch in my glass. I thought about Sci's report of that two-second phone call made from the landline inside my house to Tommy's cell phone at around the time of the murder.

That call was bad for me because it seemed to establish that I had been in my house when the crime went down.

But I hadn't made that call.

I hadn't called Tommy, so ... had he called himself from my phone to make it seem that I had been home?

Or had Tommy commissioned a hit?

Had Colleen's killer called Tommy from my house to tell him that Colleen was dead? Job done. Had Tommy been right outside on the beach, and that's who Bobbie Newton saw, thinking Tommy was me?

I sat on that barstool, but in my mind I was driving to Tommy's house. I wanted to confront my brother, to beat the truth out of him. And then I wanted to keep beating him until he didn't look anything like me. So that, guilty or not, he could never play my double again.

But Justine was right.

I needed proof. Without it, the semen in Colleen's body would be enough evidence to convince a jury that I was her killer.

I emptied my glass, left cash on the bar, and took the stairs down to the fifth floor.

I turned toward my room and again I noticed the woman who had been sitting at the bar a half hour before. Now she was on the far side of the elevator bank, twenty feet away. Her back was turned to me and she was fumbling in her handbag as if looking for her key.

I had twenty-twenty vision, and as a pilot I'd been trained to see anomalies from the air: a puff of dust, a moving shadow, a glint of steel ten thousand feet down in the dark.

I noticed this woman, but I blocked out that something was wrong with her attitude, her posture, her looks – something.

I walked away from her. I put my card key into the slot, opened my hotel room door – and felt a stunning blow to the back of my head.

I went down.

When I came to, the pain radiating from the back of my head was dazzling. I recognized the sunburst patterns on the carpet under my chin. I was on the floor of a room at the Beverly Hills Sun.

I closed my eyes, awoke to the shock of ice water in my face. The woman I'd seen at the bar and then again in the hallway was stooping over me, her hands on her knees, and she was cursing. I didn't understand her thick Irish accent, but I knew her eyes.

They were Colleen's eyes.

I said, 'Colleen,' and she began cursing again. Through the pain, and as my vision cleared, I saw that although this woman resembled Colleen, she was older.

'Siobhan?'

The cursing intensified.

I pulled myself up into a sitting position and screamed back into her face, 'I don't understand you. Shut up, shut up, shut *up*.'

'Aym nah shuh'in' up, Jack-o,' Colleen's sister shouted into my face. 'Nah 'til ye tell me why you kilt 'er.'

Chapter 49

I'd been beaten twice in the past twenty-four hours and both times by people who had loved Colleen. First Donahue had clocked me. He'd also apparently told Siobhan where to find me. And now I'd been clobbered by Siobhan.

The couch was a beauty, eight feet of down-filled cushions. I took a seat and put my feet up on the coffee table next to the sap Siobhan had used to knock me down.

Siobhan was tough, but she brought me a pillow, then took a bottle of water out of the bar fridge and gave it to me. She sat in the chair across from me and stared at me.

'Start talkin',' she said.

I did. I told her repeatedly that I hadn't killed Colleen. I explained where I'd been when Colleen had been shot, and I told her how much I cared about her sister.

'You made love to her,' Siobhan said accusingly. 'Colleen called to say you took her to bed before you left Los Angeles. Do you deny it?'

'No, I don't.'

'You were fooling with her.'

'I loved her. Just not enough to give her what she wanted,' I said.

I thought about Colleen's last birthday. We'd gone to dinner at Donahue's, sat at the same table where I'd sat with him last night. Donahue and a gang of waiters had brought out the birthday cake and sung to Colleen.

She had started out very happy that night.

I had known that, after a year of going out, what Colleen wanted for her birthday was a ring.

I had let her down. The best I could do had hurt her, terribly.

'You loved her? Then I don't understand "not enough,"' Siobhan said. Her lips trembled. Tears slid down her cheeks. 'Why would you have taken her to bed if you meant nothing by it?'

'Why did you sap me?'

'I had to do it.'

I paused to let her words stand alone. 'I missed her, Siobhan.'

I wanted to say more, but nothing I said would make sense, even to me. It had been a mistake to sleep with Colleen. If I hadn't gone back to her hotel with her, maybe she'd still be alive.

Siobhan struggled to interrogate me through her grief.

'And so, if you didn't kill Colleen, who did? Aren't you supposed to be good at this sort of thing – investigating murders?'

Siobhan was sobbing now.

I stood up, reached out my arms to her.

She shook her head no.

'It's okay,' I said. 'It's okay.'

She came to me and I held her as she cried.

'Find the bastard. You owe that to Colleen.'

'If it can be done, I'll do it.'

'I miss her,' Siobhan choked out. 'I loved her so much. She and I were best friends. Never a cross word. No secrets. I don't know how I'm going to go on without her.'

'I'm so sorry, Siobhan. Losing Colleen – it's a terrible thing.'

My voice cracked and then both of us were crying. It had been years since I had let myself cry. Sadness for Colleen swept through me. Holding her sister felt to me like saying good-bye to Colleen again.

Maybe Siobhan felt as if Colleen were saying a last good-bye to me.

Siobhan pulled away from me but gripped my arms tightly as she looked up at my face.

'You really did love her, didn't you, Jack? So why didn't you do the right thing by her?'

'I thought I did. I set her free.'

Chapter 50

Del Rio's office smelled of pepperoni pizza.

It was after nine, and he and Cruz had been working on the Beverly Hills Sun murder all day and now well into the night, comparing and contrasting the five murders that had been committed in California hotels in the past year and a half.

The first two killings had been six months and a hundred miles apart, so no one thought they were linked.

Victim number one, Saul Cappricio, was found strangled in Jinx Poole's San Diego hotel. Victim number two, Arthur Valentine, was discovered decomposing at the Seaview, a third-rate hotel in LA.

By the time the third victim, Conrad Morton, had been found garroted in the San Francisco Constellation, also a Poole hotel, the cops were looking for a connection – but even with several police departments involved, or maybe *because* three departments were involved, no viable suspect had turned up.

To date, five businessmen, including Maurice Bingham, ages thirty-five to fifty-one, had been strangled with various types of ligatures in their hotel rooms. The men had not worked for the same companies; all had different occupations, lived in different cities. Three were married and two were not.

Right now, Del Rio was at one computer cross-checking phone logs. Cruz was at a second computer, examining credit card charges.

Cruz said, 'Bingham used the same escort service as Valentine, who also charged up six hundred bucks for two hours of patty-cake.'

Del Rio leaned back in his chair and rubbed his eyes. 'All of them used hookers. Not the same service, though. Is that a lead or is that just what road warriors do?'

'I feel a business trip coming on,' said Cruz.

'Crap. Me too.'

'It's a lead,' Cruz said. 'The escort services are a lead, not a coincidence. Maybe a hooker with a thrill for the kill is moving from one place to the other.'

Del Rio could see how the next few days were going to go: interviewing prostitutes and johns and widows. He turned off his computer and threw the pizza box into the trash. He put on his jacket.

A list of escort service names and numbers chugged out into the printer tray.

Del Rio said, 'Get the lights, will you, Emilio? I'll meet you here tomorrow morning at eight. We'll stop first for coffee.'

Chapter 51

Mitch Tandy was poking around the side of the house, looking for anything out of place. He wanted to find something tangible that could link Jack Morgan to the Molloy murder.

He thought about the glove in the O.J. Simpson investigation, found near Simpson's property line. The glove was conclusive evidence, but through a freak of prosecutorial incompetence, it had ended up helping the defense.

If it doesn't fit, you must acquit.

The Simpson investigation had been the shame of the LAPD.

Never mind. This was today.

Ten guys from the crime unit were out on the beach. Divers were doing their thing in the shallows, looking for metal. Inside, CSIs were going over the house again.

Jack Morgan was smart, but he wasn't perfect. And if he'd overlooked anything in his cleanup of the crime scene, Tandy was sure something that could indict him would be found.

Tandy heard Ziegler call out to him.

'I'm over here,' he answered.

Ziegler joined Tandy where he stood inside the stucco fence that separated Jack Morgan's house from the raging river that was the Pacific Coast Highway.

Tandy asked, 'Find anything?'

'No.'

Tandy said, 'He leaves his spunk in her. Doesn't even use a rubber. That's risky behavior. Like suicidal.'

'Or it's his brother's spooge.'

They'd been over this before. The complication of twin brothers with identical DNA. The kind of thing that could introduce 'reasonable doubt' into a jury deliberation. When they'd interviewed Tommy, he'd had an alibi for the time of the murder. His wife said he was home. Swore it. Unshakably.

Still, she could have been lying.

'Tommy or Jack. It was one of them. And only Jack has a motive.'

Ziegler said, 'What's that over there?'

'What?'

Ziegler pointed at a disturbance in the mulch at the base of a bougainvillea vine, hidden in the shade of the fence.

Tandy used his foot to push away the pine bark.

For a long moment, they both stared.

'I'll get the camera,' Ziegler said.

Tandy nodded, stooped down, and continued to stare. This was the evidence they needed. The rush was indescribable. It was why, with all the

140

endless footwork, dead ends, and bureaucratic hassles, he just loved being a cop.

Moments like this one.

The idiot had left the smoking gun behind.

Chapter 52

I headed into my office at eight the next morning, still with a headache pounding like a jackhammer into a spot directly behind my right eye.

Cody was on the phone, but when I passed his desk, he held up his hand, signaling me to wait. He said into his headset mic, 'Yes, sir. I'll see if he's in.'

He scribbled on the back of an envelope, 'Chf Fescoe.'

'I'll take it,' I said.

I went to my desk, snatched the phone off the hook, and said, 'Mick?'

'Jack. This is a heads-up. Call your lawyer.'

'What happened?'

'Tandy and Ziegler found your gun.'

His words were like a fastball to the gut. I felt sick. I lost focus. My mind skipped over the events of the past three days as I tried to make sense of what he was saying.

Words came out of my mouth. 'Found it where?'

'In your front yard. Buried under a vine.'

'*Planted*, you mean. I reported it missing the night Colleen was killed.'

'I understand that, Jack. Fact is, it's your gun, a

custom Kimber, registered to you. Your prints are on it.'

'Only my prints?'

'Yes.'

I sat down. Cody brought in my Red Bull, set it down on a coaster that he positioned just so. It took him a little too long to leave. I stared at him until he exited and closed the door behind him.

'Jack?'

'I'm still here, Mickey. Say again. Where exactly did they find the gun?'

'Under some mulch, just inside your gate. Your Kimber is a .45, same caliber as the slugs that killed Colleen Molloy.'

'The killer used gloves,' I said. 'That's why only my prints are on the gun. He left it where the cops would find it.'

'I hear you. Ballistics is running a comparison now,' said my friend the police chief, not committing himself. I pictured him: a big man, six-four, wide smile, me standing with him and Justine six months ago, cameras flashing and Mickey Fescoe thanking us for catching a killer.

He'd certainly trusted me then.

Fescoe's voice softened. 'Are the slugs taken from the victim a match to your gun, Jack?'

'Maybe. Probably. I still didn't kill her. If I wanted to get rid of my gun, would I actually be that dumb? Mick. I'm asking you. Would I really bury the murder weapon outside my front door?'

'Call your guy Caine. Do what he tells you.'

'Thanks for calling, Mick.'

'No problem. Don't leave town.'

'I'm staying at a nice hotel. Got everything I

want right there.'

'Are you okay?'

'What? Sure. I'm okay for a guy who is being set up to take the rap for a murder I didn't commit. I'm absolutely fine.'

'I'll take you out to dinner when this is all over,' Fescoe said.

I told him it was going to be a pricey meal.

Cody came in again as I hung up. He said, 'Sorry,' went behind me, turned on my computer, and called up my schedule.

I stared at it blindly.

Cody said, 'We're all set up in the conference room, Jack. Meeting starts in fifteen minutes.'

Chapter 53

A chasm opened between my thoughts and my perceptions. Everything outside myself – people walking past me in the hallways, my phone ringing in my pocket, laughter coming up from the stairwell – all of that seemed far, far away, having no relationship to me at all.

I crossed the floor, opened the conference room door, saw a circle of twenty-five men and women seated around the table, all partners in Private Investigations Worldwide, all here for our biannual operations meeting.

I knew every one of the people sitting at the table. Had been to some of their weddings, stayed in some of their homes.

They expected me to reveal plans. Make decisions. They expected me to *lead*.

But I wanted to be anywhere but here. Nearly all of the twenty-five had been in the military, the law, or law enforcement before they'd joined Private. I knew that when the shock burned off, I wasn't going to be able to hide my rising panic from these first-class private cops.

Cody took a chair behind mine, and Mo-bot, who's fluent in several languages, sat next to Cody.

All conversation stopped as I pulled out my chair and sat down. There were some greetings, smiles, twenty-five pairs of eyes locking in on my face.

The unspoken question floated overhead in twenty-five thought balloons.

Did you kill Colleen Molloy?

Are you a murderer?

I had imagined Colleen's death so many times at this point that it felt as though I *had* been standing by the bed when bullets from my gun drilled into her chest.

Fescoe's call ten minutes ago had turned my mental imagery into something immediate and real. The cops had found my gun. They were running the ballistics now. And I knew with near certainty that sometime soon I would be charged with murder in the second degree.

I said, 'Good morning,' squared the printout of the agenda in front of me, tapped the table with my pen.

I brought my colleagues up to date on the investigation into Colleen's death and said, 'The person who killed Colleen is a pro. That person is trying to incriminate me – and doing a good job of it too. He did his research. He knew Colleen was in Los Angeles, knew her movements and mine. He got into my house, killed her, and left without making any obvious mistakes. The police felt they didn't have to look further than me. Why would they? The killing happened to my friend, in my bed, and she was killed with my gun.

'It was a beautiful setup. I don't know who killed Colleen, but I have some ideas, and we're going to bring him down. Please see me if you have any thoughts or if you can give me any help. Tell your staff and your clients that I'm innocent, and you can take my word for that because you all know me and I'm telling you the truth.'

'Jack, excuse me. What are these ideas you have?' asked Pierre Bonet, our director from France.

'I'm not going to discuss them until I have something solid.'

I asked if there were any other questions, and then I looked down at the agenda.

'Ian, you're up first. You want to talk about expanding the London office into Glasgow...'

I set my expression to 'listen,' although I could actually make no sense of what Ian was saying. He was reading from a chart projected on a screen when the door swung open and Tandy came in, Ziegler right behind him.

I felt sudden, pure terror, as if thugs had just broken in firing automatic weapons. Fescoe had given me no time to call my lawyer, no time to even clear the room.

'Excuse me, Ian. Mitch, let's take this outside,' I said to Tandy.

'That won't be necessary,' Tandy said. 'Please stand up, Mr. Morgan. Turn around and face the wall.'

There was no way out. Nowhere to go. I told Cody to find Caine and Justine, and I followed Tandy's orders.

Cuffs locked around my wrists. Tandy stuffed an arrest warrant inside my breast pocket and read me my rights, his voice the only sound in the otherwise stark silence of the conference room.

Tandy wanted to make sure he was humiliating me as much as possible.

I had time to say to my colleagues, 'I'll be talking to each of you very soon,' before Ziegler gave me a little shove and I was marched out of the room in the custody of two homicide dicks from the LAPD.

Chapter 54

Tandy grabbed my left elbow, Ziegler hooked my right, and they walked me down the winding staircase that opened into the reception areas on every floor. Clients and would-be clients, staffers moving between floors, all of them saw that I was under arrest.

Their faces mirrored my shock.

'We've got a car waiting,' Ziegler said. 'It's not your usual ride, Jack. But it has an engine. And wheels.'

'You didn't have to do it this way,' I said. 'But

I'm pretty sure you know that.'

Tandy laughed. The son of a bitch was having a very good day. When we reached the ground floor, Ziegler held the front door open and we exited out onto Figueroa.

Clearly, the media had been alerted by the cops. The morning sun cast a flat bright light on the eager faces of the press surging toward me. Bystanders crowded in from the fringes.

Tandy cracked, 'Hey, there's no such thing as bad publicity, Jack. I read that in *Variety*.'

Cody was waiting for me at the curb. He was very close to tears.

'Justine and Mr. Caine are heading out to TTCF,' he said to me. 'They'll meet you there.'

The Twin Towers Correctional Facility was the supersized prison complex that had replaced the LA Hall of Justice after the quake of '94. It was known as the busiest prison in the free world, consisting of an intake center and three jails on a ten-acre campus.

The horror stories of the brutality at TTCF were legendary. If you couldn't make bail, you could lose your health, even your life while waiting months to see a judge. This was true whether or not you were guilty of anything.

'What should I say to people?' Cody was asking.

'Say that I've been falsely charged and that I'll have a statement for the press as soon as I'm back in my office.'

'Don't worry, Jack. Mr. Caine will get you out. He's the best.'

Cody was trying to reassure me, and I wanted

to reassure *him,* but I had nothing comforting to say.

I wished now that I hadn't listened to Justine, that I had gotten to Tommy and beaten the crap out of him. He was a cagey bastard, but he couldn't stand up to me. Not in a fair fight. He would have told me something.

Reporters called my name, shouted, 'What's your side of the story, Jack? What do you want people to know?'

Tandy pushed my head down and folded me into the backseat of the unmarked car. As I ducked under the door-frame, I turned my head and glanced up at our offices.

Mo-bot was on the second floor, leaning out an open window with a video camera.

She was filming everything.

She saw me look up at her and gave me a thumbs-up. I was filled with affection for Mo. I smiled at her for a second before Tandy slammed my door. He went around to the other side and got into the backseat next to me.

Up front, Ziegler started the engine.

He waited a good long minute or two for an opening in the traffic while reporters banged on the doors and windows. And then the car took off.

I didn't see a crack of hope.

They had me, and if they could they would destroy me.

Chapter 55

Tandy and Ziegler broke a path through the thick clots of gangbangers between the street and the chain-link fence surrounding the prison building. A guard opened the gate, Tandy spoke, and we were led through a number of checkpoints until we reached an interrogation room on the ground floor.

This small gray room was a gateway to the grand cesspool of the men's jail, a hellhole built to hold a quarter of the eighteen thousand inmates warehoused here at any given time.

I expected to see Eric Caine waiting for me, but I should have known better. Twin Towers was a daunting, 1.5-million-square-foot maze, and defense attorneys were not welcomed here.

Ziegler closed the interview room door, blew his nose into a tissue, and lobbed the wad across the room into a wastebasket.

Tandy said, 'You need anything, Jack?'

This was his good-buddy act, which was somehow more threatening than when Tandy was showing me the sadistic SOB he really was.

I said, 'I've got nothing to say until I see my lawyer.'

'Sit down,' Ziegler said.

He shoved me in the direction of a metal chair, and as I stumbled toward it, Ziegler stuck out his foot and I went down, chin first, on the

149

linoleum floor.

Tandy helped me to my feet, saying, 'I'm sorry, Jack. Len didn't mean to do that. It was an accident.'

Even cuffed, I could have gotten in a groin kick Ziegler would have remembered for a couple of months, but I knew what would happen to me after that.

'Sure, what else could it have been?'

Tandy said, 'You're not getting mouthy with us, are you, Jack? That wouldn't be smart.'

Ziegler and Tandy hoisted me to my feet and angled me into the chair. I wondered who was behind the one-way glass and if Fescoe knew I was about to be worked over.

'I've got to admit it,' Tandy said. 'We sent your lawyer on a little detour, kind of a runaround. It'll take him a while to find you, but we did it for your benefit. We've got information you're going to appreciate.'

'Ah. I get it, Mitch. You're going to help me.'

Tandy walked behind me to a spot where I couldn't see him. Ziegler sat two feet away from me. He cleaned his nails with his pearl-handled pocket knife. Len Ziegler was a vain man. He worked out. He dressed well. But there wasn't much he could do about his weak chin and his little pig eyes.

'Listen, Jack,' Ziegler said. 'This is as close to a slam dunk as the LAPD has ever seen.'

He listed the physical evidence they had against me, then said, 'You made a phone call to your brother at around the time the victim bought it. We talked to Tommy. We leaned on him. Hard.

He says all he got was a hang-up call. But here's the thing, Jack. You established your presence at the scene.'

'Why'd you make that phone call?' Tandy asked. 'That's a mystery to me. Did you dial by mistake? Do you have a guilty subconscious?'

'I don't understand that phone call either,' I said. 'I didn't call Tommy. As soon as I saw what happened, I called 911. Mitch, given your theory of the crime, why on earth would I have called Tommy?'

Tandy said, 'Well, I asked Tommy about that. I spent a couple of hours with him. He has a good alibi and nothing good to say about you. Frankly, and I tell you this as a guy who's been a cop for twenty years, you are so cooked, I don't know when I've been happier. Len, have you ever seen me this happy?'

'I think when you hit the trifecta at Santa Anita you were over the moon, but it's a close call.'

'One Fine Day. That was that filly's name.' Tandy laughed at the memory, then said, 'I'm just an intermediary at this point; you know that. It's the chief who asked me to help you out.'

Ziegler folded his knife and put it in his back pocket. 'Fescoe said to tell you, if you save the city the cost and trouble of a trial, if you make a statement detailing what you did, Mickey will take care of you. He said he would do that. And to remind you that he and the DA are the best of friends.'

'I didn't kill Colleen.'

Tandy put his hands on my shoulders and tipped my chair over backward. I went down, and when my head was on the floor, Ziegler tapped it with the toe of his shoe. It was just a *tap-tap-tap*, but I felt cold all over. I thought how a kick at my head could sever my spine, what's called an 'internal decapitation.'

I wouldn't come back from that.

Tandy was speaking to me, apologizing about the chair falling over.

'Let's cut the bull,' I said from where I lay on the floor. 'I'm not making a statement. There's a set bail for murder on the felony bail schedule. When Caine gets here, we're going to pay the million bucks, and then I'm leaving.'

Tandy stooped so he could look me in the eyes.

'There's no set bail for murder with special circumstances,' he said.

'What are you talking about? What special circumstances?'

'Colleen was pregnant when you killed her, Jack. That's special circumstances. *Murder times two.*'

Chapter 56

I could barely absorb what Tandy had told me.

Colleen couldn't have been pregnant. She wasn't showing. Besides, she would have told me. Right?

Ziegler picked up the chair. Then he and Tandy hauled me back into it.

'You're *lying*,' I said. 'Colleen wasn't pregnant.'

'How do you know that?' said Ziegler. 'You get the autopsy report? We did. It'll be a while before we get the DNA, but it doesn't matter who the daddy is. She could have been pregnant by anyone. It's still murder of her kid.'

Tandy patted my shoulder.

I turned my head to look at him.

'Jack, are you with us? I haven't been running the video recorder, but I'm going to turn it on now. You should tell us the truth while there's still time.'

Tandy ducked out and sure enough, the video camera in the corner of the ceiling focused with a whirr. A little red light blinked.

Tandy came back into the room with a yellow pad and a Bic.

'Ready, Jack? Because this is it. Once we say bye-bye, no one can help you. Not even Fescoe.'

He had just slapped the pad and pen down on the table when Eric Caine, my friend, a Harvard Law grad, and the head of Private's legal department, stormed into the interrogation room.

Caine was a big man, prematurely gray, and like me, he played college football. Normally, Caine was a man of measured responses, dry humor, and self-control.

But now he was raging. And that made me feel good.

He shouted at me, 'Did you say anything, Jack?'

'Nope. The detectives have done all the talking.'

Caine walked over to me, turned my head from side to side. 'You're bleeding.'

He said to Tandy and Ziegler, 'Beating a prisoner is illegal. Not only is a lawsuit coming straight at you, but that beating automatically throws out anything he said.'

'He said he's innocent,' Ziegler scoffed.

'Big barking dog,' Tandy said to Ziegler, eyeing Caine. 'Woof woof.'

'I want my client checked out by a *doctor*,' Caine said. 'I mean *now*.'

Chapter 57

I was shuffled between cops to the Twin Towers infirmary, where a nurse swabbed my cuts and scrapes with alcohol. She put a bandage on my chin.

I was thinking about Colleen, that if she had been pregnant, it was impossible for the baby to have been mine.

Except for our good-bye tryst a week ago, I hadn't seen Colleen in more than six months. I mean, I would have been able to tell if she'd been six months along, right?

Still, as Tandy said, the murder of a fetus was a special circumstance when tacked on to murder. Yes, I would be denied bail. In fact, I could spend the next year in this sewer before I went to trial.

I refocused my eyes as a few feet away Tandy explained to the doctor that I had tripped and, since I was cuffed, hadn't been able to break my fall.

'And what about the bruise on the back of his head?' the doctor asked. The doctor was a late-middle-aged white man. If he'd graduated any-where in the top 99.9 percent of his class, he wouldn't have been here.

'Jack is one of those masters-of-the-universe types,' Tandy joked. 'Doesn't like being detained. When I was putting him into the back of our car,' Tandy twisted his body to show exactly how I had rammed my head into the door-frame, 'he bumped his head.'

The doctor asked me, 'Is that how it happened?'

Saying no would have been a mistake. A few years back, an inmate had complained to an ACLU monitor that no one in his pod had been allowed a shower in three or four weeks. He was beaten. His leg was broken. The ACLU got involved, but for all I knew, that inmate was still here awaiting trial.

'It happened as the detective said. I was clumsy.'

'Duly noted,' said the doctor.

'May I have an aspirin?'

Tandy nodded. 'Give him an aspirin, Doc. Our farewell gift.'

Caine said, 'Shut up, Tandy.'

I wanted to seriously hurt Tandy. I hoped I would live long enough to do it. Tandy and Ziegler waved bye-bye and slithered down the hallway.

Caine said to me, 'Hang in, Jack. I'm working on one thing. Getting you out. I've never let you down before and I won't now.'

A nurse took my vitals, then gave me a mental-status test, checking to see if I was crazy. Or had plans to hang myself. Or commit murder.

From there, I was taken into a large open room, stripped, and given a military-style physical. I grabbed my butt cheeks and coughed on command, let the guard do a cavity check.

I was declared good to go and escorted back to intake with a young sheriff-in-training who struck up a conversation with me. He said he was hoping to get out of here by five today. He was picking up his folks at the airport.

He took my watch, phone, wallet, belt, and shoelaces. My fingers were pressed onto an electronic ten-printer. I stood in front of a height chart holding a number to my chest. I turned to my left, turned to my right, as requested by the bored man with the camera.

I did what I was told, but I was swamped with a lot of feelings beginning with the letter *D:* depressed, demoralized, degraded.

All around me, people puked, screamed, threatened, spat, and seemed to be begging to be knocked around.

I wanted to shout, *I'm not one of these guys. I'm innocent.*

It would have been like shouting down a hole that went clear to the center of the earth.

And my morning was just beginning.

Chapter 58

I was walked through the building to the men's jail, where I was strip-searched again and issued a 'roll-up,' a pair of orange pants and matching shirt, and plastic shoes. Then I was given a prisoner's tour of the facilities on the way to my cell.

The jail was made up of hundreds of two-tiered pods, each with dozens of holding cells, each pod meant to hold thirty men, but as I was walked past, I could see each pod was double booked and held more like fifty living, crying, coughing, desperate men.

My cell was the size of a walk-in closet, six by eight feet, with two narrow metal slabs and a stinking, clogged toilet.

I was the fourth man in that cell.

I sat on one of the slabs.

The overhead lights glared. There was no window, no way to tell the time, but it seemed to me that at least ten hours had gone by since Fescoe's phone call to me at Private.

A rank-smelling man, somewhere between twenty and forty years old, sat on the bench next to me.

He said his name was Irwin, and he wanted to talk. He told me he'd been in holding for five days. He'd been caught with cocaine and a teenage girl in his car two blocks from a school. Still, Irwin, I thought, had less to worry about than I did.

He had a festering wound on his arm, another on his neck. He told me about the mystery-meat sandwich for lunch and the dinner burrito, the kind you get at gas stations.

I had missed both.

He asked if I had a good lawyer. I said I did, then I leaned back against the wall. I didn't want to attract any kind of attention. I was drowning in a riptide of despair that didn't make total sense to me.

I'd been through marine boot camp and then a war. I'd killed people. Friends had died. My parents had died. I'd been wounded in action. In fact, I'd died and been brought back to life. All of that.

And yet the one thing I couldn't remember feeling before was an utter lack of hope.

Nothing I said mattered.

I had no access to anyone. No moves to make.

I was at the mercy of people who wanted me put away. Even Fescoe had let me down: confess or else.

Irwin moved to the other slab, and another unwashed desperado took his place next to me. He seemed like a decent guy. Had a couple of kids, a wife, had gotten into a bar fight. Said he hadn't been able to make bail. He had a bad cough. Sounded like TB or maybe lung cancer.

I feigned sleep. I made a mental list of people who hated me. It was a long list of guys I'd busted, thwarted, fired, or exposed.

Tommy's face kept coming to me, and then I was awakened out of a murky dream. The lights were all on. One of my cell mates was grunting on the can. But what had awakened me was the voice booming over the public-address system, naming which people would be bused to what court.

Irwin said, 'This is what they do at four a.m. Like it? Court isn't until nine.'

My name wasn't mentioned.

They hadn't called my name.

I closed my eyes, and sometime later a guard hit a buzzer and the door to my cell slid open. The guard said, 'Jack Morgan? You need to get dressed for court.'

Chapter 59

Caine had enough clout to get me bumped to the front of the line, and I was transported from the jail to the Clara Shortridge Foltz Criminal Justice Center on West Temple. I was brought into the holding cell outside the courtroom, chained to three other guys, one of whom was about eighteen years old and pale with fright.

There was air-conditioning.

It was a miracle. I thanked God.

I sat for hours as my fellow prisoners left and came back. And then I was separated from my cellies.

Caine came to meet me, put both arms around me, and held me in a hard hug. He whispered, 'Remember who you are. Look alive.'

I smelled bad, like the unwashed men in my

cell. I was wearing yesterday's clothes and had numerous cuts and bruises and a day-old beard.

I said to my lawyer, 'Okay. I think I can fake that.'

I followed Caine into the courtroom. It was paneled, civilized, but it still reminded me of old prints of Ellis Island, where refugees were processed after three weeks in the hold of a ship, not knowing what would become of them.

The judge was the Honorable Skinner Coffin. I'd never met him, but I knew who he was. He was in his fifties, reputed to be touchy and opinionated. Justine had once said that he excelled at 'creative interpretation of the law.'

I didn't know if that was good for me or bad.

While Judge Coffin was in conversation with his bailiff, I scanned the gallery. There was a low rumble of people whispering, shifting in their seats. Babies cried. I heard my name. I turned to see Robbie Pace, the new mayor, coming toward me.

I remember thinking how clean he looked in his blue suit, his face shining from a recent shave. He leaned close and said into my ear, 'I wrote to the judge. Put in a good word. I think you're going to be okay.'

'Thanks, Robbie.'

'No problem.'

Doors opened at the front of the courtroom, and Fescoe entered, came up the aisle. He stopped to speak to Mayor Pace, looking at me over Pace's shoulder while they chatted; Robbie's head bobbed in agreement, then Fescoe nodded at me and went to the back of the gallery.

The doors opened again, and Justine came through them, a stunning picture of grace, fresh as a new rose, her smile weighted with sadness. She came up to me. Stopped short of hugging me. Contact was expressly forbidden.

'We're all with you, Jack. Everyone at Private. We're reaching out to street contacts, sifting through everything we've found, and we will keep at it until we've got something useful. Are you all right?'

'It's good to see you.'

'I wish I could say the same. I know how bad it is in there.'

I thought, *You can't really know – and you should thank God for that.*

I said, 'So you don't have anything?'

'Not yet. Tommy has an alibi.'

'So I heard.'

'His wife. He was home with her that evening.' I sighed.

'We're still digging,' said Justine.

'I'm okay,' I said.

'I know.'

Why had I slept with Colleen?

Why hadn't I resisted that impulse?

Justine wished me luck, and then the bailiff called out a number. Caine said, 'That's us. Let's go.'

Chapter 60

The assistant district attorney was Eddie Savino, still in his twenties, dark, handsome, and on his way up – at least he gave that impression.

Savino said, 'Your Honor, Mr. Morgan murdered Colleen Molloy, one of his girlfriends. He shot her three times in the chest. We recovered his DNA from inside the victim, to put it delicately.'

The ADA smirked, shot a glance at the gallery, didn't get a reaction, and went on.

'And the special circumstance in the charge is that Ms. Molloy was six weeks pregnant.'

'Go on,' said the judge. 'And can the flourishes, Eddie. There's no jury. Just me.'

'Yes, Judge,' said the ADA. He smiled charmingly. 'The murder weapon was a .45-caliber handgun registered to Mr. Morgan, concealed in some bushes about fifteen feet from his front door. The bullets from that gun are a positive match to the bullets extracted from the victim's body.'

Judge Coffin looked at me squarely for the first time, as Savino kept talking and ticking off items on his fingers.

'Jack Morgan is rich, he's armed, and he's dangerous. He's also a pilot. He not only flies planes, Your Honor, he owns one. If that doesn't define "flight risk," I don't know what does.

'The people request that Mr. Morgan be remanded over to the Twin Towers Correctional

Facility while he awaits trial.'

Everything Savino had said about me was true – except for shooting Colleen and being a flight risk. My mood was changing. I had gone through terror and self-pity and was now working on getting very mad.

Judge Coffin said, 'Mr. Caine. Talk to me.'

Caine said, 'Nice speech on the part of Mr. Savino, Your Honor, but my client is not a flight risk. He wants to defend himself against these heinous false accusations because he's not guilty of anything. The cops rushed to judgment, and Mr. Morgan is bearing the brunt of their laziness.'

Coffin said, 'Just the facts, please, Mr. Caine. I've got another hundred people waiting to be heard today.'

'Sorry, Your Honor. Facts are, Mr. Morgan is a war hero. He's a pilot like the bald eagle is a bird. He was a captain in the Marine Corps. He flew transport helicopters in Afghanistan and was awarded the Silver Star. Mr. Morgan is a personal friend of the chief of police and the mayor, both of whom vouch for him.

'And there's more, Your Honor. Mr. Morgan employs over three hundred people. Whatever a pillar of the community is, Jack Morgan fits the definition.'

'Bottom line it for me, please, Mr. Caine.'

'Bottom line, Your Honor, Mr. Morgan came home from a business trip and found his former girlfriend dead in his bed. It was a setup. He called the police.

'If my client had actually committed a murder,

163

he is more than capable of getting rid of any evidence of the crime. He lives alone. He had thirteen or fourteen hours before he was expected at the office the next morning. In that time, he could have gotten rid of the body, sanitized the scene, established an alibi. Hell, he could have invited twelve people out to dinner at Spago and still had time to get rid of the evidence and then get on a plane to Guadalajara.

'So what are the cops saying? He killed the girl, left her in his bed, buried the gun in a pile of mulch fifteen feet from his door? That's nuts, Your Honor. If he was going to fly to Mexico, why didn't he do it?

'Because Jack Morgan didn't kill Colleen Molloy. He called the police and he cooperated with them fully. Those are the actions of an innocent man.'

Chapter 61

Caine had done a powerful – correction, a *phenomenal* – job. My gratitude to him was so overwhelming, I almost broke down. But Judge Coffin was deadpan. He appeared to be unmoved by Caine's speech.

Coffin said, 'Mr. Morgan, you're charged with felony murder with special circumstances. How do you plead?'

'Not guilty, Your Honor.'

The judge said, 'Uh-huh.' Then he leaned over

his laptop and poked at the keys.

Judge Coffin was a two-finger typist, and while he hunted and pecked, noise rose from the gallery like a typhoon boiling up the coastline. A fight broke out in the aisles and sheriffs put it down. The judge banged his gavel four times and glared.

There was silence and then Judge Coffin looked down at me.

'Mr. Morgan, do you intend to flee?'

'No, Your Honor.'

'Okay. Well, I'd say we have an unusual situation, Mr. Morgan being an upright citizen who called the police to report the crime. Still, we've got special circumstances.'

The judge scratched his chin. He had our attention.

'I've found a precedent in *Meyer versus Spinogotti*.'

Savino looked puzzled. 'Wasn't that an abduction case, Your Honor?'

'Bingo, Mr. Savino. Pregnant victim. Mr. Caine, I want Mr. Morgan's plane disabled and secured so that it cannot be moved. Mr. Morgan, you will surrender your pilot's license and your license to carry a weapon; also your passport.

'When those conditions are met, find a bail bondsman who will put up twenty million dollars and off you go.'

The gavel came down.

The bailiff called the next case. Caine said to me, 'Don't worry, Jack. I'm on it. You'll be home tomorrow.'

Was Caine right? Or was he just giving me false hope?

A deputy was at my side. He jerked my arm, and I walked with him out the back door of the courtroom. I turned just as the door closed. I was hoping to see Justine, but I saw Fescoe.

He was in a huddle with Tandy and Ziegler and Eddie Savino. I could tell by the looks shot in my direction that they were discussing me.

It was a fair guess that the prosecution was disappointed that I might make bail.

I was loaded into the holding cell behind the courtroom, where I was chained again to three other men. I sweated in silence for six hours, then returned by bus to the men's jail, where I was shooed into my cell.

We had a new cell mate.

Another talker.

The new guy's name was Vincent, and he looked like he'd been sleeping over a grate. He got rolling fast and told me about what he called 'an almost criminal imbalance in the real estate market' that wouldn't straighten out until 2015 at the earliest. He talked about the boomers, the pressure they'd put on all things related to the economy and the current entitlement programs. We wouldn't see a bull market until we were wearing orthopedic shoes, he said.

He still had a sense of humor. It was admirable.

'You're in finance?' I asked politely.

'I drive.'

'Drive?'

'A cab. I didn't pay a couple of tickets. They pulled me in here for that. You believe it?'

'I'm sorry to hear it.'

'When we get out of here, if you need a cab, just

166

remember 1-800 Call Vin.'

I said, 'Sure. I can remember that.'

I thought about Justine, the way she'd looked at me in the courtroom. I'd felt the pain and her deep disappointment. I thought about lying with her under cool sheets in a big bed.

Early the next morning, the first sound I heard was the loudspeaker, feedback screeching, the blasting voice echoing across the pods.

This time my name was called.

Chapter 62

Caine was waiting for me on the freedom side of the chain-link barrier. He put an arm around me and hurried me quickly through the seething throng of bikers and gangbangers outside the jail.

The car was waiting for us. Aldo sprang from the front seat and moved fast to open the back door for me.

'You okay, Jack?'

'No worse than if I got hit by a car and slept it off for a couple of days in a drainage ditch,' I said.

Aldo grinned. 'Oh, man, that's bad. But we've got you now. Listen, there's coffee for you in back.'

Had it only been five days since Aldo had picked me up at the airport and driven me home? It felt like at least a decade had passed.

Caine got into the backseat beside me, and the Mercedes shot out into the stream of traffic.

'I want to stop home and change.'

'The hotel would be better, Jack. They just took down the tape around your house an hour ago. No one's been inside to clean. Cody brought some clothes to the hotel.'

I nodded, thought about my blood-soaked bed. My house forever colored by that blood.

There was a newspaper on the seat beside me. A big photo on page one. It took me a second to realize that the shackled man standing in line for the TTCF bus was me.

The headline read 'Morgan Freed on Bail.' The subhead was 'Accused Killer Walks on Twenty Million Bail.'

The lede paragraph was about Colleen's murder, then a few lines about Phil Spector, Robert Blake, O. J. Simpson. Other LA killers.

'When's the trial?' I asked Caine.

'We don't have a date. Not yet,' Caine said. 'And we don't want one too soon.'

I knew what he meant. All we had in our favor was me telling the cops I didn't do it. Another way of saying we had jack shit.

The car waited for me outside the Beverly Hills Sun. I went up to my opulent, gilded room. I stripped down, stood under the six shower heads in the travertine marble stall. Those streams of clean hot water almost resurrected me.

Thirty minutes later, about noon, I walked through the doors of Private and loped up the stairs.

Cody's workstation was vacant, but there was a client pacing the open space outside my office. It was Dewey Arnold, lead attorney for Hamilton-

Price, the biggest sports agency in the world.

'Dewey, come in. I wasn't expecting you.'

'I don't need to come in, Jack.'

'No?'

I had been headed toward my office, but I stopped, turned around, and looked into Dewey Arnold's craggy face.

I had known Dewey since I was a teenager. His firm had represented me during my one-season shot at professional football. Hamilton-Price had been my father's client. Hamilton was still friends with my uncle Fred, who co-owned the Oakland Raiders.

Hamilton-Price had been with Private for the past five years.

'Let me just say it, Jack. You're fired. We don't want to work with you anymore.'

'Dewey. Come in. Let's talk about this. I'm not guilty of anything. It's a–'

'I've heard. It's a frame,' he said. 'We don't care. We don't like the stink. I settled up with accounting and I'm putting out a press release this afternoon. We're moving our business to Private Security.'

'You're going to my brother?'

'Out of loyalty to your family. Hamilton said to tell you good luck.'

If you say the word *luck* and put a lot of power behind that *ck* sound, spit comes out of your mouth. I wiped my cheek as Dewey Arnold stalked toward the elevator.

Chapter 63

I turned away from Dewey Arnold and saw a large black woman coming out of my office. She was pretty, late twenties, a good 225 pounds, five foot eleven in flats. She wore a white blouse with some lace in the V neck, kelly-green pants. There was a scared look on her face – but, then, the shower hadn't washed away the past few days. I still looked scary.

More to the point, I didn't know her.

So what was she doing in my office?

'I'm Valerie Kenney,' she said. 'Val. I'm Cody's replacement.'

She stuck out her hand and I shook it, but I didn't get it. Cody had said he'd stay for another week. He'd told me that I would interview his top three candidates.

'Cody wanted to break me in. Give me some training while he's still here,' Valerie said. 'He's setting up some meetings for me right now.'

'Please come into my office,' I said.

I showed Val Kenney to the seating area. 'I'm sure Cody would have told me about you, but I haven't had a phone for a couple of days.'

'Being without a phone. That's hell, isn't it?'

I laughed. First time in a while.

'So what's your story, Val?'

She summarized her life, hitting the high points. She had rehearsed it, sure, but it wasn't too pat. Val was from Miami; her mother still lived in the Gables. She'd gone to Boston University, graduated four years ago with a bachelor of science degree.

'I took criminology postgrad at the University of Miami,' she told me. 'My mom needed me at home to help her with my brother for a while. He was a teenager, you know, out of control. Do you remember when you came to Miami and gave a lecture on crime detection?'

'I do.'

'I was in the front row.'

'Sorry. There were a lot of people there.'

'Oh, that's okay. But you really made an impression on me, Mr. Morgan.'

'Jack.'

'Jack. So how am I doing?' she asked. 'Am I still hired?'

Second time I'd laughed. I guess I must've missed laughter if I was counting.

'Let's see how it goes,' I said. 'Keep talking.'

Val told me she'd done a stint with Miami PD in the back office, got her master's at night, and told her mother that she was going to move to LA one day and work for Private.

'That last part's a lie,' I said.

She grinned. 'It's what you say on interviews, "I always wanted to work here." But damn it, I did. I do.'

'Have you moved to LA?'

'Yes. I'm a big one for bold moves.'

First time she'd looked nervous in fifteen minutes, since Dewey Arnold told me good luck like he was wishing I'd get the plague.

171

'When Cody answered my e-mail, I got on a plane and flew out to meet him,' Valerie continued. 'Speaking of e-mail, you've got a lot of it. Phone calls too. Three clients resigned – I cued up their contact info on your computer. And there are about five meetings I should rebook for you, if you're ready. Mr. Del Rio, urgent. Ms. Poole, urgent. Should I go on?'

'You know what has happened to me?'

'Yes.'

'Solving Colleen Molloy's murder – we're going to be working nights. Weekends. You've got an advanced degree. Are you sure you want to answer phones?'

'Yes. And I can do anything you need me to do. This is a dream job, Mr., ah, Jack. I'll work my butt off. That's a promise. You're looking at a former scholarship student. I got into the best schools on scholarship.'

Her hands were clasped tightly together in her lap. She was leaning toward me, hopeful.

I had to smile. She was smart and she was motivated, but was she as good as her act?

'When you think I'm ready, we'll talk about me moving up to investigation,' Val Kenney said.

I had a murder rap hanging over my head. I had to take a chance that the smart and motivated Ms. Kenney could watch my back while I did whatever I had to do to save my life.

I reached out and shook her hand again.

This time I said, 'Welcome to Private.'

Part Three

CUT TO THE CHASE

Chapter 64

The movie was being shot north of LA, just outside the town of Ojai, on a ranch-style property set back from a winding country lane.

Del Rio stood in the shade of an avocado grove, watching the crew set up the first shots of *Shades of Green*. A few yards away, Scotty leaned against the white horse fence that separated the avocado trees from the drive, the lawn, and the eccentric-looking house, maybe a hundred years old.

Right then, eight-fifteen a.m., the crew was adjusting the lights, the sound level, the camera angles, focusing on the blue Ferrari parked in front of the house.

Danny Whitman was in the driver's seat, and his costar, sixteen-year-old Piper Winnick, was sitting beside him. The two were joking around, getting into the personalities of the characters, two young spies who'd fallen in love despite the odds, seeing as Danny's character was marked for assassination.

Del Rio was reminded of the characters in one of those Bourne films starring Matt Damon and an actress whose name he didn't know. Unlike the brunette in that Bourne movie, Piper Winnick was a honey blonde. She wore her shining hair shoulder length and was dressed in a yellow sundress with a straw hat shading her eyes.

Danny Whitman wore a blue polo shirt, jeans,

and a baseball cap, and he was nuzzling his costar, who was fake-pushing him away, calling him '*stupido*,' the two of them laughing.

What Del Rio liked was how there were no other houses visible from this property, that the situation was under control. He lit a cigarette. He wasn't hooked, but there were times when it just felt good to exhale and watch the smoke blow away in the breeze.

Del Rio watched the actors, thinking the film was pretty much guaranteed to be next summer's blockbuster – if Danny didn't go to jail. Or maybe the film would be even more of a box office bonanza if he did.

The director was talking now, telling the couple to take their places. They got out of the car and went into the house of many crazy additions, just as three of Danny Whitman's handlers ambled up from the road.

Scotty left his post at the rail, came over, and stood next to Del Rio.

He said, 'Of the three of them, I only like Schuster, the manager. I think he likes Danny for real. Barstow, Danny's agent? He doesn't like anybody. Merv Koulos. I understand him. He doesn't try to hide that it's all about money.'

Del Rio said, 'It's all about the money for all of them, Scotty. Just different shades of green.'

The three men came up to the investigators, Schuster saying, 'You're the guys from Private, right?'

Del Rio thought Schuster looked happy for good reason. He'd waited a long time for the cameras to roll, and today was the day.

Barstow said, 'You can get something to eat if you want. The chow wagon is behind the barn.'

Del Rio said, 'Thanks, but we're good.'

He was thinking how it was great to get a softball job once in a while. Everything under control.

Chapter 65

Fifty feet away from the avocado grove, the director's assistant called, 'Quiet please. Let's have quiet.'

Someone clapped the boards, said, 'Take one.' And the AD said, 'Four, three, two and ... action.'

The camera was focused on the front door, Danny coming out of the house followed by Piper. Danny turned to Piper, saying, 'You gotta understand, that guy is crazy.'

'Cheesecake. I mean fruitcake,' Piper said in an Italian-accented voice.

They got into the car, Whitman saying, 'Try to keep it straight, okay?'

Winnick said, 'I know; cheesecake is girly pictures and fruitcake is cuckoo. And keep my head down.'

The star said to his movie girlfriend, 'I'm fruitcake to let you come with me. If anything happens to you, Gia–'

The girl laughed, said, *Stupido,* as Danny started the snazzy car. He gunned the engine. Piper yelped and flew back against the seat as the sports car shot toward Sisar Road.

It was traveling way too fast.

That was not in the script.

The crew and the bystanders stood and gaped as the car blasted through the open gate and kept going. The director yelled, '*Cut,*' but the car didn't stop.

Instead, Danny took a hard left onto the two-laner, and the car became a vivid blue streak, getting smaller until it vanished from view and they couldn't hear the engine anymore.

The director yelled, 'What the fuck? What the fuck is going on here?'

Schuster, standing next to Del Rio, was punching numbers into his cell phone. Merv Koulos did the same.

'Danny. It's Merv. Damn it,' said Koulos. 'Danny, call me. This isn't funny.'

'He'll be right back,' Scotty said to himself. He turned to Del Rio. 'He just likes the car and the girl. He's going to turn back in a second. He's just goofing around.'

'I hope you're right,' said Del Rio.

Del Rio's contentment was gone, replaced by a feeling like a cold wind blowing through his rib cage. He opened his cell phone, dialed Justine, and when she answered, he said, 'We're on the job for one hour and we lose the damned kid. Yeah, right, Danny. He took off at a hundred twenty in a three-hundred-thousand-dollar sports car. Brace yourself, Justine. He took the girl with him. Piper Winnick. No. Nope. If he said where he's going, no one here got the memo.'

Chapter 66

It was late afternoon, nearly five.

Justine and Scotty had spent the day looking for Danny. They'd been to his house and Piper's house in the Hills. They had contacted both sets of friends and families and were only now leaving the studio after talking to everyone who had an opinion on Danny's disappearance – which was everyone period.

Half the people they talked to said they thought Danny was irresponsible, immature, just didn't understand the consequences of his actions.

The other half guessed that Danny understood the consequences full well, that his disappearance was a publicity stunt mimicking the movie plot. Several people suggested that Danny's agent, Alan Barstow, had put Danny up to it.

In any case, Justine knew that soon the police would be looking for a blue Ferrari and two young movie stars.

Justine told Scotty to strap in, then she drove off the Harlequin Pictures lot with tires squealing, heading toward Beverly Hills.

As she drove, Justine beat on the steering wheel with her palms in frustration, furiously trying to make sense of Danny's insane and dangerous escapade. He couldn't claim that he'd had one of his blackouts when he'd driven that car off the location with Piper Winnick riding shotgun.

What had she missed?

Was he a narcissistic child?

Or was he a psychopath?

Either way, he was self-destructive.

Danny Whitman, the kid with everything to lose, could go to prison for twenty-five to life.

And that was if he hadn't hurt Piper.

Justine sped through a yellow light, saying to Scotty, 'You heard me tell him "Play it straight. Don't go anywhere with the opposite sex."'

'You have to turn in two blocks, Justine. Maybe you want to get over into the left lane now–'

'He agreed to our terms. I keep asking myself, is he crazy? I mean, is he actually crazy?'

Scotty stomped on an imaginary brake on his side of the car as Justine took a hard left through a red light.

Justine said, 'See, I liked him, Scotty. I liked him a lot. Tell me that address again.'

'Three forty-five North Maple. Should be about three blocks down. I take responsibility, Justine, but I don't know what I could have done differently. We had to stay out of the shot, which went all the way out to the road.'

'You couldn't have known. I mean it, Scotty.'

The building coming up on their right was blocky, about fifteen stories high. Justine turned the car down a ramp on the east side of the building and took the car deep into the dark underground garage.

A few minutes later, she and Scotty were giving their names to a woman behind the reception desk of the Barbara Crowley Talent Agency.

Chapter 67

Piper's Winnick's agent, Barbara Crowley, came out to the reception area within a minute of being buzzed. She was an attractive woman in her early forties, with short gold-and-silver hair. She was wearing an expensive black suit, gold bangles, and black nail polish.

Justine noted that Crowley had chewed off her lipstick and looked ragged for such a well-put-together woman.

'Have you heard from Danny?' the agent asked Justine.

Justine said, 'No. Not yet.'

She introduced Christian Scott, then she and Scotty followed Crowley down a hallway lined with large framed photos of movie stars, the photos signed to Crowley with gratitude and love.

When Justine and Scotty were seated in front of Crowley's desk, she closed her office door and said, 'I'm worried for Piper. That's not exactly right. I'm frantic.'

'You think Danny would hurt her?' Justine asked.

'Could he? Would he? Is he just a regular kid turned into a movie star or is he something far worse? Danny was hospitalized a while ago. Were you told about that?'

'No one told us,' Justine said.

'Well, let me do it. Danny checked himself into

Blue Skies for a "tune-up," stayed out of sight for a couple of months.'

Justine knew about Blue Skies. Tommy Morgan had spent time there for his gambling addiction.

'Rehab, isn't it?' Scotty asked. 'Exclusive place for the addicted.'

'Not just addiction. Celebrities, others who can afford it, go there for R and R,' said Crowley. 'I was told Danny's problems were stress related, and when he checked out two months later, Merv Koulos assured me that Danny was absolutely fine. He had just needed some rest.

'So I met with Danny,' Crowley continued. 'He seemed sober and sane or I never would have let Piper take the job. Then, when Katie Blackwell said she was molested, I told Piper I was going to cancel the contract, but she wanted to work with Danny, and I mean really. Her parents wanted her to make the film.'

Justine said, 'Do you remember when Danny was at Blue Skies?'

'About six months ago, I think.'

The phone on her desk rang, and Crowley leaped for it. She turned her body away from her visitors as she said, 'Yes, yes, I'll be happy to. Now is fine.'

She hung up the receiver.

'The police are here,' she said to her visitors. 'Piper's parents called them. I'm sorry about that, but Danny *has* kidnapped Piper. I won't sleep until we have that child back with her family.'

Chapter 68

Justine had dropped Scotty off at his surveillance assignment in the warehouse district, then forced herself to call Tommy Morgan. It felt a lot like walking over broken glass. At night. In a hailstorm. With a stick in her eye.

He was still in his office and had taken her call.

'Tommy, I've got a question.'

'Sure. What do you need?'

'Were you at Blue Skies while Danny Whitman was there?'

Tommy had said, 'Ahhh. I can't talk now, Justine. How about dinner?'

She'd had to say okay, and added that Private would pick up the tab.

Now they were at Providence, one of the top restaurants in the country, a modern place, elegant but not sexy. That's why Justine had chosen it. She wanted Tommy to feel flattered and well treated, without giving him any false signals. He'd hit on her before.

They were at a table in the corner, candlelight flickering, wineglasses in their hands. Providence was known for its fine seafood. Even red-meat lovers agreed that wild salmon with thin shavings of mushrooms could taste far better than steak.

Tommy was having a sirloin and apparently enjoying it. He sat back in his chair and looked at Justine, smiling as he chewed.

Justine sipped her wine, struck once again that Tommy looked exactly like Jack. He had the same dark blond hair and hazel eyes, identical build and posture – but in all the ways that counted, Tommy was precisely Jack's opposite.

Where Jack was altruistic, Tommy was craven. Where Jack would give a person his full attention and really listen, Tommy would fix his eyes on you and try to manipulate you, find weaknesses to use against you.

He said, 'I don't know how much I can tell you about Danny Whitman. He was a weird little dude. And we weren't buddies. Why do you want to know?'

'He's a client.'

'Does Jack know that we're having dinner?'

'He will when I put in my expense report.'

Tommy laughed, and Justine waited him out. Then she asked again, 'Why was Danny Whitman at Blue Skies?'

'Depression, I think. He looked depressed, but he could have been there for other reasons. He saw his shrink and he kept to himself.'

'But you talked with him?'

'Jeez, Justine. We didn't open up our hearts,' Tommy said. 'Celebrities, you know. They keep to themselves if they've had enough experience with people selling their stories to the tabs. And now my turn. How is Jack? I haven't heard anything since he went off to jail.'

'He's out now.'

'Why do you think he killed Colleen?'

'Come on, Tommy. You know he didn't kill her.'

'No, Justine, you come on. I think he did it.'

'He had no reason to do it. None.'

'Maybe he just snapped. You don't know that Jack has a temper? I tell you from firsthand experience, he can throw a punch that cracks your jaw in three places.'

Tommy took off his jacket, made a production of rolling up his right sleeve. He showed Justine an old scar about five inches long, just above his elbow.

'This is from the time he broke my arm,' Tommy said, 'over who got to ride in the front seat.'

Tommy was vile. She hated him. She knew to keep her thoughts to herself, but he'd given her an opening, so she took it.

She smiled and said, 'I hope that really hurt.'

'Man, you still love the guy.'

Justine signaled to the waiter for the check.

'Anything else I can help you with?' Tommy asked. He was smirking.

'Sure, leave Jack's clients alone. And confess to the police that you murdered Colleen or that you had her killed.'

'I can't do that, sweetie. I can't confess to something I didn't do, just to make you happy. But I would do a lot of other things to make you happy. How about letting me take you out on what's referred to as a "real date."'

'This was our date, Tommy. First, last, and only.'

Chapter 69

I was waiting for Jinx at the bar on the pool deck, having a long, tall Perrier on the rocks. I was enjoying how the sunset was painting pink light on the pool, when she slid into the seat next to mine.

'Hi, Jack. Sorry I'm late. I got stuck at the office.'

'It's okay. I like it here.'

Jinx smiled. 'I've heard you've been having a rough time in the last few days.'

She smelled sweet, like jasmine. She was wearing midnight blue, a silk tunic, tight pants, gold sandals on adorable feet. Her diamond necklace caught the light.

'Jail is an enriching experience,' I said. 'I got to see the other side of the fence. Take it from me, the grass wasn't greener.'

'You look like you took a beating.'

'Part of the enrichment program.'

I'd meant to get a laugh, but she reached out and touched my bruised jaw. I let her do it.

'I tripped,' I said.

'A bad trip, looks like.'

I smiled at her. She put her elbows on the bar, asked the bartender for a gin and tonic. It was an unguarded gesture, and I saw her through it. She was right there, the woman who had asked for my help because she was being haunted by killings – and because she could lose everything she had.

I said, 'We're working on your case, Jinx, but if you want to take your business elsewhere, I understand. More than that, there's no charge for the time we've clocked.'

'The cops are hopeless,' she said.

'You mean the cops are hopeless *too*.'

'This time last month, there was standing room only at this bar.'

'We'll keep working if that's okay, Jinx. If we don't get results, you don't owe us anything.'

'You're making a compelling case for me to stay with Private.'

Finally she smiled. 'I should admit something,' she said. 'I like you, Jack.'

I had an awkward moment because I wasn't sure how to respond. Whatever she was thinking, friendship or more, it wasn't a good time for me. It was the worst.

'Jinx. Listen, I'm checking out of the hotel in the morning.'

Jinx stiffened at what she took to be a rebuff. She said, 'Was everything satisfactory?'

'Yes. I just have to get back to my house. My life.'

'Of course.'

She stood up and said, 'Iggy, Mr. Morgan's drinks are on the house. Jack, I've got some calls to make. Stay in touch, okay? And take care of yourself.'

I watched her walk across the deck, and when she was inside, I left the bar and went to my room.

I could list four or five reasons why I didn't need a romantic complication right now. But there was no reasoning with the strong pull I felt toward Jinx. I wanted to help her as much as I wanted to help myself.

If she'd stayed at the bar for another minute, I would have told her that I liked her too.

Chapter 70

Cruz parked the Mercedes fleet car under the one streetlight on North Western, a seedy block in the heart of Hollywood. Metal security doors had been rolled down over the surrounding storefronts: Quality Market, Lupita's beauty salon, AAA discount mufflers. Iglesia Cristiana Fuente de Salvación, a church housed in what looked like a former appliance store, was also closed for the night.

Across the street, a yellow neon sign showing a cocktail glass turned on its side and the name Havana marked an otherwise nondescript cinderblock building. Cruz undid his ponytail, fingercombed his hair, replaced the band, then got out and set the car alarm. He straightened his jacket.

The muscle at the club's door was in his thirties, shaved head, small metal-framed glasses, bulked up. Cruz said, *'Buenas noches.'*

The bouncer said, 'You have a reservation?'

'I'm Emilio Cruz, here to meet a lady called Karen Ricci. She told me she was leaving my name at the door.'

The bouncer looked Cruz over, took a long thirty seconds. He said, 'You packing?'

'I'm licensed.'

'Doesn't matter. No guns.'

Cruz sighed, took his gun out of his shoulder holster, shook out the ammo, and handed the gun to the bouncer. The bouncer put the gun in a box attached to the top of a pedestal, handed Cruz a ticket with a number, and opened the door.

Cruz entered a vestibule. There was a narrow flight of stairs and he climbed it, thinking about his gun. The stairway opened into a small room featuring one piece of furniture, what looked to be a hand-carved wardrobe, an armoire.

A hostess was standing beside the wardrobe. She was in her late twenties, Hispanic, big brown eyes, very trim, and wearing a tight pink satin dress. Definitely his type. Although she barely looked at him. Most women at least *looked*.

She opened the wardrobe door, said, 'You go through here and then down the stairs.'

Cruz asked, 'I go through the closet?'

The woman nodded. '*Si.*'

Cuban shirts were hanging on the pole, making a curtain.

Cruz pushed the guayaberas aside and saw that the closet was a cleverly concealed doorway that led directly to the top landing of a spiral stair-case. Latin music and loud chatter came up from the bar below.

As Cruz headed down, he took in the dark saloon, richly colored in red and gold, and had the feeling of being sent back in time to a Cuban

189

rum bar, circa the 1920s.

Electric-candle chandeliers lit the place with soft, flattering light. Small tables at the perimeter of the room were occupied, but most of the customers were packed around the white-marble-topped bar, the back of it stacked with rum bottles, maybe seventy different brands.

As Cruz reached the bottom step, he saw that behind the bar was a hallway leading to a cigar bar, designed to look like a back alley in Havana.

Just then, raucous applause broke out.

A dancer came onto a small stage, the spotlight right on her, making gold sequins glitter. She tossed her hair and began to move sensually to a Caribbean beat.

Cruz stood at the sidelines, searching the crowd until he saw one woman drinking alone at a table near the fire exit. He worked his way through the mob, and when he got to her table, he said, 'Karen Ricci? I'm Emilio Cruz.'

She said, 'Have a seat.'

Cruz pulled out a chair and sat down. Karen Ricci was dark haired, a natural beauty wearing no makeup. It took Cruz a moment to realize that she was in a wheelchair.

'You have my package?' she asked.

Cruz opened his jacket so she could see the edge of the envelope peeking out from his inside breast pocket.

He closed his jacket and said, 'May I buy you another drink?'

Chapter 71

A waiter came over and said to Karen Ricci, 'Papa's daiquiri, as usual?' Karen said yes, and the waiter asked Cruz, 'You like rum? I recommend you try the Bad Spaniard.'

Cruz nodded, and when the waiter left them, Karen said, 'There's a whole egg in that drink.'

Cruz shrugged, put on his bashful smile, and said, 'I like eggs. Why'd you pick this place to meet?'

'The guy at the door?'

'The bouncer?'

'He's my husband,' she said.

All that Cruz knew about Karen Ricci was what his source had told him. She had worked at an escort service called Sensational Dates for the past two years. She took calls from johns, arranged the dates, and charged their credit cards.

A john name of Arthur Valentine had been strangled with a wire at the Seaview hotel back in 2010, the second victim in what would become a string of five murdered hotel guests in three California cities.

Karen Ricci had been questioned about Valentine's death by the LAPD because she had booked the escort who had given Valentine his last ride.

When Cruz had spoken with Ricci two hours ago, she had agreed to tell him everything she knew about the hotel killings for a thousand dollars cash.

Now Cruz tasted his drink, set the glass down on a napkin, and said, 'Okay, Karen. What have you got for me?'

'Something the police don't know. You'll get your money's worth, don't worry, and I'll save you some time and trouble. The escort didn't kill the john.'

'She was a suspect?'

'For a while, yes. One of the last known persons to see the victim, whatever. She said she'd had sex with the guy and they didn't arrest her. They had no evidence of anything but the date, but they harassed her. She couldn't work without cops tailing her, scaring off business.'

'So do you know who killed the john, Karen? Because if you do, please cut to the chase.'

'Oh, you think I want a grand for saying the hooker didn't do it?' The woman laughed, took a slug of her daiquiri. She refilled her glass from the shaker.

'Here's what I think, Mr. Emilio Cruz. You need to talk to the escort, because she knows something that can help you. It's what you're paying for. Her name is Carmelita Gomez. Say you know me.'

Cruz took out the envelope, plucked out two hundred-dollar bills, and passed them under the table as the exotic dancer on the little stage took off her top and shimmied her pasties for the crowd. Cruz leaned closer to Karen Ricci. 'You get the rest after I meet this woman.'

'You already did,' Ricci said. She tilted her chin toward the staircase.

'Upstairs? At the closet door?'

'That's her,' Karen said. 'She gets off work at four.'

Chapter 72

Cruz swallowed the Bad Spaniard, including the egg, and said, 'I'll be back.'

He put a twenty under his empty glass and went up the stairs.

Carmelita Gomez was still standing by the armoire when Cruz came through the curtain of shirts. He did all the talking, telling her that Karen Ricci had said to tell her he was okay. That he needed information for cash. And that he'd be waiting for her outside the club at four a.m.

He gave her his cell phone number and said, '*No llegues tarde*. Don't be late.'

Cruz got his gun back from the doorman, then got in the car and headed south.

Del Rio and Scotty were in the surveillance van on South Anderson Street near the corner of Artemus. Cruz parked, slapped the van's door, got in the back.

Cruz briefed the guys on Carmelita Gomez, and they told him that a whole lot of nothing had happened to the thirty million in drugs stolen from the Mob. That the West Coast boss, Carmine Noccia, was paying for the surveillance but was cracking his knuckles and grinding his teeth, making phone calls to Jack, getting crazy.

Del Rio said, 'What I think is that this warehouse is a safe house. They'll move the van when they have a delivery secured. Or else the warehouse has become a drugstore. Those pills could be leaving here a few bottles at a time.'

Cruz let Del Rio and Scotty sleep, took a shift watching the warehouse. He, Scotty, Del Rio, and Justine were working their major cases while Jack spent all day and all night trying to get his ass out of the bad case against him.

Cruz would be happier when Jack was free, when he was back working with them, and he hoped it would happen before the top guys at Private burned out.

Cruz shook Del Rio awake at 3:35 and got back into his fleet car. At four on the nose, he parked again on North Western under the light, across the street from the sign reading Havana.

The street was emptier and more desolate than it had been six hours before, except for a bunch of rowdies having after-drinks fast food at the Tacos El Patio.

Cruz was thinking maybe he'd go in there and use the bathroom, when the door to Havana opened and a woman in jeans, black cardigan, and black Converse lace-ups came out to the street. He flashed his headlights, and Carmelita Gomez crossed to the car. She glanced up and down the street as she slipped in the passenger side and closed the door.

Chapter 73

Carmelita Gomez smelled like flowers and cigar smoke. She turned her dark eyes on Cruz. It was like looking at the business end of a couple of nines.

'Karen just told me you wanted to talk about that dead john last year. She's got a big mouth,' Carmelita said.

'You told her about it, right?'

'The guy was dead. I'm the last one who partied with him. Cops wanted to know. Everyone wanted to know.'

'And now I want to know, but I'm paying for the information. I'll keep you out of it.'

'Give me the money first.'

'That's not how it works,' Cruz replied.

The girl opened the door and had one sneakered foot on the pavement when Cruz said, 'Wait.'

She got back in and looked at him, not saying anything.

'Here's three hundred,' Cruz said. 'With the two I gave your friend, that's a total of five hundred. Half down. Now, Carmelita, you have to talk if you want the rest.'

The girl put the money inside the neckline of her top and said, 'The killer is a limo driver. He drives the girls to their dates. Then he comes back and kills the johns.'

'Do you *think* that? Or *know* that?'

'When I was at Sensational Dates, I was friends with one of the drivers.'

'Name?'

'Joe Blow.'

Cruz's hand moved fast, like a snake, to the girl's neckline. He had his hand on the money when she grabbed his wrist and said, 'It doesn't matter what is his name. He's dead, okay? He OD'd.'

Cruz pulled out the rest of the money, held it in front of her eyes.

Carmelita sighed.

'These drivers. They are a bad group. Ex-cons. Illegals. They make their own hours. Many times, they use their own cars. When the calls go out for a driver to take an escort somewhere, they hear over the radio where the girls are going and they choose the jobs they take.'

'I need a name.'

'The driver who took me to the Seaview the night Arthur Valentine was killed? He was a guy called Billy Moufan. He and I told each other our secrets.'

'For instance.'

'Billy told me one of our drivers had killed the john at the Moon. He didn't name the name. Just said to be careful.

'Then my date was found dead. Later, Billy OD'd. I didn't tell the police anything. They don't protect party girls, you understand? Maybe Billy OD'd. Maybe someone did it to him. All I know is what Billy told me. The killer was a driver who worked for Sensational Dates in the summer of

2010. Did you know that? No. If you are a good detective, maybe you can find this driver.'

'I'm going to try.'

'*Bueno*. Now give me the rest of the money.'

Chapter 74

Justine grabbed at the ringing phone on her nightstand, fumbled it, dropped it, scrambled for it under the bed.

When her hand was around the phone, she squinted at the caller ID. It said only, 'Incoming call,' and she didn't recognize the caller's number. She glanced at the clock. It was just after four a.m.

Justine said into the phone, 'Hello? Hello?'

She heard sobbing. 'Hello, who *is* this?'

'It's Danny.'

'Danny. Where are you? What's wrong?'

The crying continued, and between the sobs, Danny gave Justine an address in Topanga Canyon.

'Please come fast,' he said.

Justine said she'd be there in twenty minutes. She disconnected the line, then called Del Rio. He picked up on the first ring, said he'd meet her at the Topanga Canyon address and that he needed coffee bad.

Justine said, 'Get two. Black for me.'

She dressed quickly, got into her Jag, and sped away from her house.

She followed Old Topanga Canyon Road, eventually taking a left onto a small road that fed into even smaller roads, her headlights barely piercing the black of that early moonless morning.

When she found Portage Circle Drive, Justine slowed the car and looked for house numbers until she saw 98 on a mailbox.

She turned at the rutted driveway, her headlights lighting the tree trunks crowding it on both sides until the driveway emptied into a clearing. There was a rustic cabin set back into the wooded lot and a blue Ferrari parked in front.

Justine braked her car and buzzed down the windows. She heard nothing but insects chirping, saw one light shining through the front windows, coming from a room toward the back of the house.

Justine retrieved a flashlight from the door pocket, then got out of her car. She touched the hood of the Ferrari. It was cold. She went up a path of broken stone to the front door, which had been painted a bloodred color and had a brass knocker under a peephole.

Justine knocked, calling Danny's name.

There was no answer.

She knocked louder and called again, with no response. She was about to walk around to the back of the cabin when a car pulled up to hers and stopped. Rick Del Rio got out.

It was more than a little spooky here, and she was very glad to see him. And his gun.

'What's going on?' he said.

'Damned if I know,' said Justine. 'The car is here, but I don't think anyone is home.'

Chapter 75

Del Rio said to Justine, 'Go around back. I'll meet you there in a minute.'

Del Rio tried the doorknob, which turned easily in his hand. The door swung open, and with his light shining into the house, he crossed the threshold.

He shone his beam around the main room and took stock. The house was one of those magazine-type decorated cabins with Native American rugs on the terra-cotta floor, bright blankets and pillows on the leather couches in front of the fireplace.

Embers glowed in the grate. He saw empty wine bottles on the floor and jars of wildflowers on the windowsills.

Del Rio called out, 'Is anyone here?'

There was no answer.

There was a light on in the hacienda-style kitchen, another designer-inspired room, bright with Mexican tiles. Iron hooks hung from the beamed ceiling, holding pots and pans. There were dishes in the sink and plates with remains of chocolate cake sitting on the counter.

He could almost see Danny and Piper cutting up right here.

Del Rio found the bedroom down a short hallway. The bed was king-size, made of birch saplings, and took up most of the room. He noted the rumpled sheets, the pillows that had fallen between the mattress and the wall, and the calico quilt in a heap on the floor.

Piper's sundress, the one that she had worn for her scene that day, was over the back of a chair. Feminine underthings were on the seat and a pair of flat shoes was underneath it.

Didn't need to be a genius to see that sex had happened here. In fact, the entire place had the look of a nonstop party. Too bad Piper was sixteen and Danny was twenty-four.

Del Rio continued his quick tour of the cabin. The bathroom was empty. Damp towels were hanging over the shower curtain rod. He opened closets, found men's casual clothes and shoes.

Relieved not to find bloodstains or any other signs of violence, Del Rio returned to the kitchen and exited by way of the back door.

The deck cantilevered out over the canyon. It was furnished with a grill and comfortable chairs. Beyond the deck, a spot of light bobbed along a trail and then was blocked from view by a thicket of trees.

Del Rio went down the steps to the path through the scrub dotted with trees. He walked fast, ducking under branches, and caught up with Justine.

She spun, startled by his touch on her shoulder. 'Find anything, Rick?'

'Looks like the kids were having a good time. That's it.'

'How could Danny be so stupid?'

'Call him. Now,' Del Rio said.

Justine did. 'Danny. *Danny*, where are you? It's Justine.'

Her voice echoed across the canyon. Del Rio said, 'Listen.'

He heard a man's voice saying, 'I'm *here*,' coming from far along the path. And then there was the sound of car doors slamming behind them, back at the cabin.

Chapter 76

There was zero visibility.

Del Rio thought that the night was so black, even dawn couldn't break through the moonless and overcast sky.

While Justine went back to the cabin, Del Rio pushed ahead, following the narrow path through oak and sycamore and chest-high scrub in the direction of Danny's intermittent cries, until the trail ended in a clearing.

He flashed his light around, and there was Danny, just ahead. The kid was wearing only his boxers, lying facedown on the ground, pretty much hysterical.

Del Rio went to him, stooped down, shook his shoulder.

'What's wrong? Are you hurt?'

'Nooo,' Danny cried.

His voice was slurred and he stank of booze. Del Rio saw that he was clutching a shoe, like a ballet slipper. Danny's flashlight was turned off or dead, lying an arm's length away.

'Where's Piper?'

Danny rolled onto his side and pointed to where the trail ended and the steep drop into the canyon began.

'What? She's down *there?*'

Del Rio walked a few yards to the edge, pointed his light straight down, and saw a patch of white. He was pretty sure that he was looking at Piper Winnick's splayed and broken body, a hundred yards down in the canyon.

Del Rio stared for a long moment, hoping he was wrong. The girl looked dead, but maybe she was unconscious. It was a slim possibility, but he *had* to check.

He went back to Danny, grabbed him by his hair, forced the blubbering kid to look him in the eye. 'What happened, Danny? What did you do to her?'

'I can't ... carry her out of there,' Danny wailed. 'I want to die.'

Del Rio said, 'What did you do, you piece of shit?'

The kid kept crying. Del Rio stood up and walked back to the lip of the canyon.

The canyon wall was at a treacherous forty-five degree angle to the floor. Del Rio looked for footholds, saw jutting boulders, some ledges running parallel to the ground, flat places where he could put his weight. If he watched where he was stepping, he could maybe get all the way down.

Pressing his left hand to the hill, gripping his light with the other, Del Rio started his descent, doing a good job of being a mountain goat even though his heart was slamming hard against his rib cage. He was about halfway to the bottom when, without any warning, his feet slipped across the smooth surface of a rock and shot out from under him.

Del Rio twisted his body, grabbed at the branches of a manzanita with both hands. His flashlight jumped away from him, bounced, and rolled downhill – and then Del Rio lost his tenuous hold and began skidding downward, his whole body sliding over rocks and dirt and grasses until, forty or fifty feet later, the ground came up and dumped him hard on his ass.

Chapter 77

Del Rio was scraped and shaken, but he hadn't slammed into anything on the way down. He rested for a moment, then got to his feet and made for his flashlight, which was, miraculously, still throwing light. Huffing, he picked his way across the rough terrain and closed in on young Piper Winnick.

She was on her back, her arms flung out like broken wings. Her white cotton nightgown was ripped and dirty, hiked up to her breasts, exposing her panties. She was wearing one shoe, a match to the slipper Danny had been holding in his hand.

Del Rio knew Piper was gone, but he hunched down beside the girl and put his hand to her neck.

He couldn't find a pulse. He listened to her

chest. No heartbeat. Her body was still warm to his touch. He didn't want to accept it, but Piper was dead and that was a sin. No other word for it.

Del Rio wanted to straighten her limbs, cover her body, close her eyes – acts that would destroy the crime scene, which this almost certainly was.

He flashed his light over Piper's face, tracked the dried blood to a wound at her temple – and saw that her skull was crushed there, caved in.

He used his light and his camera phone to catalogue the skull wound, the bruise on her arm, scrapes on her thighs, the blood trailing down her pale skin, indications that Piper had been alive when she'd gone over the cliff.

Playing his light up the canyon wall, Del Rio saw dozens of big rocks, any one of which could have cracked Piper's skull.

Danny. That fucking kid.

Screwing young girls wasn't enough. He'd moved up a few levels to physical aggression. Had Piper tried to get away from him, made a misstep, and fallen? Or had Danny shoved her over the edge on purpose?

Del Rio remembered the way Piper had looked yesterday morning, giddy with life. He could still see her in that yellow dress, holding on to her hat, saying her lines in a girlish voice with an Italian accent. He remembered the look of joy on her face when she got into that fast car with Danny.

He tried to remember what Danny had looked like when he'd floored the accelerator, but he couldn't picture him. Del Rio had been looking at the girl.

Del Rio imagined getting his hands on Danny, knocking his teeth out, breaking the bones in that too-pretty face. He was twenty years older than Danny, but he could still do some damage to a wimpy piece-of-crap kid like that.

Del Rio stood up. He had tears in his eyes as he looked at Piper's body. Her last minutes had been filled with fear and pain. A nice young girl like that.

'You were having a good day, Piper. A good life. I'm sorry this happened to you.'

Del Rio opened his cell phone and dialed Justine.

Chapter 78

Bugs circled Justine's dying beam. She whacked her flashlight with her palm, and the light flared briefly, then dimmed again.

Damn it.

Justine was pissed at herself for taking Danny's Mayday call seriously. He'd gotten her and Rick out of bed at four a.m., and now where was Danny?

Run off again with Piper.

Justine was wearing espadrilles, the wrong shoes to be hiking up this obstacle course of a path that started at the back of the cabin and led to only God knew where.

Add that to Danny's management team: Schuster, Barstow, and Koulos were following her single file, murmuring too softly for her to make out what they were saying to one another. Except that she'd heard her name a couple of times, so she knew they were talking about her.

Blaming her for Danny Whitman's escapade.

The unbelievable nerve.

The Whitman job was not worth what Private was being paid, not even close, and she was going to do something about that when she got hold of Jack.

Her cell phone rang, an incongruous bar of upbeat music. It had to be Rick saying that he'd found Danny. She hoped that whatever the problem was, it was minor or solved or both.

She dug in her jacket pocket and got her phone in hand just as the path emptied into a clearing. The faint circle of her flashlight beam revealed a heap on the ground.

It was *Danny*.

He was half naked, barefoot, sitting with his arms locked around his knees, rocking and keening.

What was this now? Was Danny having a tantrum or was he actually in trouble?

Schuster broke past her and ran to Danny, calling his name.

Barstow barked, 'Can I have that?'

He snatched her flashlight out of her hand and jogged over to where Schuster had pulled Danny into his arms and was crooning to him, 'What's wrong, buddy? Where does it hurt?'

Justine's phone was ringing again. She turned her back on the group and put the phone to her ear.

Del Rio was panting and his voice was ragged.

'The girl is dead. I'm coming up the canyon right now. Don't let Danny leave.'

'What girl? You mean, Piper? Rick? *Are you there?*'

Del Rio had clicked off.

Chapter 79

Justine sensed movement behind her and she whipped around. Merv Koulos was right there, standing so close she could smell Tic Tac on his breath.

The producer's homely face was crumpled like a paper bag and he was shouting at her, 'Do you see this, Dr. Smith? Danny is having a breakdown. We hired you people to watch him, and now I've got a mental case on my hands. My crew is showing up on set tomorrow, and you think Danny's going to be up for that? Every day that we don't shoot is three hundred grand right down the–'

'We've got a bigger problem, Mr. Koulos. Much bigger.'

'You're telling me? I'm going to sue you for criminal negligence. I'm going to sue you *personally.*'

Justine saw Rick's light bobbing as he reached the top of the incline. She left Koulos in midrant and went to Rick.

He was winded, trying to catch his breath. He gasped, 'Looks like Piper was killed by a blow to the head. Could have happened as she fell down the cliff. I can't tell if she was pushed or what.'

Danny pulled away from his agent and lurched over to Del Rio.

'Pushed? She wasn't *pushed*,' Danny wailed. 'We were sleeping. I woke up and she was gone. I went looking for her. She was supposed to be *asleep*...'

Barstow's face showed shock. His voice was high, bordering on hysteria when he said to Danny, 'I know, Danny, I know. Come back to the house with me. We'll get some clothes on you. I've got Xanax. We'll take care of this. Come on, Danny.'

Justine stood still, blinking in the dark, trying to absorb Rick's terrible news.

Piper Winnick was dead in this remote place, and no one had been with her but Danny.

Justine didn't know Piper, had never met her, but she'd met Danny. And she had contracted for Private to keep him at close range.

He'd ditched them. That was a deal breaker, and she thought that was defensible in court – but what was terrifying her now was the possibility that Danny was capable of violence, and she hadn't seen that.

Had her ego gotten the best of her? Had she missed a signal that had cost a girl her life?

Schuster and Barstow were trying to move Danny back up the trail, but Danny was resisting, shouting at them that he didn't want to leave Piper alone.

Koulos was back in Justine's face. He raged, 'And now, because he got away from you, Piper is dead. My movie is dead too. I'm ruined. Ruined.'

Justine was still holding her phone, but her hand was shaking.

'You making the call?' Rick asked her.

She nodded and dialed 911.

Chapter 80

Justine had just opened her front door when her phone rang. She hit the light switch in the foyer. Rocky barked, ran to her, and threw himself against her thighs.

She tousled his ears, tossed the car keys onto the console, and checked the caller ID on her phone. It was Danny's manager, Larry Schuster.

What did he want now? Was this another threat to sue?

She was still shaking from the sickening events of the past few hours: the dead teenage movie star, the threats from Mervin Koulos, and the pitiful arrest of Danny Whitman, who'd kicked and screamed until three cops managed to stuff him into the cruiser.

Justine said hello into the phone.

'Do you still work for us?' Schuster asked.

'You're kidding, Larry. Danny broke our contract when he drove away from the set–'

'He drove away from the set, but he's innocent of everything else.'

'Larry, I'm sorry for Danny and sorry for you, but we're out of this. It's time you got lawyers involved.'

'Just talk to him. Let him tell you what's going on.'

'Larry, he's told me. He feels like someone else is running his life, but as I understand it, no one told him to run off with Piper Winnick this morning – and now she's dead.'

'They're seeing each other. They're *involved*. They went to sleep and when he woke up, she was gone. He didn't push her off that cliff. He went looking for her and he found her down there.'

'Maybe the studio's lawyers are good enough to settle the rape case, Larry, but if Danny were my client, I'd get the best criminal-defense attorney in California. There should be a dozen five-star cannons who would love to defend Danny Whitman. Geragos, Tacopina–'

'I'm at the medical services building at Twin Towers,' Schuster said. 'The police left Danny alone for a minute and he took a head-first run at the wall in the interrogation room.'

'Are you *kidding?* How badly is he hurt?'

'It's a pretty good concussion. He's depressed. He was in love with Piper. Do you understand?'

'I *don't* understand, Larry. What do you want from me?'

'You're a shrink. And Danny trusts you. He asked me to get you, and I said I would try.'

'I'm a shrink, but I'm not *Danny's* shrink.'

'I told the cops that you *are* so that I could get you in to see him. Will you just talk to him? Maybe you can make some sense of this, Dr. Smith, because I know Danny very well. I've seen him every day for the last four years, and I'm telling you, Danny didn't kill anybody.'

Justine was exhausted, stressed out, sleep deprived, and now she was conflicted too.

Should she go see Danny because he was still her client and he had asked for her?

Or should she wait until she'd spoken to Jack and Private's lawyer, Eric Caine?

Nefertiti rubbed against her.

Justine bent to pet her cat.

Everything about Danny Whitman was bothering her. Was he a psychopath? Was that why neither she nor Larry Schuster had seen Danny's potential for violence? Or was he a lamb, as innocent as Schuster said?

For her own peace of mind, she had to know.

'Dr. Smith?' Schuster said.

'I'm here.'

It was an hour's drive to Twin Towers in traffic. Getting past the bureaucracy at TTCF could take all day, and she still might not get to see Danny.

'I'm being paged,' said Schuster. 'I've left your name at the main gate.'

Chapter 81

In the four hours since Justine had last seen Danny Whitman, he'd been transferred from Lost Hills, the best jail in the state, to TTCF.

He was now in the Twin Towers medical services building, which was packed to the walls with prisoners, many of them mentally unbalanced.

She'd worked in places like this one. They were

never good.

After being patted down again and sent through a metal detector again, Justine stood in the doorway and looked around.

The rectangular room had armed guards on both sides of the door, bars in the small high windows, fresh industrial-green paint on the walls, and a pervasive, almost punishing odor of disinfectant.

She located Danny in one of the hospital beds, two down from the glass-enclosed nursing station. He had two black eyes, wore a paper robe and a gauze turban, and he was handcuffed to the bed rails.

Justine had been told that she had fifteen minutes with Danny, no physical contact permitted, and that if she broke that rule, her meeting with Danny would be terminated immediately.

Danny looked up when she came toward him. He appeared happier to see her than she had expected. She hardly knew him. What did he think she could do for him?

Justine pulled a plastic chair up to the side of the bed. 'We don't have much time, Danny. Can you tell me what happened?'

'Piper and I were in love, but we couldn't tell anyone because of her age, and listen, the paparazzi–'

'I'm sorry, Danny. The short version, okay?'

Justine was assessing him. Did he comprehend? Was he lucid? Was he truthful? Was he living in this time and place or in a world of his own creation?

'Yesterday morning when we were setting up in

the Ferrari, Piper said to me, "Too bad we can't just get out of here," and I was thinking with my heart. We'd never spent the night together... It was a great opportunity... I drove to the cabin I bought last year under a fake name. Oh, God. If I'd used my brain, she'd still be alive.'

He was crying again.

'Danny. In twelve minutes, I'll be thrown out of here, so please talk to me. Did you have a fight with Piper?'

'Oh, no. We had a wonderful day. We partied until we both passed out in bed. I woke up – maybe something woke me up. Piper wasn't there.'

'Then what happened?'

Danny dried his face with the sleeve of his gown and went on.

'I went out to look for Piper. It was totally dark outside, but I saw a car parked next to the Ferrari. It was right in the flower bed. No car should have been there. Then I saw a flashlight moving through the trees, and I started walking up the trail and calling Piper.

'All of a sudden, the light disappeared. I heard the car start up behind me, and I thought maybe Piper was having regrets, that she had called for someone to pick her up. But then ... I found her shoe at the edge of the drop. I thought, "No, she can't be down there," but when I looked over the edge ... I knew there was nothing I could do for her. I called you. I called everyone.'

The guard came toward Danny's bed and said, 'Time's up.'

Danny looked directly into Justine's eyes. 'I swear to you, Dr. Smith, I didn't do that to Piper.

213

You have to believe me. Someone is doing something to me. I don't know what it is and I don't know who's doing it. But that car I saw at my cabin? Whoever owns it is the one who killed Piper.'

Chapter 82

Carmine Noccia's father was a thug; so was mine. Carmine and I had both gone to Ivy League schools, we'd both served in the Corps, and both our fathers had given us the keys to the family business.

Beyond that, Carmine Noccia and I had nothing in common.

Carmine was a third-generation killer, never caught, never even charged. The FBI had him on their watch list, but they had no evidence to support their certain knowledge that he'd had three people murdered.

There'd been no fingerprints. No smoking guns. No surveillance tape.

Snitches had been killed before testifying.

Carmine's father, the don, was ready to retire, and Carmine was rumored to be stepping into his job – and more. According to the stories, the Noccia family was expanding east in the coming year, from their Vegas hub to Chicago.

It was unprecedented in Mob history for a satellite organization to return to its roots, but Noccia had brass and his father had raised him to accomplish big things.

The hijacked van stuffed with thirty million in pharmaceuticals had been the first major move in Carmine's expansion plan, and now that same van was standing in his way. And because six months ago I'd reached out to Carmine to protect my brother from a lesson he might not have lived to regret, I was in bed with a mobster. On a first-name basis.

Noccia called me at around three in the morning. He didn't say hello. He said that his distributors, having paid for the drugs, were very *unhappy*.

He'd made this point to me before.

I said, 'We're on the job, Carmine. I didn't need the wakeup call.'

'We don't have clocks around here,' he said.

Another way of saying that my time was his time. I brought Noccia up to date on the plan going forward, and he hung up without saying good-bye.

I fell back to sleep.

I was running after Colleen, trying to tell her that I was sorry, but she wouldn't stop running away from me. The phone rang again.

This time my caller was my good friend Lieutenant Mitchell Tandy.

'I'm in the neighborhood, Jack. I'd be happy to stop by if there's anything you'd like to tell me.'

'I told you, Mitch. I didn't do it.'

Tandy laughed pleasantly and hung up.

By the time Justine phoned to report on Danny Whitman's arrest on suspicion of murder, I was wide awake.

Chapter 83

I checked out of the Sun and drove to work, keeping the car to ten miles below the speed limit. Tandy tailed me to Figueroa Street, gave me a two-blast salute from his horn when I turned into the underground garage below my office building.

Mitchell Tandy was a hyena.

I walked into my office at half past seven, caught Justine's second call that morning. She told me that Danny Whitman was in the hospital at TTCF.

I cringed just thinking about that place. It was like an ice-cold hand gripping the back of my neck: a bad feeling, and it was impossible to shake off.

'What do you think, Jack?' Justine said. 'Should we cut Danny loose? Or should I work with him and his cast of sidekicks until I know whether or not he killed Piper Winnick?'

'Sounds to me like you think he's innocent.'

'I'm leaning that way. He thinks someone is screwing with his head. Gaslighting him. Who would do that? What would they get out of it?'

Justine was the heroine of lost causes. When she got it wrong, she'd say, 'Princess Do-Good strikes again.' But her instincts *were* good. The worst you could say about Justine was that she put in too much time on her cases and got too emotionally involved.

That said, if she could prove Whitman innocent, that would be a point for Private. A point we needed.

'It's your call,' I said.

I got into Cruz's report on his interviews at a Cuban club in Hollywood, and when Val Kenney came in at eight, I asked her to break down the report and flag items for follow-up.

While Cody and Val worked outside my office, I put some time in on *California v. Jack Morgan*, found out a couple of things about Colleen Molloy that she hadn't told me. I was digging into that when Val came in. 'I've got something on the woman Cruz met with last night,' she said.

'Carmelita Gomez?'

'Karen Ricci. The woman in the wheelchair.'

'Go on.'

'Before she was Karen Ricci, she was Karen Keyes. She did a five-year stretch at the women's jail for extortion. There was a riot and she got clubbed. That's how she ended up in the wheelchair. She's out early for good behavior.'

Val was putting her time with the Miami PD to good use. I was about to tell her to follow up on Ricci, but she wasn't done yet.

'I've got something else, Jack. The story Carmelita Gomez told Cruz isn't right. She said that a driver named Billy Moufan tipped her off.'

'He was Gomez's driver, right?'

'That's what she said. She told Cruz that after her john was killed at the Seaview, her driver, Billy Moufan, told her that a limo driver might have done it, that this same limo driver may have killed the john at the Moon.'

217

'But no one named Billy or William Moufan has ever been issued a chauffeur's license in California. I can't find that name in any database, no matter how I spell it.'

'So you're saying she lied to Cruz.'

Val said, 'At best, she was concealing the name of the driver who tipped her off.'

I asked Val to brief Cruz, then Cody buzzed me, saying Jinx Poole was on line one.

I took the call.

Jinx said, 'Can you have dinner with me, tonight, Jack? It's important.'

Chapter 84

At one-fifteen in the afternoon, Del Rio and Cruz were parked inside the big lot under the shadow of the 96th Street bridge. The lot was a mile and a half from LAX, bounded by the eight-lane Sepulveda Boulevard and a loop of the Sky Way. Limos, taxis, and other commercial transport continually streamed in and queued up under alphabetical signs, waiting to enter the airport.

They were watching one guy in particular, Paul Ricci, a bouncer from Havana, married to the tipster in the wheelchair. Ricci was shooting the bull with three other drivers.

Ricci glanced at the Private fleet car, then opened the door to his own car and got a sandwich out of a cooler. He called out to one of the other drivers, 'Baxter. You got any Grey Poupon?'

Baxter laughed, said, 'I'll give you a little brown poop-on. How's that?'

Watching this from inside the Mercedes, Cruz said to Del Rio, 'That's him. Ricci is the one in the cheap suit and the chauffeur's hat.'

Del Rio put on his jacket, said to Cruz, 'Can you see my gun under this?'

Cruz said, 'You look like you're packing even when you're sleeping.'

Del Rio said, 'That's good, because I want Ricci to freeze in place. I don't want to chase the guy. I kinda twisted my foot when I was rock climbing.'

Cruz said, 'Aww. Face it, Rick, you're getting old.'

Del Rio told Cruz that he wasn't old and that he could still beat the crap outta anyone his size.

'You don't have to do that, Rick. I'll protect you,' said Cruz.

Del Rio gave Cruz an evil look.

Cruz laughed, tightened the band on his pony-tail. When it was the way he liked it, he said, 'Ready, pardner?'

Together, Cruz and Del Rio walked over to where the four men were standing under the D sign.

Two of them, including Paul Ricci, were limo drivers. The other two wore uniforms of 'The Air Shuttle Guys.' The shuttle guys were fat, no problem. But the limo driver standing next to Ricci was ripped and young. Looked like he'd done some time.

Cruz said, 'Paul Ricci?'

All conversation stopped.

Ricci puffed himself up. 'I'm Ricci. Wha'chu want?'

Cruz said, 'Don't you remember me?'

He opened his jacket and showed the guy his gun, the one he'd had to give up outside the club.

Ricci looked at the gun, pivoted, and, his hat flying off his shaven head, took off toward the exit at a fast run.

Cruz shouted, 'We just want to *talk* to you.'

The guy ran pretty fast.

'Shit,' said Del Rio.

Chapter 85

Paul Ricci, limo driver by day, bouncer by night, weighed two hundred pounds, a lot of it muscle. He steamed past the small administration building at the entrance to the parking lot, took a hard left on the sidewalk, and got his speed up on the side street.

Cruz took off after him.

Cruz was smaller but faster and was closing in on Ricci, who was running alongside a high vine-covered fence, heading due north toward Sepulveda Boulevard.

Cruz did not want to end up on the boulevard. A foot chase through eight lanes of traffic was a pileup waiting to happen.

Cruz shouted, 'Ricci. Stop,' but Ricci ran out into traffic, showing some good open-field moves as he wove between fast-moving cars.

Horns blared, first at Ricci, then because traffic had slowed. A moment later, Cruz had lost sight of him.

Cruz stood in place for a few seconds, taking in nice deep breaths of diesel fumes, trying to see everything at once. Vehicles of every size and shape obscured his view, and now he was getting mad.

What was wrong with the guy, running like that?

Then Cruz saw Ricci's shiny head. He was across the road at the base of the staircase leading from Sepulveda up to the Sky Way. There was no place to go once he got to the top, but Ricci was going anyway. Asshole.

Cruz waded out into the roaring traffic, holding up his cop-like badge so that cars would slow for him, calling out, 'Ricci, for Christ's sake. *I'm not a cop.*'

Cruz got across Sepulveda as Ricci was climbing the upper section of the switchback. Ricci turned his head, saw Cruz gaining on him – and lost his footing. He grabbed the handrail too late and went down, giving Cruz the chance he needed to close in.

Cruz took the stairs like Rocky and caught up with Ricci. 'Okay?' he asked. 'Is this enough running for one day?'

He reached to give the guy a hand up, and Ricci took the help. But as soon as he was on his feet, he swung at Cruz's jaw. The bouncer was off balance, and Cruz easily ducked the punch, then he returned the favor with a punch of his own.

Cruz's fist connected beautifully with Ricci's jaw, and Ricci went down again, this time for the count.

'California light-middleweight champ, 2005,' Cruz shouted to Ricci. 'That's who you're fighting with.'

Right then, Del Rio drove the Mercedes up the sidewalk to the base of the stairs.

He got out and straightened his jacket.

'The relief column has arrived,' he called out to Cruz.

Del Rio joined Cruz and Ricci on the steps, where a couple of people passed them without making eye contact.

Del Rio said to Ricci, 'Listen, douchebag. We don't care about your life story, okay? Just tell us what we want to know and we're gone.'

Ricci rubbed his jaw. 'You're not cops?'

Cruz said to Del Rio, 'You believe him?' Cruz put out his hand and helped the guy up again. 'Listen, Paul. We're not cops. We don't want to hurt you or anyone. We paid Karen and Carmelita for information about five murdered johns in the LA area. We didn't get it.'

'What information? What information?'

The guy was still panicky, and now Cruz was thinking that one of the people walking up to the Sky Way might have called the police.

He said, 'Carmelita said a driver named Billy Moufan had told her that one of their drivers was the killer. She said that Billy OD'd. But there's no such person as Billy Moufan and there never was. The thing she didn't say is that you drive a limo. Big oversight. Are you "Billy Moufan"? Do

put a lot of time on her tab.

'I think we're getting somewhere,' I said to Jinx.

The waiter took our order, and when he left, I told Jinx about Cruz's night at Havana and about Del Rio and Cruz confronting a limo driver under the Sky Way earlier today.

'We have a pretty good idea how to find this Tyson Keyes. If he knows who killed the johns, we're going to find out.'

'Why were Karen Ricci and Carmelita Gomez holding back his name?'

'Ricci was afraid of him,' I told her. 'Apparently Keyes is abusive. I don't know why women marry men like that. And I don't understand why they stay with them.'

'My husband was abusive,' Jinx told me. 'It's complicated. I've been wanting to tell you about it.'

'Tell me,' I said.

Jinx sipped her drink. She had said she wanted to tell me, but I could see from her expression that it wasn't an easy story to relate. I sat next to her and waited her out.

'I killed him,' she said. 'I want you to know that I killed my husband.'

Chapter 87

Nothing about Jinx Poole said 'killer' to me. She was smart, cool, a respected businesswoman, and her admission sounded literally, factually, un-believable.

Yet I believed her.

Still, I was just about shocked out of my shoes – and I didn't hide it.

'Jinx, you can't tell me that you committed a felony. I'm not a lawyer and I'm not a priest. I can be subpoenaed. Forced to testify.'

'I don't even understand why I want to tell you,' Jinx said to me. 'But I feel I must. I want you to know about my husband's death from *me*.'

I didn't like this setup. I hardly knew Jinx Poole. Why was she confiding in me? The question jumped into my mind for the first time: Did she have something to do with the hotel murders?

'My husband was Clark Langston,' she said. 'You've heard of him?'

'He owned some TV stations in the nineties?'

'Yes, that was him.'

Despite my warning, Jinx began to tell me her story. She described meeting Clark Langston twenty years before, during the summer between her freshman and sophomore years at Berkeley. She was waiting tables at the Lodge at Pebble Beach.

'Clark had a boat, a plane, vacation homes in

226

Napa, Austin, and Chamonix. He was so charming, like George Clooney, maybe. Rich and handsome and funny – and he always had friends around him. He was *magnetic*, you know what I mean? I was a kid. And I fell for him, Jack. I fell very hard.'

Jinx kind of lit up as she described what she had thought was only a fantastic summer romance. Then Langston told her that his divorce had gone through. He proposed, offered her a big diamond ring and a big life to go with it.

'I married him that September,' Jinx said. 'My parents told me to wait, but I was nineteen. I thought I knew everything. I knew nothing. I left school and became Mrs. Clark Langston and got all that came with that.'

Jinx stopped talking. She swallowed, made a few halting starts. She was having trouble going on, but after a moment, she did.

'A few months into our marriage, he started putting me down in public, flirting with other women, telling me to fetch things for him. Actually, it was worse when we were alone. He drank every day. Until he was stupefied.

'I had never known a real drinker, Jack, and Clark was an angry drunk, a violent drunk. He'd wrench my arms behind my back, shove me against a wall, and rape me. Soon the only kind of sex we had was rape. That's how he liked it.

'One time, he had his hands around my throat, had me bent back over the sink and was screaming in my face about how worthless I was. There was a knife on the drainboard, and suddenly it was in my hand, pointed at his back – I didn't realize that I had grabbed it. It was the first time murder actually occurred to me.'

'Did you tell anyone about him? What he was doing?'

'No. You didn't do that in his circle, and I no longer had a circle of my own. No one would have believed me anyway. And sometimes, this is the crazy part, I saw the man I loved – and I still loved him. Imagine that.'

'I'm sorry to hear this, Jinx. It's a bad story.'

The waiter brought our meal, asked if we needed anything else. I told him we were fine, but my appetite was gone.

Jinx said to me, 'When we'd been married for about two years, we went to a wedding far off the beaten track, if there's ever been a track to Willow Creek Golf and Country Club.

'Clark was in his element. He gave a toast and he also gave the new couple a car as a wedding gift.

'When the bride danced with Clark, I saw embarrassment and fear on her face. I'd worn that look myself. Hell, I'm wearing it now. I realized that the bride had also been victimized by my husband, but she'd been luckier. She'd gotten away.

'We were driving home when Clark got lost. We had a GPS, one of the first, but I didn't know how to work it, and Clark was crazy hammered, taking hard turns at high speeds, driving up on the shoulder of the road. It was at the end of the day in a remote rural area.

'Clark said, "Get out the map, Fluffy. Can't you do anything?" I got the map out of the glove box and started to read him the directions back to the freeway – and that gave him a big idea. He told me to give him the directions in the electronic voice of the GPS. To do an imitation.'

I nodded, told Jinx to go on.

'There was a sign for Whiskeytown Lake. Clark said, "Whiskeytown. Sounds like my kind of place." I started talking like the GPS. "Turn right. In one. Mile. Turn right. In one half. Mile."'

'Jinx turned to me, looking small and young and vulnerable.

'I've never told this much of the story to anyone before. I'm sorry, Jack. I think I've made a mistake.'

I thought she *had* made a mistake, but now I was with her on that twisting road and I couldn't see around the corner.

Had Jinx stabbed her husband?

Had she strangled him with a wire garrote?

'It's okay,' I said. 'You're safe with me.'

That was when I realized that my point of view had shifted.

I wanted to hear Jinx's story.

And I wanted her to be okay.

Chapter 88

Jinx looked haunted as she told me about Clark Langston's life and death, still afraid of her dead husband. Maybe she still loved him too.

'We were on a dirt road that circled the lake,' she said. 'Boaters were packing up their gear. The road turned into a rut, overgrown with grass and weeds, and in every way deserted.

'I was still doing my GPS voice,' Jinx continued. She smiled, but it was a nervous smile. 'This laughable pretense of control over my husband was inspiring me, Jack. We were now locked in a crazy game of chicken. And he was goading me, saying, "You think I don't know what you're up to?"

'I don't know how he knew it, but an idea had occurred to me – that maybe I could get him to crash his Maserati. I wanted to hurt him. I wanted him to die, and if I died too, it was all right.

'I said, "Take the next left." That was the road to the national recreation area.'

I sat back in my seat and watched her face. I imagined this power struggle twenty years before, the tyrannical older man and his bride who fantasized about getting even. Emotionally, Jinx was still back there.

'It was still light enough to see,' she said to me. 'I told him to take the next turn, which was onto

230

a boat ramp. He did it, and we took the ramp going forty.

'I lost my nerve. I screamed, but Clark was having a high time scaring me, making me sorry that I'd dared him. He laughed at me, Jack. He pressed his foot down even harder on the gas.'

'Did he realize where he was?'

'I'll never know. He might have thought he could stop the car in time and misjudged the distance. Maybe he thought that his quarter-million-dollar car would fly. All I know for sure is that he never braked.

'I undid my seat belt,' Jinx told me. Her head was lowered. She was rushing now, trying to get the story over with.

'I had the door open, and I jumped before the car hit the water. I went numb for a while after that. I heard nothing, saw nothing, thought only of reaching the shore, which wasn't far away.

'I didn't look back. I walked for a while, got a ride, told the police that my husband had lost control of his car.

'When they pulled the car out of the lake, Clark was still wearing his seat belt. His blood alcohol was three times the legal limit, and his death was ruled accidental. No questions.

'I went to the funeral. I cried. Then I moved to LA. I took back my maiden name, and I got my degree.'

'You bought a hotel.'

Jinx said, 'Yes. Right after I graduated. I bought a hotel with the two million dollars stipulated in my prenuptial agreement. I borrowed a lot more. I renovated the whole place, reopened it as the

Beverly Hills Sun, and then I bought the other two. I was in a frenzy. I needed to work, to prove to myself that my life was worth something. That I didn't need Clark's love – or his disdain.

'Jack, what I did at Whiskeytown Lake – I wanted him to die, then I made my wish come true.'

She had started to tear up, but she wouldn't let herself go. She said, 'I've been feeling that the killings in my hotels are payback for Clark's death, for the money I got from him.'

'Jinx, did you make your husband a drunk, an abuser, a rapist? Did you make him drive off that ramp?'

I was continuing in this vein, but she stopped me. She put her hand on my chest. She was struggling to get something out.

'I'm afraid ... to trust myself again ... to be with a man.'

She was leaning against me.

'I feel like I want to hold you,' I said.

She looked up at me, her eyes full of tears. 'I need to be held.'

I took her into my arms, and at last she cried.

I hadn't expected to feel close to her. I didn't even welcome the feeling, but it was undeniable. I liked Jinx a lot.

Chapter 89

It was just after midnight. Except for a plastic bag blowing around the street and the odd car lost in the wrong neighborhood, absolutely nothing was happening on Anderson and Artemus.

The Private fleet car was a gray 2007 Chevy sedan, parked on Anderson, just south of Artemus, where the guys had a view of the entrance to the Red Cat Pottery, as well as the loading docks on Artemus.

Del Rio was at the wheel, Cruz riding shotgun, Scotty in the backseat. Everyone was very quiet.

Cruz said, 'Call Jack.'

Del Rio got Jack on the line and told him where they were. They exchanged thoughts on how to steal a fortune in illegal pharmaceuticals on behalf of the Vegas Mob without getting caught, without getting thrown in the clink for twenty years, with no help from Carmine Noccia.

Del Rio said, 'It's getting late, Jack. That Oxy is going to leave the warehouse one box at a time. In another few weeks there's going to be an empty van in there and Noccia is going to break heads. He's going to start with yours.'

Jack gave Del Rio the go-ahead, and Del Rio hung up.

Cruz started the car and drove to Boyd, a dead-end street parallel to Artemus, where he found a space among the delivery trucks and panel vans parked all along the length of it, both sides of the street walled in by cement-block warehouses colorfully tagged with spray-painted graffiti.

Del Rio twisted around in his seat. 'Scotty. You're up. Let's rock 'n' roll.'

Scotty took a slug off his water bottle and said, 'I'm liking the window below the stairs.'

'Make it quick,' Del Rio said.

Scotty pulled on a pair of work gloves, turned the dome light to the 'off' position, and opened the back door.

Del Rio said, 'Wait a second.'

When the taxi had passed on Anderson, Del Rio told Scotty to go. Scotty was wearing black from neck to toe and was almost invisible except for the shine coming off his blond hair. Del Rio and Cruz watched as he reached the top of the alley and crossed the street, still in view of the Chevy.

Then Scotty disappeared.

A half minute after that, an alarm shrieked, and seconds later, the back door of the car opened and Scotty got in, saying, 'Did you time me?'

Cruz laughed. 'You were quick, yo. Like in those films where they stop time and the one guy, runs between all those frozen people, you know?'

Del Rio said, 'Let's see how fast the cops answer the call.'

Four minutes later, the first sirens came up South Anderson and stopped out of sight. From the proximity of the squawking car radios, Del Rio figured they were outside the roll-up gates at the loading dock.

The three investigators ducked down in their seats, Del Rio assuring himself that so far no crime had been committed. Scotty had only rattled a window until the alarm went off. They waited for more cars to arrive, but only the two cruisers showed up.

When the cops had left, Del Rio and his team did the same thing: set off the alarm, then waited for the cops to come and leave again. Then they did it once more.

Chapter 90

Justine woke up to a racket.

Rocky was going nuts *and* bananas, barking, his toenails clacking as he got traction on the hardwood floors in his scramble toward the front door.

Justine looked at the clock. It was just before seven.

What the hell was this? In between Rocky's barks, she heard her doorbell ringing insistently.

She threw a robe on over her silk PJs and walked to the foyer, thinking it had to be Jack. Who else would dare? She peeked through the peephole, then opened the door to Danny's manager, Larry Schuster.

His clothes were rumpled, his patchy beard was coming in – in sum, he looked like he'd slept in his car.

'I'm sorry about the time, Dr. Smith. I have to

talk to you.'

'Call me Justine. Did something happen to Danny?'

'No, he's still in the hospital. I was driving around all night. I finally came to a decision.'

'Here's an idea, Larry. I'll be at the office at nine. Why don't you meet me there?'

'This will only take a few minutes. Please. It's important. I can't take a chance that someone sees me and thinks I told you what I know.'

'You'll never eat lunch in this town again?'

Schuster smiled. 'Exactly.'

Justine told Schuster to come in. She led him to the kitchen, asked him to make coffee and to take a seat at the counter. She went to her bedroom and reappeared a few minutes later, dressed for work.

Justine took a carton of milk out of the fridge, then poured coffee into mugs.

'Sugar?'

'Yes, please.'

Justine put the sugar bowl next to the milk. She fed her cat and her dog and told Schuster to start talking.

'There were other girls.'

'There were other girls what?'

'Besides Katie Blackwell, three other girls in the past year threatened to sue Danny for unwanted, um, sexual contact.'

'Shit,' Justine said. 'You should have told me this before I took the case, Larry. This is a contract breaker, as if we didn't already have enough reason to tell you and Danny good luck without us.'

'Please don't do that,' Larry said.

'I was a shrink in a mental hospital, did you know that?'

'Yes. That place in Santa Monica. Crossroads.'

'That's right. So I know a thing or two about mental disorders. But the way Danny keeps fooling me makes me think he's delusional. He believes his own stories.'

'No, he's telling the truth. He was loyal to Piper. He didn't have sex with those girls.'

'Then who did? This crap about someone else running his life could possibly get Danny some kind of insanity deal, but I wouldn't count on it. You should prepare yourself. Danny is looking at prison for a very long time.'

'He didn't molest those girls and he didn't murder Piper either.'

'Larry, unless you say, "I know he didn't do it, because I killed her," I'm not going to believe you.'

Schuster said nothing. He just stared at her.

'Did you kill Piper, Larry?'

'No. No. I'm sorry. I was just thinking whether it's all right for me to tell you what I think–'

'Tell me, damn it. Or get the hell out of here and don't ever call me again.'

'Alan Barstow.'

'Do *not* make me drag this out of you.'

'Alan Barstow paid off those other girls. And he tried to pay off Katie Blackwell. Alan stands to make many, many millions on Danny and will do whatever it takes to keep him as a client.'

'Why would he kill Piper? What's his motive?'

'Piper didn't like Alan. She was trying to get

237

Danny to change agencies. If Piper got between Alan and Danny, Alan would have been dangerous. He's a very scary dude. You should seriously check him out, Justine. I think you should put him on a skewer and fire up the grill.'

Chapter 91

Justine drove the car around the lake with the Vegas-style fountain set in front of the enormous black glass building in Century City. The Monolith, as it was called, was home to Creative Talent Management, the biggest, most influential talent agency in Hollywood. And the world.

Nora Cronin sat beside Justine in the passenger seat.

Early in the year, Justine had worked for the DA's office to help the LAPD catch a spree killer who had been terrifying the city and running the cops into the weeds.

The Schoolgirl Killer had been Lieutenant Nora Cronin's case, but despite her initial outrage that the DA had assigned Private to work with her, she and Justine had meshed brilliantly, as if they'd worked together for years.

Nora touched up her lipstick as Justine drove into the garage, took a ticket from the machine, then cruised around the subterranean car park that consumed more square footage than the town where she was born.

'You know what's freaky? More money passes

through this building than we spend annually on national defense.'

Nora was big, built like a tank, and she had a good, hearty laugh, which she let loose now.

'You're too funny, Justine. Actually, I can't wait to see the inside of this place.'

'Yeah?' Justine said. 'I think we're in for a real gladiator-style face-off with an egomaniacal, money-driven jerk who may also be a killer.'

'We might not be able to pull this off. I'm just preparing you. If he says to leave, we've got to go.'

'Come on, Nora. A cop and a shrink are going to tag-team him. He'll talk. He'll beg us to listen to him.'

Nora laughed again. 'What a pair you have, Justine. Anyway, this place may be the colosseum, but we only have to take down one lion. Only one. Here, take this.'

Nora reached down to the floor, picked up a file, and passed it to Justine, who stashed it in her briefcase.

'Let me do the talking,' Justine said.

'Fine,' said Nora. 'I'll be your bodyguard.'

Justine laughed. 'Perfect,' she said. 'I've always wanted one of those.'

Chapter 92

An elevator took Justine and Nora from the car park to the Creative Talent Management lobby, a vast, marbled space hung with imposing works of modern art. Glass-faced staircases fooled the eye and suspended disbelief, rising thirty feet through the reception area ceiling, itself made of glass.

The space was meant to impress and intimidate – and it did both of those things to Justine. She'd laughed about CTM as the black hole of greed, but now she felt the force of the place. The might of the money.

And she and Nora were on their own.

Justine gave their names to a receptionist, signed a log book, and she and Nora took seats at the periphery of the room to watch the show.

Actors practiced their lines, gesticulating in the corners; messengers came and went; groups of well-dressed people entered the agency through doors that blended so perfectly with the surrounding walls there didn't seem to be doors at all.

Tom Cruise came through in one of those groups.

Ethan Hawke left the building.

Fifteen minutes after they had arrived, a young man floated down one of the invisible staircases. He was wearing a white linen shirt, dark pants, and a smug expression. Approaching Justine and Nora, he said, 'I'm Jay Davis, Mr. Barstow's assistant. Alan is ready to see you now.'

Justine lifted her briefcase, feeling like she was carrying a dirty bomb, thinking, *I doubt Alan is ready for this.*

When they entered his office, Barstow was standing with his back to the door, shouting into the mic of his headset, 'I said no, you dumb prick. Lily Padgett will *not* do a screen test. You made the deal and if you dare to break it, we'll sue you for breach. We'll take everything you've got including the sweat on your balls. Yes. A network series. Jerry Bruckheimer. She turned him down. Do you get me now?'

Barstow clicked off the phone, turned, and saw the two women come into his large, transparent corner office. His smile was bright and cold, like winter sun on a frozen lake.

'How's Danny?' he asked, shaking Justine's hand. 'I hope you have good news.'

Justine introduced Nora as her partner and they took seats around Barstow's coffee table, where they had a view of a Frank Stella construction the size of a barn wall, and a panoramic view out the window of West Hollywood and Beverly Hills.

But Justine was scrutinizing Alan Barstow.

He had acne scars and thinning hair and narrow shoulders, but he had swagger to spare. That came from being a top earner at CTM, from making millions upon millions every year.

Justine sat forward in a five-thousand-dollar armchair, put the Waterford crystal goblet she'd

241

been sipping water from down on the Brazilian cherrywood table, and said, 'Alan, we think we know who is responsible for Piper Winnick's death, but we need your help.'

Barstow pressed a button on the arm of his chair and said, 'Jay, no calls.' Then, 'I'm all yours.'

Justine said, 'We think Piper was killed by someone who was jealous of her relationship with Danny.'

'No kidding. That's bizarre.'

'A few people knew about Danny and Piper. You, Merv Koulos, Larry Schuster, Danny's friend Kovaks, and his assistant, Randy Boone. But Danny's relationship with Piper wasn't public knowledge. Neither was his cabin in Topanga.'

'So obviously someone close to Danny did it.'

'Yes. We think this man expected Piper to be grateful to him for getting her the part in the film and attracted to him because he's a powerful guy, and he was furious that she ran off with Danny. So it makes sense that he drove to the cabin, woke Piper up, and got her to take a walk with him on the trail. We surmise that he argued with her. That things got physical.'

Barstow broke in. 'Justine, are you making a pitch or do you want my help? Who the hell did this to my boy?'

'Someone who likes young girls, Alan. A man who has a real passion for young girls.'

Justine took the folder out of her briefcase, opened it on the table, turned it toward Barstow, and fanned out the pages.

Justine said, 'This is what we're going to show the police. And I have a feeling these mug shots are going to find their way to the Internet. Millions will know that Alan Barstow is a sex offender. That's you, Alan. You're the real deal.'

Chapter 93

Barstow sputtered, 'Whoa-whoa-whoa. Where did you get *this?*'

A shiver danced up Justine's spine. She watched Alan Barstow's face as he stared at his mug shots and the rap sheet listing his arrest for sex crimes against minors. His arrogance was gone, replaced by more primitive stuff: fear, anger, and confusion, emotions that made people turn violent.

Justine said, 'There's software now, Alan. It can match faces to sex offenders in any police data-base, even if the crime happened ten years ago in New Jersey. Even though you changed your name.'

'So *what?*' he said, pushing the file off the table. 'You're saying *this* means that I killed Piper? Are you fucking kidding me? Look, you. The only interest I had in Piper Winnick was *financial.* That's *all.*'

He grabbed a copy of *Variety* off the coffee table and showed Justine the headline, 'Shades of Red.'

Barstow shouted, 'The film is dead. A great slamming summer movie is dead. You know what I got for a year of busting my nuts? Absolutely *nothing.*'

The angrier he got, the more relaxed Justine

became. As long as he only yelled.

'Calm down, Alan. I'm not saying you *planned* to hurt Piper. I'm saying you were insulted. You tried to tell her who *you* were and who *she* was. Things got out of hand. She pulled away from you–'

Barstow cut her off. 'Dr. Smith, you are totally, I cannot say this strongly enough, *totally* out of your tiny little mind. This meeting is over. If you repeat a word of this crap, I'll sue you for slander, for defamation, for anything our legal department can throw at you.'

He got up from his chair, went to the door, and said to his assistant, 'Jay. Show these people out. No. Call security.'

Barstow turned to Justine and Nora. 'You have one minute to leave the premises.'

Nora said, 'LAPD trumps corporate security anytime.'

She unbuttoned her jacket, showed Barstow the gold badge hanging from a chain around her neck.

'We're testing Piper Winnick's clothing. If we find your DNA on that girl, you're cooked. Meanwhile, we have a witness who claims that you drugged Danny Whitman as well as the girls who accused Danny of sexual misconduct. Our witness says you had sex parties, Alan. Your guests were young girls, drunken girls, you sick son of a bitch.'

Men in khaki uniforms trotted up the hallway. Barstow strode to the doorway, pulled open the door, and said to the head security guy, 'Sorry, Roger. My mistake. Everything is under control.'

He closed his door, pulled down the blinds, and returned to the sitting area, but he didn't sit down.

Barstow said, 'You're a cop? You're supposed to *say* you're a cop. This is entrapment. You haven't read me my rights. I'm not saying another word without my lawyer.'

Nora got up and stood toe-to-toe with the raging Barstow.

'You're all wrong, Mr. Barstow. I don't have to identify myself, and you only get your rights read if you're in custody.'

Barstow's eyes darted from Nora to the door, to Justine, back to the door, looking for a way to save himself.

'Don't wreck my life for this,' he said. 'I didn't kill Piper. I may have invited girls to my house for Danny. I may have served liquor. Some girls maybe woke up in bed with Danny and thought they'd had sex with *him.*'

'That's not a confession. That's a "maybe."'

'But I did *not* push Piper off a cliff. Not accidentally, not on purpose. I had nothing to do with her death.'

Nora said, 'Mr. Barstow, you're under arrest on suspicion of murder and a few dozen lesser charges that will keep you in custody while we check out your story. You have a right to remain silent. Anything you say can be used against you in court. It's time to call that lawyer. I think you'll find that you have a morals clause in your contract, in which case CTM is going to cut you loose. But play it out. See what happens.'

Barstow turned desperate eyes on Nora.

He said, 'Wait. If I can help you get Piper's killer, can we make a deal?'

Deals were what Alan Barstow did. He was finding hope in his comfort zone.

Nora said, 'If you have information that leads to the arrest and conviction of Piper Winnick's killer, I'll do my best to help you.'

'Okay,' Barstow said. 'I'm cooperating with you. I'll put it in writing. If we can all relax, start over again. I think I know who killed Piper. It wasn't me. And it wasn't Danny.'

Chapter 94

Justine was back at the Topanga Canyon cabin, this time in sunlight, standing with Dr. Sci and Nora Cronin a few yards from the flower bed where fresh tire tracks had been pressed into the earth.

A car had parked among the flowers recently, just as Danny had said. And Danny had also said that whoever killed Piper had to have been driving that car.

The LAPD's tire track specialist aimed his Minolta at the tread marks and fired off a few shots. He put a scale down next to the impressions and fired off another few rounds.

'Thanks, Stan. We're good for now,' said Nora.

Dr. Sci was as excited as a kid on his birthday. 'This is a beautiful thing, Justine. What a great tread mark.'

The LAPD had two big Leica scanners back at the lab.

Sci was using Private's state-of-the art, handheld ZScanner 700 CX, which captured images in three dimensions, in full color, with self-positioning in real time. There was no scanner anywhere that could top it.

Nora said, 'I don't care if you show off, Sci. But gloating is just uncool.'

Sci laughed. 'Just sayin', you're going to thank Jack for spending the fifty grand on this.'

'If we catch the dirtbag because of your scanner, I'll kiss Jack on the mouth, okay?'

Sci grinned. 'If it's okay with Jack, it's okay with me.'

The 3-D scanner looked something like two hairdryer heads fused onto one handgrip. Sci laid down a net of small positioning markers in the tire track, then passed the scanner above the track in one continuous motion. As he did so, the image transferred to the laptop Justine had set up on a nearby tree stump. Every ridge, wave, and detail of the tread mark appeared right on her screen.

Nora came over to watch as Justine ran the image through the software that compared the image to six thousand distinct patterns in the TreadMate database.

Justine held her breath as the computer stopped at a tread mark identical to the image Sci had scanned. The word *match* flashed onscreen.

'We have a hit,' she said.

Sci joined Nora in looking over Justine's shoulder.

'An N-spec,' Sci said. 'That's a Porsche stand-ard tire. Justine, may I?'

Sci tapped the laptop keys and found what he was looking for.

'The N-spec tires have a special tread design. Yep, it's got a thin groove around the outboard shoulder. I'm gonna say it's the tire of choice on the Porsche 911.

'Hey-hey. Look at this,' Sci continued. He pointed to a flat mark near the image that wasn't part of the tire track. 'This is a partial shoe print. Part of the toe. The guy stepped in the dirt when he got out of the car. Too bad he backed over the rest of the prints on his way out.'

'Can you run that?' Justine asked.

'Even if we could identify the type of shoe, it's not enough to give us a size or idiosyncratic wear patterns.'

Justine was thinking back to way early yesterday morning.

She had started down the trail behind Danny's cabin in the direction of his cries. Del Rio had caught up to her, and then they'd heard car doors slamming behind them.

Del Rio had gone on ahead while Justine had gone back to the cabin. When she got there, she spoke with each of the men who'd arrived to help Danny: Schuster, Barstow, Koulos.

She hadn't been looking at cars, couldn't make a positive ID on any vehicle she'd glimpsed at four a.m. in the dark.

Still, she thought one of those cars had been a Porsche.

What model? Who had been driving it?

She couldn't say. But all the cars had parked in the gravel driveway. If one of those three men had arrived earlier, while Danny was sleeping, if he had been in a hurry and parked his Porsche beside the Ferrari, not behind it, in the flower bed...

Justine said, 'We can get a match the old-fashioned way.'

'Justine, there's no way,' Nora shouted at her, right there in front of Sci and Stan and every other tech within earshot. 'I can't get a warrant based on a tire track that could match any of six jillion Porsches in LA.'

Justine stood speechless, not used to having a rule book, not used to be shouted at either. Of course Nora was right. But there were other ways.

'Can you look at traffic cam footage, Nora? Can you do that without a warrant?'

Chapter 95

It had taken Justine two minutes on the DMV database to learn which of Danny's handlers owned a Porsche 911. After that, she and Del Rio had gone looking for the car in logical places and hadn't found it.

Now Del Rio parked the fleet car in the circular drive of a six-million-dollar, ten-thousand-square-foot Mediterranean-style house in Bel Air.

He took his gun out of the glove box, slipped it

into his shoulder holster, and said, 'Justine, there's no point in getting worked up. As my old cell mate used to say, "If you can't find what you're looking for on the street, go into someone's house and take it."'

'Great. We're taking advice from a convict.'

'And you're taking advice from my cell mate too.'

Justine laughed. 'No offense, Rick. I don't think of you as a jailbird.'

'I'm honored. You ready to risk your life and reputation?'

'Maybe. I mean, let's go.'

A young Hispanic housekeeper came to the door under the portico, smiled pleasantly, said, 'I'm sorry. No one is home.'

Del Rio held up his badge, opened his jacket to show the woman his nine. He said, 'It's okay, miss, we're authorized to do a quick search and seizure.'

'We're painting the great room,' the young woman wailed.

Justine said, 'Don't worry. We'll be careful not to step in anything. Where is the master bedroom?'

Some other day, Justine would have enjoyed the house tour of the first-class chef's kitchen, the loggia and pool, the screening room, the master bedroom that looked like a set from a James Bond film and was equipped with more high-def, high-tech gizmos than the Situation Room at the White House.

Justine expected a tidy closet in the master suite, but this one was a mess. Expensive clothes were hung haphazardly and draped over hooks. Heaps of shoes were under the racks, all types, in no particular order.

While Rick stood in the bedroom doorway, Justine used gloved hands to pick through the shoes. She was looking for a rubberlike sole that could match the three inches of usable shoe print Sci had found next to the tire tread.

Justine paused, trying to sort the shoes in her mind before diving in, and then she saw what she was looking for, a pair of ASICS GEL-Kayanos, the current trend in men's conspicuous casual footwear.

She plucked the left shoe off the heap and turned it over. She called to Rick, and when he came to the closet, she showed him the bottom of the shoe.

'The good thing about transfer is it works both ways. The shoe makes an impression on the soil. And the soil – see it?'

'I see a dark crumb of something.'

'I see a happy day for Dr. Sci.'

Justine sealed the shoe in an evidence bag, starting as she saw that the housekeeper was now standing behind Rick at the entrance to the closet.

'You get me in trouble,' she said.

'No, no,' said Rick, using his very patient, even fatherly voice. 'You don't tell anyone that we were here. This is a top-secret investigation, covered by the California Seal of Silence. Understand?'

They were leaving North Bentley Avenue when Justine's phone rang. It was Nora.

'You have something?' Justine asked. She put

Nora on speaker for Rick's benefit.

'We've got the Porsche at six stoplights from two to two-thirty this morning, traveling from Bel Air to Topanga Canyon. He was driving fast and leaning over the wheel, so we got close-ups of his mug.'

'This is good, Nora. And I think we have a cherry on top for you.'

Chapter 96

I was dressed in my best, had on the nice after-shave Justine had given me, and was driving the Lambo at a pretty good clip from the office toward Beverly Hills. Justine was sitting beside me and urging me to go faster.

She was edgy, and she was talking to me like I was hired by the hour.

I got onto the 110. Although it was largely ignored, the posted speed limit was fifty-five. I nudged the accelerator until I was going a shade over sixty, and still Justine was applying the whip.

'If we get pulled over,' she said, 'don't worry. I've got a friend in the LAPD.'

'I'm the one who's out on bail, Justine. Bail can be revoked. Let's not push my luck, all right?'

Justine said, 'Uh-huh,' looked at her watch, then stared through the windshield. I knew she wasn't seeing anything on the freeway. She was inside her head, thinking back, projecting forward.

'Justine. Hello. It's me. Jack. I'm right here.'

'I'm running it all through my mind again,' she said, her voice heavy with exasperation.

'Okay.'

'Danny could have finished the film, but he's so messed up, it would have been a joke. It would have been panned. And a bomb at the box office meant certain bankruptcy.'

'Piper's death killed the film.'

'Yeah. Who would've guessed that could be a good thing?'

I left Justine to her thoughts, dwelling on other fights we'd had, how I hated them, how much I wanted things to be all right with us. Christ, I missed her. I wished she missed me.

After a one-minute mile on the freeway I got off and took a route through the streets of Beverly Hills that saved us a couple of minutes, finally taking a right onto North Crescent Drive, which brought us to the entrance of the famous pink-stucco, five-star Beverly Hills Hotel.

As I handed my keys to the valet, Justine called to Nora Cronin, who was getting out of her own car. Unmarked police cars pulled up to the hotel entrance, and I heard Nora telling the valets to leave the cop cars right where they were.

There was a poster on an easel near the front door; a life-sized photo of Piper Winnick, draped in black crepe, the dates of her birth and death beneath her young and angelically beautiful face.

Justine and Nora spoke briefly under the porte cochere, then Justine broke away from Nora and said to me, 'We're late, Jack. But not too late.'

I gave her the crook of my arm and together we

walked up the red carpet that ran between pairs of square columns and up three steps. Still on the carpet, we entered the dazzling hotel.

Chapter 97

Justine tried to see everything at once as she entered the Crystal Ballroom.

It was a sumptuous place, a grande dame of a room; round, pale, decorated in an art deco style, looking much as it had when the hotel was built in 1931.

Justine did a visual check of the exits, the walls of silk-draped windows, the tall French doors leading out to the Crystal Garden. And she checked out the tables under the magnificent chandelier.

There were celebrities at every place: movie stars both young and old, fashion designers, and talk show hosts. Piper's parents were near the stage, and Danny's people were at a table in the center of the room. Larry Schuster was there, and Alan Barstow, as well as Danny's entourage and their dates and wives.

If she and Nora didn't screw this up, Danny Whitman could be out of jail tonight.

Across the room was a large stage, the wall behind it forming a backdrop for a Piper Winnick slide show. Still shots from Piper's films and endearing candid photos from her childhood flashed by. Four-foot-tall vases of white roses

flanked the stage, and there were candles every-
where.

Mervin Koulos stood behind the podium at
center stage.

He looked impressive today: a six-foot-tall, perfectly groomed Hollywood producer of a shattered
picture with an untraditional, non-Hollywood
ending.

One of his stars was dead. The other star was in
jail. And he'd figured that this disaster would be
his salvation.

Justine walked along the left-hand wall toward
the steps to the stage. Nora Cronin advanced on
the stage from the other side of the room.

Meanwhile, Merv Koulos was telling a story
about Piper, and he was having a hard time getting his words out.

He said, 'I'll never forget when Piper was cast
in the role of Gia in *Shades of Green*. She said to
me, "Merv, it's been a lifelong dream of mine to
work with Danny Whitman."

'Lifelong dream,' he choked, his voice cracking.
'Imagine that. She was just sixteen.'

Justine and Nora had both reached the stage,
but Koulos saw only Justine, who had walked
right up to the podium and touched his arm.

Koulos started. He looked bewildered.

He put his hand over the microphone and said,
'Dr. Smith. What is this?'

Justine said, 'Merv, I want you to say this into
the mic. "I'm sorry, I've been called away. It's an
emergency."'

Koulos kept his hand over the mic and whispered, 'Whatever the hell you think you're doing,

it can wait. If you didn't notice, I'm giving a *eulogy*.'

'Merv. Look to your left. See that woman in the blue blazer, waggling her fingers at you? That's Lieutenant Cronin. Homicide. She needs to speak with you, urgently.'

Koulos scowled. The buzzing of conversation rose up from the tables. Koulos spoke into the microphone.

'Ladies and gentlemen, Mr. and Mrs. Winnick, I'm very sorry for the interruption. This is some kind of prank, and it's in very poor taste. Will someone please call security?'

Nora crossed the stage. She had her badge in her hand and three uniformed officers following her as she came toward Koulos. She said, 'Mr. Koulos, please put your hands behind your back.'

'Are you crazy?' Koulos peered out into the audience. 'I need help here. Alan? Give me a hand, will you?'

All conversation died – then Koulos panicked.

He broke away from the podium, knocking the microphone to the floor. He ran toward the stage door, but the cops were quicker and they brought him down, pulling back his arms for Nora, who clapped on the handcuffs.

The fallen microphone carried Koulos's desperate cries for help and Nora Cronin's response.

'Mervin Koulos, you're under arrest for the murder of Piper Winnick.'

Now the audience panicked too. Women screamed. Chairs went over.

Koulos yelled at Nora over the recitation of the Miranda warnings. 'So much hell is going to rain down on you. You'll be a meter maid by the time I'm done with you. If you're that lucky.'

Justine watched the cops drag Koulos to his feet. Then she turned away and walked down the stage steps, her job done.

As she moved toward the exit, she thought about greed: how Koulos had lived too large, had borrowed too much, had put every penny into this film starring Danny Whitman, a guy too damaged to bring it off.

But Koulos had an insurance policy on the film in the form of a completion bond worth a hundred million dollars.

He wouldn't be collecting that money now.

Jack was waiting for her near the door. He put his hand to her waist and walked her out.

'Well played,' Jack said to Justine. 'Well played and well done.'

Part Four

DEAD END

Chapter 98

It was eight p.m.

I was standing just inside Private's front entrance, saying good night to my friend and attorney Eric Caine. He hadn't said so directly, but he had let me know that without new evidence, my defense in the case of *California v. Jack Morgan* was looking bad.

As I closed the door, a storm came up out of the blue. Rain slashed against the floor-to-ceiling windows of the building and haloed the headlights of the traffic streaming along Figueroa.

Caine ran to his car, and I headed up the winding staircase to my office, where I planned to put in another four or five hours of work on my own behalf.

As I climbed the quarter-turn span between the third and fourth floors, I saw Justine coming down.

She was still wearing the black dress she had worn to Piper Winnick's memorial service, and seeing her sent a jolt to my heart, as it did every time.

I said, 'Hey.'

Justine returned the hey and kept going down the stairs. I stopped and said, 'Justine, did you eat? Let's go out and celebrate your Koulos bust—'

'No, thanks anyway, Jack. I'm wiped out. I can't wait to get home.'

'Are you sure linguini marinara and some good wine wouldn't beat being home alone? I need to talk to you.'

'Not tonight, Jack. Ask Cody to fit me into your schedule tomorrow.'

She started to pass me on the stairs, and I didn't like it. She wasn't tired so much as she didn't want to deal with me. As though I were a guy standing behind her in line at Starbucks, breathing down her neck and yakking into his phone at the same time.

I said, 'Then spare me a couple of minutes now. Are you going to take that job offer? I have to know.'

Justine sighed, shifted her weight, adjusted the strap on her shoulder bag.

'They're matching my compensation plus fifteen percent.'

'So you've made your decision?'

'I like Private. I like my job.'

'Stay, Justine. I'll match their offer and more.'

'Thanks. Let me think about it overnight.'

'You're mad at me, Justine. I understand. But will you please talk to me? I want to talk about ... us.'

Justine gave me the subzero look that I remembered well from fights we'd had when we lived together.

'There is no "us," Jack,' she snapped, 'and I'm not sure there ever was. But I still give a damn. So as your friend, I want to say don't ever take your eyes off Tommy.'

After the memorial service, I'd tailed Tommy's car from his office to his house, watched him tinker with a sprinkler and then go inside for his home-cooked meal.

His phone was tapped, his car was bugged, and right now, Mo-bot was monitoring the live feed from the 'spy eyes' I'd personally trained on his home.

I said, 'Short of implanting a device in his skull, there's not much more I can do.'

'Tommy hit on me again, Jack. I don't take him seriously, but you should.'

Again?

Tommy had hit on Justine *again?*

I felt a knife slide into my gut. Not just because Tommy was still trying to beat me at girls, but because Justine had filed the edge of this news so that it would really cut deep.

I said, 'Did you go out with him?'

'When you were in prison. Strictly business. At least it was for me.'

'Nice one, Justine. Thanks for keeping me in the loop.'

Justine said, 'See you tomorrow,' then she took the outside rail and walked past me.

I stood on the staircase until I could no longer hear the sound of her heels striking metal treads.

Point taken, Justine.

Parting shot duly noted.

Chapter 99

I drank down a Red Bull in the break room while I waited for coffee to brew. I thought of a few comebacks for Justine – mostly why she should forgive my completely unpremeditated good-bye tryst with Colleen.

I'm human. I'm sorry. I couldn't possibly be more sorry.

Why couldn't she forgive me?

I went to my office, booted up my laptop, opened files in the 'Colleen' folder, and revisited facts that Colleen had never told me.

Item: Right out of high school, Colleen had married a man named Kevin Molloy. The marriage was annulled six months later, but Colleen had kept her married name. In the year that Colleen and I had dated, she'd never mentioned an ex-husband, not once.

Had Molloy followed her to LA?

Did he still love her?

Item: A businessman named Sean McGough had paid Colleen's way to the USA in 2009. McGough was still in Dublin, had not left Ireland in three years. Who was McGough to Colleen? And why had she also failed to mention him?

Item: Mike Donahue. Colleen had said he was like an uncle to her. As with Molloy and McGough, I had put Donahue's life through an electronic sieve. Donahue had gotten his American

264

citizenship in 2002. He'd gotten two DUIs in LA and another in Seattle, where he was supporting a boy of seven. He hadn't married the child's mother.

If Donahue had wanted to kill Colleen, it would have been easy. She'd trusted him. Still, I had never gotten any sense that he'd had a romance with her, that he'd been jealous of her feelings for me, that he was anything other than an avuncular man with an Irish pub that Colleen had frequented when she'd lived in Los Feliz. A dead end.

Another folder.

I had collected all of the personal e-mails between Colleen and me going back to the day I first kissed her. I went time-traveling for a while, got lost reading her words and mine, remembering the growing romance at the office, all the love we had made in her rose-covered cottage.

And I remembered Donahue calling me. 'Come to the hospital, quickly.' Seeing Colleen with bloody gauze around her wrists. Knowing what she'd done to herself after I'd told her it was over.

I got up, paced the hallway, made more coffee, stared out onto Figueroa. The rain had moved on. I went back to my desk and clicked on the video folder.

I'd seen all of the videos stored there, except for the one Mo-bot had shot while Tandy and Ziegler were perp-walking me out to the car at the curb.

Now I forced myself to play the video and look at myself from Mo-bot's second-story point of view.

There I was, just ripped from the Private Worldwide meeting, stumbling between Tandy and Ziegler in the blinding sunshine. The media had been shouting questions and I'd kept my eyes down.

I watched every frame – and I saw something I hadn't seen that day. Correction. I saw some*one*. Clay Harris.

Clay Harris was a Morgan family hand-me-down, not exactly harmless, almost a Morgan family curse.

It couldn't be happenstance.

Harris lived in Santa Clarita, twenty miles out of town, yet there he was, standing behind the media surge with a very good view of me.

Why was Harris lurking in front of Private the moment I was taken in for Colleen's murder? He was smiling, and I thought I knew why.

Chapter 100

Emilio Cruz didn't like it.

This was what was called a 'bad job.' Like if a middleweight found himself mixing it up on the street with a heavyweight. The best the smaller guy could hope for was not to get killed.

Cruz understood that Jack had to do this job for Noccia. The guy was lethal. He was vindictive. He killed people. And he got away with murder.

Not only was Cruz doing this for Jack, he was

266

doing it for his partner.

Rick was over forty. He was stiff. He was slow. He was going to have to scale walls. In the dark.

Scotty picked up some of the slack for Del Rio. He could do one-armed cartwheels and run like a cheetah. But Scotty was a former motorcycle cop. He'd never gone outside the law like this, and doing a job for a mobster was against everything that had made Scotty a good cop.

Right now, while Rick cruised around looking for a parking spot, Scotty was sitting behind Cruz, jouncing his knee, sending shocks through the front seat.

Cruz said again, 'Rick, we should go in through the back wall. I don't like the roof. At all.'

Del Rio said patiently, 'We know what Scotty scoped out. If we go through the wall, we don't know what we're going to find. Could be heavy crap stored against it. We could hit pipes.'

Now Del Rio was swearing because Boyd Street, where they'd parked before, was locked in. Not an empty space on either side of the block.

Cruz said, 'Ricky, I'm telling you. I don't like this.'

Del Rio said, 'There.'

And he parked in a 'No Parking Anytime' driveway that maybe wouldn't attract the attention of a random drive-by cop at this time of night. Maybe.

Before the car had come to a stop, Scotty was out the back door. He crossed the street in his black duds, his ski mask in hand. When he crossed Artemus, he ducked into the shadow of the pottery's outside staircase and, as he'd done before, rattled a window until he set off the alarm.

The alarm screamed out over a couple of square blocks, and Cruz knew that it also alerted the techs at Bosco Security Systems' control center through the phone line.

The same people who had manned the phones twenty-four hours ago were very likely on duty now. They'd received three false alarms from this address, and team Del Rio was counting on Bosco to tell the building's owner and the cops that the alarm indicated a system failure, not a break-in.

The Private investigators waited for a police response that didn't come.

Fifteen minutes later, under the pale light of a new moon, Cruz, Scotty, and Del Rio crossed Anderson and proceeded into the narrow gap between the Red Cat Pottery and the auto parts building next door.

Employing a rock-climbing maneuver called 'bridging,' they inched up the brick crevasse between the buildings.

Two cars hissed past on slick pavement as the Private guys slowly ascended to the Red Cat Pottery's roof.

Chapter 101

Scotty got a leg across the low wall at the edge of the roof, pulled himself up and over, gave Cruz a hand up, and did the same for Del Rio, who rolled onto the tar paper, saying, 'Everybody down.'

The three men hunched behind the wall, got their wind and their bearings.

Del Rio counted off a couple of minutes in his mind, then stood up, located the skein of electric lines running from the pole on Anderson to the roof, and severed them with his wire cutters, causing a blackout inside the warehouse.

The alarm was cut off, as were the motion detectors, the telephone backup, everything – but, shockingly, the alarm sounded again almost immediately.

Startled, Del Rio ducked from pure reflex, then said to the others, 'They have a battery backup. To the alarm. It's gotta be wireless.'

Cruz said, 'Let's get out of here.'

Then the alarm halted midshriek.

Del Rio said, 'That's Bosco shutting it down, thinking that's enough of this noise tonight. Emilio, we're okay. We stay put. Make good and sure no one is coming.'

A long ten minutes went by, then Del Rio got up, paced off twenty feet in from the Anderson side of the building, eyeballed approximately the same distance from Artemus, took his eighteen-volt battery-operated Sawzall out of his bag, and flipped it on.

It made a little bit of a racket, but not the kind of thing that would wake up any watchdogs in the neighborhood or even cause anyone driving by to notice.

Scotty and Cruz stood by as Del Rio sawed through the tar paper, the old layers of asphalt roofing, and the plywood below that, cutting through sheetrock that had little resistance to the blade.

Roofing fell through the opening and clattered down. They listened to the ensuing silence, and then Scotty opened his bag of tricks.

He put on his miner's lamp and took out a thirty-five-foot length of marine-grade one-inch poly line. He tied one end to a brick chimney, put some knots into the rest of it, and approached the hole.

Del Rio said, 'Take it *slow*,' and Scotty grinned, jazzed up with nervous energy.

He pulled the knotted rope taut, then lowered himself down from the roof to the kiln room, where the clay pots were fired. Del Rio followed and Cruz was last to come down the line.

As soon as his feet touched the floor, Cruz went to the office and found the wireless alarm backup system next to the circuit box. He took out the batteries and set up the cell phone signal jammer in case the wireless signal went active again.

Del Rio, meanwhile, left the kiln room and went to the back-right-hand corner of the warehouse proper, where Scotty had seen the van. But

Del Rio didn't see a van. He saw racks and racks of flowerpots.

He didn't want to believe this.

Private investigators had watched the damned warehouse, three shifts a day every day, for the past week. Had the van been dismantled, taken out in parts, or driven intact into a big rig?

Del Rio was ready to call Jack, when Scotty walked past him, catlike on rubber soles, and showed him where the van was hidden behind the racks, pretty much barricaded in.

Scotty said, 'What do you think, Rick?'

Relieved that Jack wasn't going to have to tell Noccia that the van had disappeared, Del Rio said, 'We're good.'

Chapter 102

The van was a late-model Ford transport, white with vegetables painted on it, two doors and a slider on each side, cargo doors at the back, tinted glass all the way around.

It was parked fifty feet away from and facing the roll-up doors at the far end of the warehouse. Whoever had parked the thing had meant to hide it. The driver's side and rear were against the corner walls of the warehouse. The other two sides were hemmed in by metal racks of flowerpots two deep and seven feet high.

Del Rio squeezed around to the driver's-side door and tried the handle, but the door was locked. So were all of the others.

Fucking A.

He had a short crowbar in his bag. He took it out, staved in the passenger-side window, reached in, and pulled up the handle. He brushed the glass off the seat with his gloved hand, threw his bag into the passenger-side foot well, and slid behind the wheel.

After flipping on the dome light, Del Rio looked at the ignition. He wanted to see a key dangling there. That would have been nice, but no, the only thing on the ignition was blood spatter. It was on the wheel too, sprayed all inside the windshield, and there were some bits of bone and brain matter too.

Noccia's wheelman's remains.

Del Rio looked for the keys under the mats and up under the visors. No luck. He called out to Scotty to check the tops of the tires, just in case, and when Scotty said, 'Nope. Nothing,' Del Rio opened all the doors with the lock release.

He got out of the van and squeezed past the racks of flowerpots, hitting one of them with his shoulder. The rack shimmied as if it weren't sure if it was going to fall, giving him a shot of adrenaline he didn't need.

He imagined Cruz calling Jack: 'Jack. Ricky had a heart attack, man. What should I do?'

Cruz called out, 'You okay, Rick?'

'Fine. Fine. Emilio, let's see how quick you can start this engine.'

Cruz squeezed along the racks, got into the van, and used the screwdriver attachment on his knife to remove the guard plate from the ignition tumbler. While he stripped the wires, Del Rio groped his way to the rear of the van and checked the cargo.

He counted the stacks of cartons, did the math, came up with four hundred cartons, all but one of them still sealed. Each carton was marked with the number of bottles per carton, so many pills per bottle, so many milligrams per pill. He took out one of the bottles, shook it, put it back.

This was a ton of Oxy. If there wasn't thirty million in this van, it wasn't his fault.

Scotty called to him, 'Houston. We've got ignition.'

Del Rio closed the cargo doors, came out from behind the van, and got in the passenger side. Scotty wedged himself between the seats.

Cruz put the transmission into drive and turned on the headlights. At that moment, there was the loud, brassy roar of a motor coming from outside the building. The lights in the warehouse flickered and then they came on. It was like daylight inside the Red Cat Pottery.

Fucking A, for sure.

Chapter 103

Cruz yanked the wires apart, cutting the engine. He snapped off the headlights too. He sat there, gripping the steering wheel, staring through the tinted windshield, thinking, *Sure, there was a generator.* Red Cat had a generator in case the power went out while they were making the flowerpots.

Cruz turned to Del Rio, same instant as Del Rio grabbed his arm and ordered, 'Get down.'

Cruz did what Del Rio said, thinking, *Now what?* There was roofing on the floor of the kiln room, rainwater was maybe dripping down. If that was discovered... They were walled in, couldn't even attempt a break for it.

Whatever getting caught red-handed meant, this was it. Literally. He had a dead mobster's blood on his palms. He knew what to say when they got dragged out of the van and shoved facedown on the concrete floor.

You got us. We give up.

Scotty said quietly, 'Hear that?'

Cruz heard men talking over the roar of the generator. Their voices were getting louder as they came through the office door and into the warehouse proper.

Cruz hoped that they weren't going to check the ovens, that they wouldn't look at the van. But the voices were getting closer.

'You see it? Because I sure don't,' said one of the men. 'Where's the goddamned van?'

'It's here. Stop worrying, Victor. It's hidden in the back here. Right there. Behind the frickin' racks.'

It was about the van after all. Whoever was leasing the space, storing the van, he was looking to make sure his millions were still safe. These weren't cops. They were hoods.

Cruz got his piece out of his waistband. Del Rio was doing the same.

The first voice was saying, 'Okay, okay. Just be

glad, Sammy. I want to move this thing in the morning.'

'You say so.'

'I say so. Sammy, you and Mark...'

The men's voices faded as they turned and headed back toward the office.

Cruz thought about that one guy saying Sammy. It clicked. Sammy, with the goatee and the piercings – a guy he'd known for years as an almost-dead druggy – was moving up. This was the same Sammy who had taken twenty bucks in exchange for sending a text message and said it was common knowledge that the drug van was inside a warehouse.

Common knowledge?

It was *inside* knowledge. He had fucking *known*.

Sammy's brains were like scrambled eggs. He would say and do anything for a fix.

And the guy Sammy called Victor?

Cruz thought he knew that guy too.

Cruz peered over the dash, saw the backs of the guys' heads going into the office. The office door closed, then the lights in the warehouse went out. His heart was still hammering, his palms and underarms wet.

Scotty was muttering, 'Man, oh, man.'

Cruz said to Del Rio, 'One of those guys is Sammy. Remember him, Rick?'

'Turquoise cowboy boots? Metal in his nose?'

'Yeah. Sell himself out for twenty bucks. And the one looking for his van? I think that's Victor Spano. He's with the Chicago Mob, am I right?'

Del Rio said, 'Yeah. Spano. That could have been him. We gotta wait now. Just sit tight.'

Time dragged, Cruz counting off too many minutes in the dark, smelling his own sweat, thinking of the time he'd been in a knife fight and the other guy had a gun. The time he'd been in bed with a woman and her husband came into the room.

He was thinking about his last professional fight, with Michael Alvarez, the punch that had ended his career, when Del Rio said, 'Okay. Let's do it.'

Del Rio flipped on the dome light.

Cruz twisted the wires, got a spark. The engine turned over. He gunned it.

Cruz turned on the headlights, sending two high beams into the pottery, and put the van in gear. He let off the brake, and the van rolled, nudging the racks until they tipped over in slow motion, pots crashing to the floor.

Cruz backed up, twisted the wheel, and maneuvered in quarter turns until the tires were clear of the racks.

There were two sets of roll-up doors at the Artemus side of the pottery. One set opened onto a ramp that went down to the street. The other doors opened onto a loading dock where there was no ramp. There was an eight-foot drop.

Cruz said to Del Rio, 'It's on the left, right?'

Del Rio said, 'What?'

'The doors to the street are on the left, right?'

Del Rio said, 'Make *sense*, Emilio.'

Cruz was almost sure the doors that went to the street were on the left. He stepped hard on the gas and ran the van into the thin metal of the roll-up doors, the door-frames flying right off the walls.

Scotty was saying, 'Man, oh, man' over and over again like a mantra. Cruz went through the doors, praying he was right.

Chapter 104

I was still at my desk when my cell phone buzzed. It was Del Rio.

'How'd it go?' I asked him.

'Mission accomplished,' he said. 'Which means our troubles are just starting.'

'Where's the van now?'

'We're in it. On the road.'

'Did you put the tracker inside?'

'It's under the seat. Way under.'

I said, 'Good,' told Rick to stay on the line, and called Noccia from my desk phone. I had a ringing phone in one ear, traffic sounds and Del Rio and Cruz talking together in the other.

Noccia picked up.

I said to the Mob boss, 'We've got your delivery. It's intact.'

We agreed on a place just north of Fry's Electronics Paradise in Burbank.

I said, 'Del Rio has some names for you, Carmine. The guys who jacked your van.'

'That's more than I expected,' Noccia said to me. Then he hung up.

I wanted Del Rio and his crew out of that vehicle. It couldn't happen fast enough for me. I hung in with Rick for a half hour of pure screaming adrenaline overload as Noccia got a couple of his goons out of bed and we waited for his guys and mine to meet up on the shoulder of a highway.

Rick said to me, 'My date is here,' and a few minutes later he said, 'They're gone. Headed north on Five.'

I told Rick to call Aldo for a ride, and had just hung up when the phone rang again, a 702 area code. Vegas.

'Carmine. Is everything under control?'

'Very under control. I'm going to sleep like a kitten tonight. I wired your fee into your account. Six million even.'

'Thanks.'

Noccia said, 'No problem. Good job,' and hung up.

My throat was dry. My hands were shaking. I drank down a Red Bull in one long swig and I dialed out. I got Chief Mickey Fescoe on the third ring.

I told Fescoe that a van with a fortune in illegal pharmaceuticals was headed north on 5, that it belonged to Carmine Noccia. I pictured Fescoe, my sometimes friend, shaking off sleep, jumping out of bed, dying for me to fill in the blanks.

'What did you say?'

I repeated myself and then gave him the details.

Fescoe punctuated every fifth word with *'Holy shit'* and *'You're kidding'* as I connected the dots for him. I drew a straight line between the three members of the Noccia crew who had been found shot dead on a highway in Utah to the Ford transport van holding a street value of thirty million in OxyContin.

I said, 'There's a GPS transmitter in the van. The receiver is in Fry's Electronics parking lot. Yeah. Inside a trash can under the flying-saucer marquee if you want to send a car for it.'

'I'll send someone now. I might get it myself.'

'If I were chief of police, I'd tip off the DEA. And take them down with a traffic stop, Mickey. Keep me completely out of it.'

'My thoughts exactly,' said Fescoe. 'Hey, Jack, how *did* you come into all this information?'

'I can't say.'

'Right. It's private. Sorry I asked. I don't need to know,' said Fescoe.

I said, 'Not that I'm keeping track, Mick, but don't forget that I helped you with this.'

Another way of saying *You owe me a big one.*

'I'll help you if I can,' said Fescoe.

Another way of saying *I'll help you if I can, but don't count on me if you killed Colleen Molloy.*

Chapter 105

It was a hell of a send-off for Cody.

The Bazaar was a five-star restaurant on La Cienega, a 'movable feast' that called up Spanish fiestas of the kind you only saw in movies.

We had booked the tasting room, called Saam, for our party of thirty. The furnishings were leather and Murano glass, and the food was bizarre and terrific: tapas and cheesy confections and foie gras lollipops wrapped in cotton candy.

People were lit on magic mojitos infused with end-of-the-workday relief. There were silly toasts and drunken laughter, and a couple of girls were crying and laughing at the same time.

As I said, it was a hell of a party.

But some people were missing: Del Rio, Scotty, and Cruz were out working the hotel murder case. Justine had given Cody a cashmere sweater and begged off the festivities.

I wanted to be anyplace but here. But I owed it to Cody to give him a bash worthy of how much we all loved him. He'd stepped into his job after Colleen left six months ago, filling her place without a hitch. Like he was made for it. I'd always be thankful to him for that.

I clinked my glass with a fork, and the whooping only escalated.

'Cody,' I said. 'Cody, we're going to miss you.'

There was whistling and guys yelling Cody's name. Mo-bot was beaming. Even Sci stood up and gave Cody some applause.

'We're going to miss your clothing commentary,' I said to my former assistant, 'and your impersonations of all of us, especially me.'

I did an impersonation of Cody doing an impersonation of me, running his hand through his hair, giving himself a serious look in the mirror, straightening his tie.

People roared.

I said that I had put a contract out on Ridley Scott for taking Cody away from us, but that I was grateful to Cody for finding Val.

Cody broke in to say, 'Val, stand up, girlfriend.'

And she did, laughing too, and I'm pretty sure it wasn't the magic mojitos. She was just having fun.

I said, 'Cody, you've kept us on track and you've brought us a lot of happiness too. And if the acting thing disappoints you, I'm going on the record: You'll always have a home at Private.'

I gave him the gift-wrapped camera and card from everyone at Private, and after the applause had abated, Cody wiped his eyes with a red napkin and used his foie gras lollipop as a microphone. 'Jack, I want to thank you,' he said. 'Seriously, this has been the best job of my life. You taught me more than this,' he said, grinning as he ran his hand through his hair. 'You showed me honorable leadership in action. That's what I'm going to remember most.'

I didn't know thirty people could make so much noise with their hands.

Chapter 106

Del Rio eyed the King Eddy Saloon, a bar within an old bootlegging hotel by the same name on Skid Row, East Fifth and Los Angeles Streets. This was a bad section of town, but King Eddy's attracted all types, from homeless drunks to young people with dreams who owned condos around the corner.

The building was gray with black trim, bars on the three windows around the door, a security gate attached to that, attesting to what could and often did happen in this neighborhood.

Del Rio went through the door, Cruz right behind him, like Samuel Jackson and John Travolta going into that diner in *Pulp Fiction*.

'Cold Cold Ground' was playing on the jukebox, and some people were singing along. The circular bar was jam-packed with local characters. A cheap wooden platform held the TVs, which were tuned to a basketball game. At that instant, the Lakers lost by a point.

Customers groaned.

Alongside the wall opposite the bar was a line of tables under decorative neon beer signs. At one of the tables a pair of trannies was getting crazy. From the pitch and volume of the screaming, Del Rio thought it was just a matter of moments before it got physical.

With luck, they'd be out of there before the trannies blew.

Del Rio had seen a picture of the guy they were looking for. It was a couple years old and the guy had been holding a number under his chin, but Del Rio was pretty sure he could recognize him inside his favorite hangout.

He searched the backs of heads and profiles, and then he saw the African American guy with a short beard sitting at the bar. He was eating a free doughnut and talking to the old barfly sitting next to him.

Del Rio got Cruz's attention, tilted his chin toward the guy with the beard. Cruz squinted, then nodded, and Del Rio pulled his nine.

Del Rio walked over to the guy having his beer

and doughnut, put the gun to his spine, and felt the guy stiffen. The guy stared into the mirror over the bar for a second, looked into the faces of the two men who weren't joking, raised his hands, and held them up.

Del Rio said, 'Mr. Keyes, walk with me.'

Keyes said, 'I don't want any trouble.'

'Then don't do anything stupid.'

This was Tyson Keyes, the badass limo driver who was Karen Ricci's first husband. According to her second husband, Paul Ricci, Keyes was the man who had tipped Carmelita Gomez that her john had been killed by a limo driver. Maybe he'd done more than that. Maybe Tyson Keyes had killed five businessmen who'd hired party girls for a couple of hours in their hotel rooms.

Keyes swiveled around, then got off the stool very carefully. 'I'm not the guy you're looking for, man.'

The barfly said to Keyes, 'You through with your beer?'

'He's through,' said Del Rio. 'Let's go.'

A couple of people looked up, then looked away real fast. They would say that they hadn't seen anything.

With his hands still in the air, a former limousine driver named Tyson Keyes walked slowly through the crowd, escorted out the door by a former US Marine and the former California light-middleweight champion of 2005.

Tom Waits sang his signature song on the jukebox right behind them.

Chapter 107

A message from Justine was waiting for me when I got home.

'Jack. I want to stay at Private. That's a definite yes. Also, if I was rude the other night, I'm sorry. I'm still feeling ... bruised. See you tomorrow.'

I listened to the message a couple more times, strained it for subtext, listened for hidden meanings. All I got for sure was that Justine was staying at Private.

Was there still a chance we could reconcile?

Or were we done for good?

I heard her saying *There is no 'us,' Jack. I'm not sure there ever was.*

I had showered and changed into jeans and a polo shirt when the intercom buzzed. I went to my new security system and checked the gate monitor.

Jinx was there with a tray in her hand, silver covers over the food.

She was right on time.

I buzzed her in, and when she came to the door, I took the tray and put it on the hall table.

Her face was sunny and beautiful, and her glasses were cute, the lenses a girly shade of pink. She was wearing jeans and a blue polo shirt.

Same color blue as her eyes.

Same color blue as the shirt I was wearing.

She said, 'Hey, look at you.'

I said, 'If you don't mind, I'd rather look at you.'

'Okay,' she said.

We laughed and I wrapped her in my arms, gave her a long hug.

As I hugged her, she told me what she'd brought for dinner, heirloom tomato salad and crab cakes with mango salsa. She was excited, talking very fast.

I had already had dinner at Cody's farewell banquet, but Jinx didn't know, and she wasn't going to hear it from me.

'I made the salsa myself,' she said, still holding on to me. 'Specialty of the house.'

'I have a bottle of Pinot Grigio on ice.'

'I hoped you would,' she said, grinning up at me. She had a very pretty smile.

I got the wine and we took dinner out to the deck, settled into chairs, took a few breaths, and relaxed.

We toasted the setting sun as it did a fan dance with a bank of fat gray clouds. It was all special: the view, the salsa, the wine, and Jinx, who was turning out to be very good company.

She kicked off her sandals, hugged her knees, and asked me to tell her more about myself, something that wasn't on my corporate bio.

I could give a pretty good tour of my life using the map of scars on my body, but no. Not right now. I was thinking of a football story, something funny, when a musical ringtone came from the living room. Jinx's phone.

She said, 'I'm not answering that.'

'Good.'

When her phone rang the second time, it broke the mood for real. I closed the sliding glass doors, but we could still hear the phone when it called out again.

Jinx said, 'It might be... Let me just get it. I'll be right back.'

I stared out at the surf as Jinx opened the doors. I liked Jinx, was enjoying whatever this was, a date or just getting to know her.

I thought about telling her that I could make her cell phone disappear, that I could demonstrate my famous forward pass and send it into the ocean.

I thought she would laugh.

But then I heard her say in the next room, 'Please. Just tell me.' And then, 'Oh, no. No. I'll be right there. Don't touch anything.'

Jinx returned to the deck, a look of panic on her face.

'Someone else was killed in my hotel, Jack. Another man is dead.'

Chapter 108

I stood with Jinx just outside the Fellini Room on the second floor at the front of the hotel. It wasn't the best location or the priciest room, but there was easy access by way of the stairs from the lobby.

The distraught young guy standing with us in the hallway was the manager, 'Mr. Knowles.' His face was red, his lower lip quivered, and his eyes were swollen.

I looked beyond him into the room and saw a murder scene horrifying enough to shake up a kid with a degree in hotel management. It shook me up too, and I'd been through a war.

A man lay dead, half on the bed, half on the floor. A homemade wire garrote with two wooden handles had been pulled so hard around his neck an artery had been severed. The victim's blood had splashed onto the unmade bed before he died.

'That's Mr. Albert Singh,' said Knowles. 'He checked in at one a.m. Had the "Do Not Disturb" light on all day. He didn't put any charges on his bill.'

Mr. Singh looked to be in his twenties, was wearing briefs and a white T-shirt. He had a wedding band on the ring finger of his outstretched hand.

'Ms. Poole, I said I'd wait for you,' Knowles was saying to Jinx, 'and now you're here. I've had enough, Ms. Poole. Here are my keys and my pass. I'll send back my uniform, but I have to go home–'

I touched his arm, interrupting his exit speech.

'Mr. Knowles. I'm Jack Morgan, Private Investigations. I work for Ms. Poole. Talk to me for a minute. Tell me what happened.'

His voice was a screech. 'Like I know? Housekeeping knocked on the door. There was no answer. The housekeeper came in and saw *this*.'

Old hotels, even those renovated in high style, weren't designed with modern security in mind. If the killer was running true to form, he'd ducked the cameras. It might actually be impossible to secure this hotel and still keep it open for business.

If Mr. Singh was like the five other men killed in this manner, my theory was that he had hired a hooker. Sometime after she'd left, he'd let the killer into his room. Maybe a limo driver pretending that he was a hotel engineer investigating a leak, or hotel security. Most guests would let the guy in.

The LAPD was working the case, and we hadn't gotten in their way. But we hadn't helped them either. We had an unproven theory.

That was pretty much all we had.

Like Knowles, I felt like calling it quits. I was sorry I had taken the job. Sorry I had let Jinx down.

'Jinx, we have to call the police,' I said.

She had her fist to her mouth. I wasn't sure she even heard me. I took out my cell phone and called it in.

Then I called Del Rio.

'I was just calling *you*,' he said. 'We've got breaking news on the hotel john killer. Come quick. We need you to talk to someone, Jack. Someone who needs convincing.'

Chapter 109

I had a clear view of the hotel's entrance through the windows of the late Albert Singh's room. Cops streamed into the Sun's driveway, and sirens wailed as more sped up South Santa Monica Boulevard.

I put my hands on Jinx's shoulders and made eye contact with her. I said, 'I'll call you as soon as I can. You're going to be all right.'

I didn't want to leave her, but Del Rio said he needed me urgently. I had to go.

I left the hotel by the rear exit, got my car out of the lot, and drove to Fifth Street. I found Del Rio and Cruz in a garbage-strewn alley called Werdin Place. A half block from King Eddy's, Werdin ran between buildings and served as a parking place for owners of the businesses on the block. The shops were closed for the night, and Werdin was deserted.

Cruz greeted me at the top of the alley. Behind him, Del Rio held his gun on a forty-ish black man who was sitting on the ground, his fingers interlaced behind his neck. He was in what we called 'Private custody.'

Del Rio said, 'Jack, I'd like you to meet Mr. Tyson Keyes.'

Keyes didn't look at me, kept his eyes on the heap of trash bags ten feet away.

Del Rio had filed a report after he'd talked to

289

the bouncer from Havana. The bouncer had told Del Rio that Keyes was a felon of the violent kind and that he knew the name of the hotel john killer.

Del Rio said, 'Mr. Morgan, Mr. Keyes doesn't want to talk to us. I told him if he didn't tell us who killed those johns, I would blow his head off, but that corporate policy dictates I get your permission first.'

I stooped down to Keyes's level. 'Mr. Keyes,' I said, 'no one will call in shots coming from this location. You know that. And here's something you don't know. Mr. Del Rio has nothing to lose. He has cancer. He'll be dead before he ever sees jail again.'

I looked past Cruz's startled expression, said, 'It's metastasized, isn't that right, Rick?'

'Right you are, Jack. I've made peace with my maker. I'm ready to go at any time.'

Keyes said, 'That's what you want? The *name* of who killed those johns? I thought you wanted me to say *I* did it. Yo, I *want* you to get that crazy bitch off the street.'

'Wait,' I said. 'A woman killed those johns?'

'You deaf, man?' Keyes asked me. 'Yeah, she's a she, all right. I was banging her while my old lady was in prison. I thought we had something going, but she doesn't like men, yo. She fuckin' *hates* them.

'One night, I was sleeping, she put a *coat hanger* around my neck. I put my gun in her ear. Told her she had to the count of three to get the hell out of my life. Then I heard one of her tricks died by a wire. See, I picked Candy up from the

Seaview the night that trick was killed, yo. She called me up without going through her service. She used me as her wheelman, you hear me? That's not right.'

'What's Candy's full name?' Del Rio said.

'You let me go if I tell you?'

Del Rio lowered his gun.

'Carmelita Gomez. She works at that Cuban club from ten to four, so, like, she can still squeeze in a few tricks on the side—'

Cruz leaned in so that his eyes were only inches from Keyes's face.

'Where can we find Ms. Gomez now?'

Chapter 110

Cruz and Del Rio were in the car in front of me, forcing me to keep to a sane speed as we headed north into the Valley.

I dictated case notes into a recorder as I drove.

I described the scene at the Sun and brought the Poole case file up to date.

The facts, as we knew them, were starting to make sense.

Karen Ricci, the woman in the wheelchair who had tipped Cruz off, was an escort service call booker. She'd told Cruz that a limo driver knew who had killed the hotel johns, and that she'd gotten that information from her friend, a former escort and current coat checker, Carmelita Gomez.

Cruz had interviewed Gomez and she'd given

him false information.

Now we had a lead from Ricci's first husband, Tyson Keyes. Keyes had picked Gomez up from her date with Arthur Valentine, the john who had been killed at the Seaview hotel last year.

If Carmelita Gomez was the hotel john killer, it was clear that she had easy access.

Twenty minutes after leaving Keyes, we found Gomez's name on a mailbox on Stagg Street, in front of one of the tan-colored stucco houses in a cookie-cutter development of middle-class homes.

Gomez's house was set back from the street, centered on a small mat of a yard. A driveway curved in from Stagg, coursed along the fence on the west side of the lot, and ended at a garage in the backyard.

Cruz and Del Rio pulled the fleet car into the mouth of the driveway, and I parked across the street.

I got out of my car and joined Cruz at Gomez's front door, while Del Rio headed toward the back. With our guns drawn, Cruz and I flanked the doorway.

Cruz rang the bell, and in a moment the porch light came on.

Cruz said, 'Carmelita, it's Emilio Cruz. From the other night.'

There was no response, so Cruz tried again. 'Look through the peephole, Carmelita. You know I'm not a cop. *No seas tonto.* Don't make me kick the door in.'

A car started up at the back of the house. I saw headlights. Everything happened very fast after that.

Chapter 111

One second, Rick was walking toward the back door.

The next, he'd flattened himself against a stockade fence so he wouldn't get creamed by an old red Chevy Impala that tore across the lawn and passed the car Cruz had parked in the driveway.

Cruz leaped from the front steps and both he and Del Rio ran toward the fleet car. Gomez seemed to have gone from zero to almost sixty in no seconds flat, but I saw her face as the Impala shot past me and made a hard right turn on two wheels.

Gomez didn't look afraid. She looked determined. Del Rio yelled to me, 'Should I call the cops?'

I shouted, 'Yes.'

I got into my car, made a U-turn, and followed Cruz and Del Rio east on Stagg, a narrow road, not a speedway.

Gomez was out in front and gaining ground, driving through the residential development as if she were both drunk and crazy. She took out a mailbox, sideswiped a couple of parked cars, and ran a stop sign.

She took another two-wheel turn, this time a sharp left onto Laurel Canyon Boulevard, scraping the side of an SUV that was headed north in her lane of traffic.

I got onto the boulevard in time to see the red car rocket ahead in the inside lane. Horns blared. The Impala weaved – left, right, back to the inside lane. Cars swerved. Hubcaps rolled across the road. Cruz and Del Rio drafted right behind the Impala but couldn't pass.

Gomez wasn't just running, she was escaping like a wildfire was burning up the street.

Sirens blared as we flew through the intersection of Laurel Canyon and Strathern Street, an area cluttered with minimall shops: a liquor mart, a flower shop, a 76 station, fast-food joints.

Then the road flattened into a straightaway that ran between two- and three-story commercial buildings on both sides.

Del Rio's call to 911 and Gomez's outlaw run had brought out the cruisers, and when Carmelita Gomez turned, six squad cars were screaming behind us. The sounds of others were in the distance.

Gomez didn't slow, stop, or falter.

In fact, the more cars pursuing her, the faster and crazier she drove.

Chapter 112

Cruz was driving the fleet car, Rick in the seat beside him, Jack's blue Lamborghini filling the rearview mirror. Ahead of them, Carmelita Gomez was sending all of their speedometer needles into the red. Cruz kept his foot on the gas, staying close, aware that if Gomez braked or plowed into another car, he couldn't stop in time.

The woman was guilty of something, for sure.

Cruz tried to get his mind around what Tyson Keyes had said about her, and he was picturing that cute but snooty woman in a whole different way.

He flashed on her standing near the wardrobe at Havana, wearing that tight pink dress, not looking at him the way women usually looked at him. At all.

He remembered her later, sitting next to him in the car, finally giving up a guy she said was her driver, Billy Moufan, saying that Moufan knew the killer's identity.

But there was no Billy Moufan. Anywhere.

Tyson Keyes had been her lover *and* her driver. And he had said Gomez was a man-hater who had sex with men for a living. How twisted was that?

A car horn blew loud and long as the speeding caravan forced a Caddy tight up against the median strip.

Del Rio said, 'Pay attention, Emilio.'

'Pay attention? I'm driving in a straight line. It's too fast, man? You want me to pull over and you drive? That's okay with me. I want to piss my pants, you hear me?'

The Impala made a sudden screaming right onto Neenach, and Cruz followed, Jack tight behind them.

Neenach was residential, a lot like the street where Gomez lived, two lines of facing single-story stucco homes fronted by low walls or small gardens, a few trees sprouting up between the houses and the asphalt.

Cruz didn't want to take his eyes off the road long enough to check the speed, but his gut told him they were going ninety down Neenach, flying toward the intersection at Haddon.

But Gomez didn't take the turn at Haddon.

There was a sound wall up ahead where Neenach Street dead-ended at the freeway. Gomez wasn't stopping. She sped into the cul-de-sac, a dead end with a semicircle of houses, maybe six of them, facing the high cement wall that separated them from the freeway.

Cruz slammed on the brakes.

So did jack and the four cruisers behind him. Cars spun and jackknifed, ran up on lawns and into parked cars. Rubber burned. There was the grating sound of metal compacting as cars slammed into garbage cans and walls.

Cruz saw the Impala leap forward in stop action. The car seemed to pause in the air, then fold up as it collided with the wall. Cruz had his hand on his door handle before his car stopped, and then he was out and running.

Rick and Jack were also running toward the crash, but Rick was yelling at Jack, 'Jack, stop. That car is going to blow.'

Jack shouted back over the noise, *I have to know if she's alive,* and kept running toward the crushed red metal that had been Carmelita Gomez's car.

Chapter 113

People came out of their houses in their pajamas and underwear, kids clung to their parents, cop cars piled up in the cul-de-sac. I knew full well that I was running toward a crashed car, but flashbacks were flooding my mind, sending me back to the worst night of my life.

I was in Afghanistan, transporting troops to base, when a rocket grenade tore through the belly of my CH-46, knocking out the rear rotor assembly and bringing us down.

There'd been a terrifying descent. The aircraft dropped into a black vortex of night. I pulled up on the cyclic, praying that I could land the Phrog upright – and miraculously I did.

As Del Rio and I scrambled out onto the sand, fuel ignited. Ordnance exploded. A column of fire burned and, through my night-vision goggles, became a green wall of flame.

We were out of the aircraft intact, but fourteen US Marines were trapped in the cargo hold where we'd taken a direct hit.

It was an honest-to-God hell on earth.

Men I knew, fought with, loved, were certainly dead, but I had to know for sure that no survivors were burning alive. I ran toward the cargo bay, and as he was doing now, Del Rio shouted at me to stop, screamed that the aircraft was going to blow.

'Jack.'

I turned to Del Rio now and shouted, 'I have to know if she's alive.'

The front end of the Impala had hit the wall head-on and compacted like an accordion.

The driver's-side door was open and the air bag had deployed and deflated. Gomez was hanging limp from the seat belt. She was bleeding from her mouth, but she was breathing.

I leaned into the door-frame and said to her, 'Carmelita. Can you hear me?'

She flicked her eyes toward me.

'Who?'

'I'm Jack Morgan, a special investigator. Did you do it? Did you kill Maurice Bingham? Did you kill Albert Singh?'

Her laugh was a wheeze, maybe an answer with her last breath. But it wasn't answer enough for me.

'You're dying, Carmelita. You don't want to go with this secret.'

I felt a hand on my shoulder.

Cruz said, 'Candy. *Dime la verdad. Pides perdón.*'

She sucked in air and said, 'God knows. I killed them. *No me necesito maldito perdón,* muthafucka. They ... got ... what they deserved.'

She lifted her hand with great effort and, looking right at me, she gave me the finger. Then her face froze, her eyes went flat, and she died.

Chapter 114

Ambulances poured into the bowl of the cul-de-sac, and uniformed cops put up barricades, instructing dazed and frightened homeowners to stay out of the street.

Sergeant Jane Campbell interviewed me beside my car.

Jane was a good cop, twelve years on the job. I had gone to high school with her brother, had had a few sandwiches at her kitchen table a long time ago.

'Looks like about thirty grand in damage,' Sergeant Campbell said, surveying my car. 'And that's just for the rear panel.'

'A police cruiser gave me a tap, but I'm okay. And I'm insured.'

Campbell smiled. 'Glad to hear it. Tell me what happened, Jack.'

'Long version or short?'

'Start with the summary, then we'll back up.'

'Okay. We got information about a case we're working. Men who were garroted in their hotel rooms. I had a theory that they were killed after having sex with a hooker. We wanted to talk to Ms. Gomez.'

'The LAPD is working that case.'

'We're on it privately for Amelia Poole.'

'She owns the Sun? On Santa Monica?'

'Right. Another guest was killed in her hotel

today, strangled with a wire. She's concerned for her guests' safety.'

'You think Carmelita Gomez was the killer–'

'We got a tip an hour ago saying she was. We went to her house to talk to her, and she fled, I mean at warp speed. We called the police immediately.'

'So why are you here?'

'We had to follow her, Jane. She was telling us she was guilty by the fact of her flight. We couldn't take a chance she'd get away. I saw her drive into that wall. She didn't try to brake. You'll see there's no rubber on the road. It was a suicide.'

'So you had a tip, chased your suspect, and now she's dead. That's what you're telling me?'

'I didn't see any other option. I still don't.'

'Emilio Cruz,' she said, indicating him with her chin. 'He said Ms. Gomez made a dying declaration.'

'She did.'

'And you'll testify to her confession?' the sergeant asked.

'Yes. I will.'

'We're going to have questions. Please don't leave town, Jack.'

'People keep telling me that,' I said. 'Do I have to worry about moving violations? Anything like that?'

'Why? So you can call Fescoe and get it fixed? Just get your taillight repaired,' she told me. 'And tell Tommy I said hi.'

I drove my car up to where Del Rio and Cruz sat in the fleet car with the engine idling.

'Is the day over yet?' Del Rio asked.

'It's done. Good job, both of you.'

I said good night and drove my injured car to the Hollywood Freeway. This time of night, it was only twenty minutes to Hancock Park.

Since my release from jail, I'd spent every free minute analyzing, researching, watching. Then I'd ruminated some more.

Jane's message to Tommy was the prodding I needed to do what my gut had been telling me to do since the beginning.

Chapter 115

I parked in the driveway of a house with a pediment and Doric columns and underwater lights turning the reflecting pool deep ocean-blue. It was the very picture of over-the-top conspicuous consumption as only Californians could do it.

Lights were on in the house.

I set the brake, climbed the walk, rang the doorbell a couple of times, and when no one came to the door, I let myself into the house.

I found my sister-in-law in the five-hundred-thousand-dollar kitchen, making chocolate pudding and watching *Goodfellas* on TV. Her back was to me.

I said, not too loud, 'Annie. Hey.'

Annie screamed and dropped the spoon. She turned, hands to her cheeks, still screaming.

'It's me, it's me. I rang the bell.'

She took a breath, put her arms out, and hugged me. 'You're a menace, Jack,' she said. 'Feel my heart racing?'

'I'm sorry.' Maybe she'd lied to give my brother an alibi, but I loved her anyway.

'Are you okay?' she asked me.

I hugged her, patted her back, said, 'I'm fine. But I've got to see Tommy. Believe it or not, I need his help.'

'He's in the barn. Go wake up your nephew. He's worried about you. Take this.'

She took a jug of milk out of the refrigerator, poured a glass, and handed it to me. 'You remember where his room is?'

Ned was asleep.

I turned on the lamp and lit up a room lined with posters: military recruitment, dinosaurs, action figures. I sat on the side of the bed, looked at the eight-year-old boy who wasn't my child but carried half my genes.

I put the milk down, touched Ned's arm, said, 'Hey, buddy. It's your old uncle Jack.'

His eyelids flew open and he sat up fast, throwing his arms around my chest. I hugged him and kissed his hair.

'How are you, buddy? How's Ned?'

He pulled back and grinned at me. 'I was digging and look what I found. Dad says it's older than he is.'

I followed his finger, saw the old glass Coke bottle on the night table. I picked it up, and admired it under the light.

'This is fantastic. It's a real antique.'

'I saw you on TV,' Ned said. I put the bottle

down, and Ned was back in my arms, talking into my chest. 'They said you killed someone. Colleen.'

'It's not true, honey. I know what people say, but I didn't kill her. I'm being framed.'

He looked up at me, questions and tears in his eyes.

'Someone *lied* about you? But *why?*'

'I don't know.'

'That's not right. That's whack, Uncle Jack.'

'He's not going to get away with it. I'm not kidding.'

'Good. Go get him. Bring the dirty dog down.'

I bumped fists with the little guy and hugged him again. Then I left the house with its elaborate coved ceilings, formal furniture, and fireplaces in every room, walked past the Olympic-sized heated pool and out to the six-bay car barn.

Tommy had a classic American car collection, a passion he'd shared with Dad. I found him under a 1948 Buick Roadmaster, a pewter-gray automobile that looked as if it had been blown from a bubble machine. It was a beautiful thing.

I grabbed Tommy's ankles and pulled him out on the dolly he'd rolled in on.

He stared at me, his expression changing as his initial fear turned to mocking anger.

'What's your problem, Jack?'

'I know who set me up, junior. I know who killed Colleen.'

Chapter 116

'Take a look at this,' I said to Tommy.

I cued my iPhone to Mo-bot's video and handed the gadget to my brother. He pushed the 'play' button, and I heard the tinny sound of reporters shouting to get my attention outside my office on a day I would never forget.

'This is you being taken to the hoosegow,' my brother said. 'That's a rough crowd.'

'Keep looking. You see someone we know?'

'Huh. Clay Harris. What's he doing there?'

'He works for you, Tom.'

'Part-time. He's a charity case, believe me.'

'So you had nothing to do with him being there?'

'Hell, no. What are you saying? That I knew you were going to jail? And that I called Clay? Why would I do that?'

'Let's go talk to him,' I said.

'Now?'

'No better time than now.'

'If you say so. I'll tell Annie I'm going out for a while. I'll meet you at the car.'

A few minutes later, Tommy met me in the driveway. He was wearing a jacket, different shoes. He walked around to the back of my car.

He ran his hand over the Lambo's left rear haunch and along the crease to the door. His jacket fell open, and I saw the gun stuck in his waistband.

'Christ,' he said. 'What the hell happened to your car?'

'I went to the supermarket. When I came out...'

'I've got a great body shop guy. I'll give you his number. But as good as Wayne is, this is never going to look the same again,' Tommy said. 'It's a damned shame.'

'Get in, will you?'

'Are you allowed to drive?'

'Get in. Try not to shoot yourself in the dick.'

Tommy got into the car. I pulled out onto West Sixth, toward the 5 going north. I figured it would be forty-five minutes to Santa Clarita at this time of night.

'Why do you want to talk to Clay?' Tommy asked me.

Clay Harris had worked for my father as an investigator, and when I took over Private, he was on the payroll.

I didn't like him, but he was great at surveillance. He could stay on a tail or sit in a vehicle for days at a time. He looked like an unemployed factory worker, could blend into a crowd on the street. And he knew his way around electronics.

But he was a cheat and a liar.

Clay Harris had fattened his expense report. He had done work on the side. And one day he sold photos of a client in a compromising position. I found out.

That's when I fired him.

Next day, Harris went to Tommy, who gave him a job.

Thinking about him now, standing in the crowd, smirking as I was marched off to jail, put

Clay Harris in a new category. He disliked me. He had the skills to hurt me. And I couldn't say murder was out of his league.

I said to Tommy, 'I want to talk to Clay about Colleen.'

Chapter 117

I took the 5, heading toward the Tehachapi mountain range linking Southern and Central California.

Clay Harris lived on a dirt road in an isolated area made up of remote ranches, parks, and forest service land. From the satellite view, I knew his house was at the edge of a three-hundred-acre parcel, marked for development then abandoned when the bubble burst in 2009. Harris's house was two miles away from any other man-made thing.

I took the 126 to Copper Hill Drive, which sent me past a minimall and then a cluster of migrant-worker housing. After the development, there was nothing to see but dry scrub and low hills, copses of native trees, and miles of flat land untouched by the hand of man.

'Here's our turn,' I said, taking a left onto San Francisquito Canyon Road.

Tommy had been talking about himself since we left Hancock Park, filling the air with self-aggrandizing stories about his bodyguard service to celebrities, the stunts the A-listers pulled. But he stopped talking as my headlights lit up the chain-link fence and signs reading 'Harris. No Trespassing.'

I slowed as the house came into view, parked on the shoulder, turned off my headlights.

The house was at the end of a long drive, placed far back on the property; a ranch-style rambler, white with dark trim and a plain front porch.

There was a clump of mature native oaks in the yard and more oaks at the fence line, but what grabbed my attention was a brand-new Lexus SUV at the top of the drive.

I knew how much Clay Harris had earned when he worked for me, and assuming Tommy hadn't quadrupled his income, the Lexus didn't fit. Unless someone had given him about seventy-five thousand dollars.

I reached across my brother and opened the glove box, took out a gun.

'I don't think you have a license for that,' Tommy said.

'Let's just keep this between us, okay, Junior?'

We got out of the car and edged along the chainlink fence, getting cover from the trees. The gate latch was open, an oversight on the part of Mr. Harris, I thought. We were still thirty feet from the porch when the motion detector found us.

Lights blazed.

A siren blared across the open land followed by a fusillade of bullets.

Harris was unloading a semiautomatic, and shots were whizzing through the trees. Then there was a pause in the shooting.

Had Clay Harris seen us? Or was he just firing in response to the alarm? Thinking coyote. Or bear. Or, *If you're on my property, you're dead.*

I whispered, 'You take the back door and I'll take the front.'

'No, Jack. *You* take the back.'

'Fine,' I said.

It wasn't fine.

I hadn't planned for a shootout.

In fact, as of right now, I had no plan at all.

Chapter 118

We were trespassing

If I called out Harris's name and he wanted to shoot me, he could get a bead on my voice and nail me. Legally.

I dropped to the ground and pulled myself across the yard with my elbows until I had reached the side of the house, out of gunshot range.

With my back to the wall, I negotiated piles of junk and brush as I made my way to the back entrance.

I held my gun with both hands, using my foot to push the door open. Hinges creaked and I stepped into a mudroom. I expected shots or at least a challenge, but I heard nothing.

A light glowed from the center of the house, and I made for it. Using the wall as a guide, I moved forward, past garments hanging from hooks, stacks of newspapers, and towers of boxed, empty beer bottles. Clay Harris was one of those people who didn't throw things out.

The mudroom led to the small, narrow kitchen. Pots and pans were piled on the table and in the sink. Garbage stank. There was an off-center door at the end of the kitchen, which led to a dining room.

I stepped around a table that was heaped with boxes of files and hoarded crap, kept moving toward the beams that framed the entrance to the living room. I peered around the corner into the larger room.

Clay Harris had his back to me. His gun was still in his hand, and his hands were over his head. He was facing my brother, who had his weapon pointed at Harris's chest.

Harris was saying, 'Tom. What are you doing? This is stupid. I'm not gonna say anything about that girl.'

I stepped into the room, gripping my own gun in both hands. I shouted, 'Clay, drop your gun.'

Harris turned, saw me, said, 'Shit,' and tossed his gun onto an easy chair.

At the same moment that the gun hit the chair, Tommy fired two shots in quick succession. Harris put his hands to his chest. He said, 'Oh, fuck,' then dropped to his knees and toppled facedown onto the floor.

I went to Harris, put a hand to his neck.

He had no pulse.

'For God's sake, Tom. I wanted to *talk* to him.'

Tommy put his gun back in his belt.

'I feel for you, I really do,' my brother said. He looked for his two shell casings, collected them, put them in the front pocket of his jeans. 'Things don't always go the way you want. You wanted to talk to Clay, and now he's dead.'

I stood up, facing my brother. 'You think I don't know what just happened here.'

'It was self-defense, Jack. That's the truth. But I guess you'll never know for sure. Did I shoot that scum because he was going to shoot me? Or did I shoot him because he would give me up?'

Tommy was mocking me, shifting his weight from one leg to the other, moving his hands up and down like they were trays on a scale.

He went on. 'Was Harris a dangerous lunatic with a loaded gun? Or was he going to tell you that I hired him to kill Colleen?'

I stared at Tommy, then looked back at the body of Clay Harris. There was an angry-looking bite mark in the fleshy part of his right hand between thumb and forefinger. The bite had been so hard, it had left a clear dental impression, a distinct bruise in the flesh where teeth had clamped down.

I took a handkerchief, the investigator's number one basic tool, out of my jacket pocket. Keeping an eye on Tommy, I used the handkerchief to pick up Clay Harris's phone.

I dialed 911.

Chapter 119

Tommy's face was knotted with anger and disbelief. He asked, 'What the fuck are you doing?'

The operator came on the line, said, 'What is your emergency?'

I disguised my voice, spoke softly with a Spanish accent. 'I heard shots fired in a house on San Francisquito Canyon Road.'

I gave her the house number and said that I'd gone inside to see if someone needed help. That I'd found one person in the house, a man, and he'd been shot.

'Is he breathing?' the operator asked me.

'No. He's dead.'

'What's your name?'

'I'm sorry. I can't say.'

I hung up the phone.

Tommy was asking me again what I thought I was doing, repeating that he'd shot Clay Harris in self-defense.

I wasn't sorry that Harris was dead, but it would have been better for me if he'd lived, if we'd gotten him to turn on Tommy and testify that they'd conspired to kill Colleen.

Tommy was highly agitated, his cockiness entirely gone. He was saying, 'Jack, let's get the fuck out of here. I've got to get rid of my gun.'

His only concern was to get rid of the gun. One thing I had to say about Tommy: He was a shit, just like my dad.

I aimed my camera phone at the bite mark on Clay Harris's hand, took three or four shots to be sure I got what I needed, frames that included both his bitten hand and his dead face. Then, I left the house by the open front door.

I disarmed the car with the remote, and my headlights flashed a hundred yards away. I walked along the dark roadway with Tommy following.

There wasn't another car traveling on this road. Not a soul.

I reached the car and got in behind the wheel. Tommy was at the passenger side, trying the door, but I'd locked it. He yanked on the handle several times, then pounded on the window with the heel of his hand. He cursed at me, sounding completely desperate.

He was still begging me to open the door as I started the engine.

'Jack. Come on. Please open the door. You know I was just horsing around. You know he was going to shoot me. You know he was worthless.'

I let the window down a couple of inches. 'Tell it to the cops,' I said. 'You're very persuasive, Tommy. They'll be here in a couple of minutes. Or you can start walking. Maybe you'll get away.'

'Jack. You don't want to leave me here. Come on. Don't do that. I'll tell them you were here. I'll say you did it.'

I buzzed up the window and pulled out onto the road that stretched from nowhere to nowhere two miles in both directions.

When I was back on Copper Hill Drive, I called Eric Caine and filled him in.

Then I just listened to what my Harvard-educated, street-trained lawyer had to say.

Chapter 120

Eric Caine sat next to me in an interrogation room at the police station downtown. He looked calm, like he'd had a good lunch, a nap, and had checked the balance on his retirement account and found that it was good.

My stomach felt like it was full of snakes.

They hadn't said why they wanted to see me, but I was pretty sure Mitch Tandy hadn't summoned us to North Los Angeles Street so he could tell me that I was a great guy.

I forced myself to think of fluffy clouds and rainbows, not that Tandy had sworn to put me in a federal prison for life for killing Colleen.

Tandy got comfortable in one of the two metal chairs across from us. Then Ziegler came in with a bulky manila envelope. He made a big production of pulling out a chair, putting the envelope down on the table, and taking his seat, snapping a rubber band on his wrist.

Like he was onstage.

Like he wanted all the attention.

What was up?

Other than the rubber band tic, neither cop gave any sign of emotion.

Tandy said, 'I suppose you know what this is about.'

'Why don't you tell us?' Caine said. 'My client has a busy schedule. I'm sure you do too.'

'Does the name Clay Harris mean anything to you?' Tandy asked me.

He knew full well that I had known Harris.

Three days had passed since I'd stared down at Harris's dead body. I hadn't heard anything about the shooting since then. And I hadn't heard from my brother.

Caine was speaking for me.

'We both know Clay Harris. He worked for Private for, what, three years, Jack? He was terminated in '09 for extortion.'

'He's dead,' Tandy said. 'He was shot in his house out in the boondocks three days ago. An anonymous tipster called it in.'

'I'm sorry to hear that Harris is dead,' Caine said. 'What does that have to do with Jack?'

The snakes writhed in my belly. Had I left a fingerprint at Harris's house? Had my car, with its crumpled rear panel, been seen by a passerby? Had Tommy gone to the police and said that I was the shooter? I'd considered these possibilities many times, but I was sure that I hadn't touched anything in Harris's house. I hadn't left any trace, I was pretty damn sure.

Ziegler opened the envelope, rummaged around, took out a sheet of paper. I'd learned to read upside down when I was three. Ziegler had a report from the LAPD's forensic lab.

Ziegler said, 'Someone took a bite out of Clay Harris's hand. The ME matched the bite mark to

314

Colleen Molloy's dental chart. Looks like she bit Harris. Probably the last thing she did before he shot her.'

I already knew what the LAPD lab knew. Sci had matched that bite mark to Colleen's charts too.

I waited for Ziegler to speak again. I guessed he was hoping I'd blurt something out, give him something on me that he didn't have already. The silence seemed to go on forever.

Caine said, 'This isn't *48 Hours*, Detective, and we don't *have* forty-eight hours. You matched the bite on Harris's hand to Colleen Molloy's teeth. You want to know if we're interested? We are.'

Chapter 121

Ziegler twisted in his seat. He'd delivered the news as if it had caused him physical pain.

'We're all interested, Caine,' he said. 'We actually want the one who killed her.'

I exhaled. It didn't matter that Ziegler and Tandy saw my relief. They had evidence that Colleen had bitten Clay Harris. Their evidence was now *our* evidence.

Apparently Tandy felt the same way. He said, 'We're going to concede that Colleen bit Harris. But, Morgan, before you and your attorney start throwing confetti around, let me say that this bite mark isn't conclusive. It doesn't mean that because Colleen Molloy bit Harris, he killed her.

You understand that, right?'

The bitterness was in his tone if not his words. Tandy had been wrong about me and that had to be killing him. I wished I could tell him that in the past couple weeks he'd funneled me through a meat grinder with a very sharp blade, that he was a bad cop, that someday he was going to pay.

I stifled myself.

'Colleen fought for her life,' I said. 'I'm glad about that.'

Caine tapped the table, half a signal to me to shut up, half a signal to the detectives to keep talking.

'So you'll be happy to hear that we also have this,' Ziegler said. He opened the envelope again and dumped out a chunk of metal. It was a hard drive. It looked like the one that was taken from my security system the night Colleen was killed.

I stopped breathing.

'What's this?' Caine asked.

'It's Jack's hard drive, with video evidence that Clay Harris carried Colleen Molloy into Jack's house. It's time-stamped with the date and hour that approximate Molloy's time of death. We found it in Clay Harris's shack of junk. And that indicates that he took it from Morgan's house and brought it home. This, along with the bite mark...'

Clay Harris had killed Colleen, but he didn't have the ingenuity to have done it on his own. And he didn't have a motive either.

Tommy had a motive – to put me in a hole for the rest of my life. But he didn't have to do the killing himself. Harris had been willing to do it

316

for a year's salary, which he'd spent on a car.

It just made sense that Tommy had directed the action from the beach outside my bedroom window and that Harris had called him as soon as Colleen was dead.

Caine said, 'My client is cleared of the murder charge.'

'We've spoken to ADA Eddie Savino,' Tandy said. 'He's meeting with the DA tonight. I think Morgan is going to be free of Molloy's murder, but here's the thing, Mr. Caine...'

I saw something I didn't like in Tandy's eyes, a flash, a warning.

'We've got another dead body,' he continued. 'Clay Harris was shot dead, and Jack, if he killed your girlfriend, that's classic motive to kill him.'

'I didn't do it,' I said.

'Are you charging Jack with Clay Harris's murder?' Caine snapped.

'Not yet,' said Tandy. 'We're watching you, Morgan. You and your brother.'

Chapter 122

Tandy's reluctance was palpable as he gathered himself to give me evidence about Clay Harris's murder. If Tandy was looking at Tommy for the crime, I had reason to hope that Tommy had left some trace of himself behind.

It got real quiet inside the interrogation room, except for the soft thwacks of Len Ziegler snapping the rubber band on his wrist. Tandy sat back in his seat, feigning nonchalance.

Finally he spoke.

'Tommy was pulled over for speeding on the night Clay Harris was killed. He was driving a new Lexus LX 570 that belonged to the victim. He'd been drinking.

'He couldn't explain to the patrol officers why he had Harris's car. He also couldn't say where he'd been for the previous few hours or what he was doing in Canyon Country.'

Last time I saw Tommy, he was outside Harris's house. Cops were on the way. He had to have gone back inside Harris's house to get the keys to the Lexus. Dumb move, Tommy. Very dumb.

'We're holding Tommy on a DUI and possession of a stolen vehicle for now,' Tandy said. 'We're not done yet.'

For a slim moment, Tandy's expression was open and I could read his mind as if it were a newspaper headline. Tandy felt sick that he had nothing against me.

Maybe he could read my expression too.

He had nothing on me. He had nothing.

There was a big celebration going on inside my head. I grinned my face off and did the touchdown dance all over the end zone. Champagne corks blew and bubbly ran down my face. The fans stood up in the stands and cheered, and I was lifted into the air.

Caine wore serenity like a custom-made suit, but his right eyelid twitched. It was a wink, just for me.

I stood up and said, 'It's been a pleasure, detectives. I'm late for a meeting.'

I walked out of the police station with my lawyer. I could stop worrying about going back to the Twin Towers, spending a year or two in court being humiliated before being locked away at Lompoc for twenty-five to life.

I was free, again.

'Fucking say something, Jack.'

I clapped Caine's shoulder and grinned at him. 'Happy day, Eric. Oh, happy day.'

Chapter 123

Colleen's friend Mike Donahue and I were at Santa Monica Airport, where I kept my Cessna 172 Skyhawk.

I'd told Donahue that I'd flown with Colleen a few times, and that she'd taken over for me when we were in the air. She had done a couple of loop-the-loops and had shrieked with laughter every time.

Now Donahue wanted to do it too.

We ducked under the wing, and I said to him, 'It's not like you see in the movies, like flying a plane is a step or two over driving a car. In a plane, you control the mixture of fuel and air that goes to the engine, you monitor exhaust temperatures, you reset the compasses. It's ninety-nine percent procedure and checklists. A minor screw-up on the ground means something entirely different when you're in the air.'

'Like what, for instance, Jack? No. Don't tell me.'

'For instance, you forget to put the gas cap on. Gas just vaporizes out of the tank. Your plane turns into a glider, and you don't want that.'

Donahue pointed, said, 'Is that the gas cap?'

'Yes.' I smiled at him. 'The cap is secure.'

We finished the walk-around, and I gave Donahue a leg up to the cockpit. I got into the pilot's seat, strapped in, and adjusted Donahue's headset so that we could talk and he could hear my conversations with the control tower.

I was cleared to taxi to the active runway, and Donahue stared straight ahead, unblinking, as we rolled.

We stopped at the end of the taxiway and I went through another checklist, reported to the tower, and began my take-off. As always, because of the way the propellers turned, the aircraft pulled to the left, so I gave it some right rudder as I built up speed.

I watched the airspeed indicator, and when we got up to about sixty, I came back a touch on the yoke.

The nose angled upward and we climbed. And I exhaled. It was a beautiful evening. The sun was going down, leaving a luminous band of sky-blue and pink along the horizon. I headed west and took us out over the ocean. Colleen used to call out the many hues of blue and green as the water went from the shallows to the deep.

I told Donahue that right here, at this altitude and distance from land, was where Colleen liked to take the controls.

'I'll think of her flying,' Donahue said to me, 'but I'll just be a passenger.'

'Maybe you'll fly some other time,' I said.

I took the plane into the clouds, and for a few moments there was nothing to see but condensation wicking across the windshield. Then we were above the castles in the air, and for a passenger and the pilot too, it was easy to put motors and magnetos and gas caps into the back of your mind, just feel the magic and the majesty of flight.

Donahue was smiling broadly as we sailed above the pastel-colored cotton balls of cumulus, and then his voice came to me loud over my headset.

'I changed my mind,' he said. 'I'd like to take a turn at the controls, boy-o.'

I told Donahue how to do a loop-the-loop, and he did as I said. He pulled lightly up on the yoke. The plane climbed straight up, curved, and flew upside down. Donahue screamed in a very manly way, then yelled into the mic, 'This is what we call ass over teakettle.'

His laughter almost popped my eardrums.

Donahue completed the loop and we were heading west again. He took his hand off the yoke and reached out to me. I matched his palm with mine, and we looked at each other, grinning like fools.

Our way of saying good-bye to our dear, sweet friend Colleen.

Chapter 124

I got home at around nine p.m., still jazzed from too much adrenaline and not enough sleep.

I locked the front door behind me, walked around the house and checked the windows, went to the newly improved security system monitor station and ran through the front- and back-door security tapes, reviewing them on fast forward. I didn't see anyone in my driveway or approaching my deck from the beach, and the log showed that the alarm hadn't gone off.

I swept the phones and the interior, and as far as I could tell, my house wasn't bugged.

There was a case of beer in the fridge and not much else. I popped the top of a Molson and swigged half of it down. I paused, then drained the rest of it.

Knowing Tommy was in police custody should have been relief enough, but I checked all the window locks, the sliders, the front door again.

Then I stripped off my clothes and left them where they fell.

The multihead shower was in the master bath, and I headed for it. The water was hot and rejuvenating. I was thinking that I was finally ready to move back into my bedroom, sleep in my new bed, new linens.

If I couldn't sleep in my bedroom, fuck it, I would sell the house.

So I tried it out.

I went into my bedroom, checked the perimeter once more, and dropped my gaze to the bed. I looked at it for a long minute and still saw just a bed, not a bad image of Colleen lying there dead.

In my mind, at least, Colleen was at rest.

I turned down the covers and turned on the TV.

I flipped around the dial, found twenty-four-hour cable news, and when I saw a talking head standing in front of a lot of flashing red-and-blue lights, I put down the remote.

The reporter's name and the station call letters were on the screen, 'Matt Galaburri, CNN.' There was a headline in small type under that: 'DEA busts organized-crime drug haul worth $30 million in Renton, Washington. Four men arrested.'

I jacked up the sound.

It had happened as I hoped it would, but I wanted to hear the details to be sure that Private was in the clear.

The reporter was excited, kept turning his head as he talked, so that half his words were lost. He was looking at a white panel van surrounded by law enforcement, both unmarked cars and those with the initials DEA on their sides.

The location was a parking lot outside a warehouse that, judging from the camera angle, looked to be on a highway. The warehouse was one of those unremarkable square buildings you drove past on your way to somewhere and never thought a thing about.

The reporter said, 'What you see behind me is mop-up of one of the largest drug busts in recent history. A spokesman for the Drug Enforcement Agency has told CNN that narcotics valued in the tens of millions have been confiscated and four men were arrested, men who are known to have strong ties to organized crime.'

He then filled in the backstory, how the van had stopped to transfer the cargo at a warehouse just south of Seattle that had been under surveillance for the past year.

There was a cutaway to a video shot earlier by a dash cam mounted inside a DEA vehicle. The scene was illuminated by headlights.

Four men were shown briefly unloading a white transport van with a vegetable decal on the side. A split second later, cars screamed into the lot.

There were loud shouts, and cops rushed the four men on foot. Two of the men ran, two put up their hands. Law enforcement agents brought all of the men down, cuffed them on the asphalt.

The video cut away again, this time to a man in a suit standing behind a podium marked with an official insignia. The lettering in the lower portion of the screen identified the man as Brian Nelson, director of the DEA.

Nelson said to the cameras, 'The officers involved in this operation saved a lot of lives today—'

My phone rang and I dragged my eyes from the screen, saw Fescoe's name on the caller ID. I thought, *What the hell is this now?* as I picked up the call.

Chapter 125

My old fair-weather friend, chief of police Mickey Fescoe, said, 'Jack. Turn on the TV. Something you're going to want to see.'

'I've got it on,' I told Fescoe. 'Looks like the DEA took a lot of illegally obtained drugs off the street.'

'That's right, buddy. I didn't say anything about your role in this. That's what you wanted, right?'

'Right. I don't want any credit. Don't say anything to anyone, *ever.*'

'I hear you, Jack. The DEA is elated. All that van needed was a red bow on top. Didn't even need that. Noccia family fingerprints are all over this deal. Can we get Carmine? I don't know, but this bust isn't going to help him any. Maybe he'll have a heart attack. Maybe someone will whack him. We can hope.'

We exchanged a few more words about the good outcome for America, and then Mickey said, 'By the way, I'm glad you're free of the Colleen Molloy murder rap. I kept my eye on Tandy and Ziegler throughout. I don't want any credit either,' Fescoe said, 'but I hope you feel that the LAPD treated you fairly.'

I said, 'I have no complaints.'

There was a beep in my ear and I checked the caller ID.

Just when I thought there wasn't a drop of

adrenaline left in my body, I got a rush of panic as I saw that Carmine Noccia was on the line.

Noccia's drugs were gone. His customers were going to go crazy, and the DEA had Noccia's men in custody.

I told Fescoe I had incoming fire and congratulated him on his part in the DEA score.

Then I switched to the second line.

As I said hello to Carmine Noccia, I was hoping to heaven that he didn't know I was behind the DEA bust. If he did, he was calling to tell me to put my affairs in order.

Noccia said to me, 'You heard about our unfortunate run-in with the DEA.' His tone of voice told me nothing.

'I just saw it on CNN. That's rough, Carmine.'

'You had nothing to do with that, right, Jack?'

'No. Of course not.'

'I had to ask.'

There was a long pause as I listened to my blood hum a very nervous tune. Then Noccia started speaking again.

'The Feds say they've been watching our transfer station. Shit, maybe someone said something and the Marzullos found out. Called in a tip.

'Either way, I've got no one to blame but myself. I should have arranged a transfer at another point, but we own that place, never dirtied it. We could get in and out fast, it being right on the highway like that. Hide the van until we could chop it up. Or so I thought.

'Anyway, it's my problem, Jack. I'm calling to tell you to keep the fee.'

Was it safe to draw a breath?

I said, 'You want me to keep the six-million-dollar fee?'

'You got the van out of the warehouse without incident, right? You handed it off to us. You gave us the names of the guys who took it. You executed the mission and so I'm paying you. That's how it works between us.'

Crap.

Classic case of good news, bad news.

Noccia trusted me. He was saying we were like brothers. That there was honor among thieves – and US Marines. The six million dollars in Private's bank account meant that Carmine and I were friends.

I never wanted to hear from Noccia again, but I didn't think I was going to be that lucky.

He hung up the way he always did – suddenly.

He didn't say good-bye.

Chapter 126

I put the phone down and tried to absorb the shock of my conversation with Noccia. I wondered if I was really safe. If Mickey Fescoe could keep my involvement in the DEA bust a secret. Or if it was just a matter of time before some Noccia hoods confronted me in a dark alley.

I wanted to call Justine.

I wanted to hear her voice. I wanted to fill her in on Noccia and my twin brother, who was in lock-up for grand-theft auto and suspicion of murder.

Justine's number was first on my speed dial. I listened to the ring, imagined the call going through. I hoped she was at home, having a glass of wine out by her pool. I hoped she'd tell me to come over.

Justine answered the phone on the third ring.

'Don't hang up, girly. I mean it.'

Justine laughed. 'Okay. You got me.'

She said she'd been cleaning out her fridge. That it was her first evening off in about a month and she had a few chores to do.

'You mind taking a glass of wine out to the pool? It's how I pictured you just now.'

She laughed again. 'Let's see. Yep. I happen to have an open bottle. Give me a second.'

I heard glassware clinking, her pit bull rescue, Rocky, barking. I heard sliding glass doors open, and then she said, 'I'm all set. What's on your mind, Jack?'

I started talking, surprised to hear what came out of my own mouth.

Maybe the phone gave us both the intimacy and the distance we needed to at last discuss what I had done and why.

'I want you to understand that I know I did a wrong thing. I can't excuse myself, especially not to you, but you can believe me, Justine. I'm sorry. I couldn't be sorrier.'

Justine said, 'Stop blaming yourself for Colleen's death, Jack. You did what you did, but you didn't kill her.'

Justine told me how much she'd liked Colleen, that she understood my feelings for her.

'I thought that you two had broken up for good.

328

And then you hadn't. Not really or not yet. That hurt me, Jack. I think it would have hurt anyone, but I'm over it now.'

I thanked her, and when the silence dragged on for too long, I told Justine about Clay Harris, how Tommy had shot him and that Tommy was currently in jail.

'Knowing Tommy, they won't be able to prove anything,' Justine said. 'He'll say he bought the car for Clay so that Clay wouldn't have to pay taxes on a bonus. Something like that. He'll say that he was taking it for a drive. I'll bet Tommy *did* buy Harris that car. I can't imagine Clay Harris walking into a Lexus showroom in Beverly Hills. I just can't see it.

'Tommy will get off the murder charge too,' she went on. 'The cops will know he killed Clay, but they'll never find his gun. You can't testify against him. He can't testify against you. Stalemate.'

I sighed.

'Jack, I'm not angry at you anymore.'

I said, 'Good.' I was on the very edge of saying I'd like to come over, when she said, 'I've got to go, Jack. I've got a dog to walk, kitty litter to change, a freezer to scrub. I may even paint my nails. You should get some sleep. I'll see you in the morning.'

I said, 'I've got some critical life-or-death chores to do myself, Justine. I'm going to run a couple loads of wash.'

Justine laughed with me. 'You do that,' she said.

I said good night.

What else could I do?

Chapter 127

Justine took Rocky for a run. She needed the exercise more than he did, wanted to flat-out drive the tension right out of her body and mind.

A half hour later, she and her doggy were back on Wetherly Drive, going up the path to her wonderful old house. It had been built in the late 1930s as a carriage house and had terrific architectural details.

More than that, the house gave off a sense of permanence, very different from the modern place she'd bought a couple of years ago with Jack.

There was no ocean to hush her to sleep here, but there were other sounds she liked as much: kids biking on the sidewalks, sprinklers chunking out spray over the close-cropped lawns, TV laughter coming from living rooms on her street. This all felt cozy and right to her.

Inside the kitchen, Justine fed Nefertiti and Rocky, and went to close the cabinet doors she had opened when Jack had called and cajoled her into having a drink and a conversation.

The ten sets of cabinet doors in her kitchen had been written on inside from top to bottom. Different pens had been used and different hands had penned little notations that told the family history of the Franks, who had lived here for three generations, right up until the time she had bought the house.

The door she was looking at now had notations from the 1940s: a baby had been born, Eleanor Louise Frank. There were stars around the little girl's name. A year later, there was a new Packard in the garage. John and Julie got engaged. Saul got polio at the age of ten. Puppies were born in a closet. There was a wedding in the backyard. And a cousin, Roy Lloyd Frank, had gone off to war.

Justine closed the cabinet door.

She had a good life. No question about it. She had a home of her own and a good job, and her life was the way she wanted it.

Just today, she'd brought in a new case: a twenty-four-year-old fashion model had inherited a fortune from her now-dead eighty-year-old billionaire boyfriend. And the dead man's family wanted Private to investigate the woman.

This was a plum job, a nine-to-five kind of case. There would be no shooting. No mobsters. No one would get shoved off a cliff. She was going to enjoy this case and until she had the time to rest, work would fill her days in a fine and satisfying way.

When the doorbell rang, Justine angrily jerked her head toward the front door. Rocky ran to the living room, threw his front legs up against the door, and whined.

He knew who was ringing the bell and she did too.

It was after ten. It was a weeknight. The man at her door couldn't open up and he couldn't settle down. He was a good boss, but in every other way, he was a waste of her time.

Damn it.

Her phone rang.

She said, 'What is it, Jack?'

'Let me in, Justine. Please.'

She clicked the phone off, went to the living room, and shouted through the door, 'Jack. Go home. I mean it. I don't want to see you.'

Her phone rang again.

She pressed the button and held the phone to her ear, slid down the wall, and sat on the floor. And she listened to him telling her what she already knew.

'Two weeks ago we were on track, Justine. I made a bad mistake, a backslide, that I deeply regret. But we were making our way back to each other after a long time apart. We were building on all of it, everything we know about each other. There is nothing we can't work out. You can't turn your back on love, Justine, not ours. Please, sweetheart. It's just me. Let me in.'

'Oh, Jack,' she said into the phone.

He loved her. Jack still loved her.

And damn it, damn it, damn it. She still loved him.

Acknowledgments

We're grateful to Captain Richard Conklin of the Stamford, Connecticut, PD and Elaine M. Pagliaro, forensic science consultant, MS, JD, for sharing their valuable time and expertise. Thanks too to our researcher, Ingrid Taylar, and to Lynn Colomello and Mary Jordan for their unflagging support.

The publishers hope that this book has given you enjoyable reading. Large Print Books are especially designed to be as easy to see and hold as possible. If you wish a complete list of our books please ask at your local library or write directly to:

Magna Large Print Books
Magna House, Long Preston,
Skipton, North Yorkshire.
BD23 4ND

This Large Print Book for the partially sighted, who cannot read normal print, is published under the auspices of

THE ULVERSCROFT FOUNDATION